# The Chamala Quest

## Mason Malone

A Doctor Liberty Belle Corcoran Novel

The Chamala Quest

Revised Edition, Published July 2018

Mason Malone Publishing

ISBN 9780991205868

masonmalone.com

# PROLOGUE

As the full moon rises above the eastern horizon, Tawaka begins his ascent up the forested slope of the mountain. The light from the stars above is blocked by a thick canopy of leaves. He travels in total darkness, navigating from memory alone, feeling with his hands and feet for familiar landmarks. The physical demands on his aging body are considerable and more difficult to ignore each time he makes the journey. A younger person would be more capable, but this is a duty which falls to him, and him alone. The responsibility has been passed down from father to son for several generations, maybe hundreds of generations and thousands of years, for all he knows. When the day comes that he can no longer climb the mountain, or if he should die, hopefully his son will be ready to take his place, so the tradition can continue. The future of the tribe is dependent on the Chamala plant and the successful harvest of its fruit.

Halfway up the slope the musky odor of fungi and bat guano wafts from the opening in the side of the mountain leading into the hidden cave. The opening is barely three feet in width and covered by thorny vines. He slides on his belly through the opening, then crawls on hands and knees to reach the central chamber, a cavernous room where the ceiling rises to a height of twelve feet. It is so dark he can't see his hand in front of his face, but that will change the moment the moon is positioned at the perigee of its orbit, the point when it is closest to the earth. He rests his tired body and lets his mind drift back to the first time he came here, when he was just a boy and his father led him up the steep slope of the mountain to the mouth of the cave.

"I'm afraid," Tawaka said to his father, when he was told to crawl on his belly through the small opening.

"I was afraid the first time, too," his father, Kiniki admitted. "But, something wondrous is about to occur."

A low crackling noise coming from somewhere in the chamber, draws Tawaka out of his reverie and back to the present. A subtle change is taking place. The air grows warmer. A shaft of moonlight enters through a fissure in the chamber's ceiling. In the center of its beam the single stalk of a Chamala plant grows out of a crevice in the cave floor and stretches upward until it is as tall as he. At its tip is a large teardrop-shaped bud. The petals

1

forming its outer shell begin to expand and separate. A glow emanates from the center, increasing in intensity as the bloom opens. Then, another stalk appears beside the first, then another, and another after that, until there is a total of eight stalks with a bloom apiece. The flowers unfurl and in the center of each is a cluster of pea-sized luminescent berries. He picks the berries and carefully places them in a special pouch he's brought with him for this purpose. The glow from the flowers fades as the moon moves away. The Chamala plants wither and sink to the cave floor. His task completed, he crawls from the cave, retraces his path down the mountain and returns to the village where he stashes the Chamala berries in his hut.

In the morning, the three-day celebration of the successful harvest will begin. Every man, woman and child in the village will participate. The tribe's elders will recount the many battles fought by their ancestors, all of which ended in victory for the tribe, due in no small part to the mystical power of the berry. The celebration culminates with the cutting of a few berries into tiny pieces and dividing the bits among the people.

As Tawaka sleeps, his son, Payou takes two berries from the pouch and hides them. If he is caught stealing them, the penalty is severe, but having something so valuable to do with as he pleases is too tempting to resist. Several kilometers distance from the village, there is a well-traveled trail. Though he is forbidden to venture that far from home, he has been there once. From a hiding place in the undergrowth, he watched with great interest as people passed by carrying all kinds of goods. They carried weapons, shields, masks and exotic foods—things he had never seen before then, and has coveted ever since. All he has to do is wait there for the right person to walk by.

# ~1~

The Global Federation of Botanists' annual symposium is a can't-miss, mark it on your calendar two years in advance, max out your credit card on airfare and a room kind of affair for its members and their guests. The venue changes from year to year, but it is always held in a lush tropical setting with varied and abundant vegetation, so when the attendees aren't listening to one of their brethren giving a presentation on plant systematics, taxonomy or nomenclature, they can enjoy the indigenous flora on a trek through a nearby rainforest.

Libby attended the year before last as a guest of Walter Adams, a member and recently widowed—only a month before—older gentleman, who spent the entire week of the event trying to coax Libby out of her panties. She managed to fend him off, but regrettably never received another invitation after that.

This year the symposium is taking place in Mahé, an island off the east coast of Africa, in the archipelago of Seychelles. And not only will she be attending, Doctor Liberty Belle Corcoran will be a featured guest speaker, which means all expenses paid, plus an appearance fee to boot. No way is she going to miss out on an opportunity like this, but it's going to take a lot of shuffling around of her busy schedule and a fair amount of careful planning to pull it off.

Her ten-acre compound in the Miranda Canyon outside of Taos, New Mexico, is the site of one of the most sophisticated botanical research facilities in the world, consisting of a laboratory, an office building, several greenhouses and grow light enclosures, as well as her living quarters. She employs a staff of ten to handle the day-to-day management of the operation and her client list includes major pharmaceutical companies, large-scale commercial farming operations and wholesale plant nurseries in twenty-seven countries.

Besides spending several hours a day in the lab examining specimens under the microscope or preparing a patent application for a new hybrid plant, she makes guest appearances on TV and radio garden shows at least once a week. On top of that she endorses a number of herbal diet

3

supplements and skin care products, which leaves her with very little spare time. The closest thing to a vacation she's had recently was last month when she slept through her alarm and didn't get up until nine, all the more reason she is going to this symposium, no matter what.

With less than a week to go before the trip, her mind is already ten thousand miles away in Mahé, thinking about a sunny beach, ocean breezes, and a tall handsome Austrian telling her how good she looks in her tiny black bikini. He called the day before while she was in the flower greenhouse enjoying the fragrance of hybrid azaleas and roses in bloom.

"Hello Libby, zis is Gunter Schneider, calling from Austria. Do you remember me?"

Her heart skips a beat at the sound of his voice. Do I ever, she almost says, but she doesn't want to appear too eager. Gunter is tall and charming with blonde hair, blue eyes, a strong jaw and a dimple on his chin. She met him at the previous symposium and might have jumped his bones the second they met, had Walter Adams not been attached to her arm like a tick the entire time she was there.

"Gunter Schneider...?" she replies, as if trying to recall the name. "Oh yes, we met a couple of years ago, in Bora Bora. Isn't that right?"

"Yes, zat is correct. I see you will be speaking at zee symposium in Mahé. I will also be there and would like to have dinner with you one evening. Zat is if you are traveling alone."

Her pulse quickens at the prospect of an evening alone with him. She inhales the aroma of the greenhouse and lets the breath out slowly to calm herself before answering, "That's nice of you to ask, Gunter, and as a matter of fact I will be attending the symposium by myself. Where will you be staying? Can I contact you there once I get in and know what my schedule will be?"

"Of course, Libby. I am staying at zee Four Seasons. You can leave a message for me, if I'm not in zee room when you call."

After disconnecting, she fist pumps the air and exclaims excitedly, "Yes!"

"Who was that on the phone?" says someone nearby. The voice is coming from Quentin, who's been napping behind a cluster of bushes since before Libby got there. "He, or she sure seemed to give your spirits a lift. I hope this means you'll be getting laid, soon. Lord knows you could use it."

She follows the sound of his voice to find him stretched out on the ground. A sky blue rose clipped from one of Libby's treasured experimental bushes rests on his chest. It has taken years to develop a plant which produces a bloom of such a rare color. Her hazel eyes flash with anger at

4

the sight of her precious flower slowly wilting on his chest. His total disregard for the time spent nurturing the hybrid rose bush appalls her, but his lack of respect for her privacy bothers her more.

"Quentin! What are you doing lurking around, eavesdropping on my conversation? Don't you have work you should be doing?"

"I'm on a break. Geez, doesn't anybody around here ever think about anything but work? I mean heck, I'm on the job twenty-four seven as it is. Now I'm supposed to be working every minute I'm here."

Libby starts to respond, but checks herself. What's the point, anyway? Talking to Quentin about something as archaic and mundane in his mind as work ethics will prove as productive as discussing quantum physics with a rhesus monkey. She's come to think of Quentin as sort of a company mascot, a kind of entertainment for her employees—albeit not as cute as one of those NBA team mascots who prance across the court between periods.

Four months earlier he wandered onto the property saying he'd work for food. She let him do a few odd jobs, expecting he'd be gone before the end of the day, but no such luck. Her mother had warned her against this very situation when as a six year old she brought home an abandoned kitten.

"If you feed it, it will never leave, and you'll have to take care of it for the rest of its life."

"Quentin, I have a ton of things I need to attend to during the next few days. The last thing I need is you underfoot. If you're not going to do something useful, then at least do your goofing off somewhere else."

"Goofing off! I can't believe that's what you think of me. After all I do for you and what do I get in return? Nada, zilch, no medical insurance or other benefits, and no paid vacation."

"Don't start with the vacation thing again. For the umpteenth time, you are not going with me. No way, no how!"

Two weeks ago he overheard Libby telling someone about going to this symposium on the island of Mahé.

He says, "You're kidding, Hawaii! I would do anything to go to Hawaii."

She says, "Mahé, not Maui. It's not anywhere near Hawaii. It's in Seychelles, east of Africa. Trust me, it's not your cup of tea. You'd be bored out of your skull after one day." That seemed to appease him, until he sneaked into Libby's office to use her computer and Google Mahé, Seychelles. Then, he started up again.

"Think about it, I could be your bodyguard. Anyone tries to rip you off and I go bam, bam, bam." He throws a series of air punches to demonstrate.

5

"Look Quentin, I don't need a bodyguard and I can't afford to pay your way. If the GFB weren't funding the trip I couldn't go myself. Besides the expense and inconvenience of taking you along, there are several other considerations. At the top of that list is the difficulty—no strike that—the impossibility of getting you on an airplane."

"What's that mean? I'm not afraid of flying."

"Maybe not, but most of the other passengers might have reservations about flying with you. I doubt you can even get past airport security, given the number of body piercings you have." She doesn't bother to mention the tattoos covering every visible inch of his body or the strange hairdo which consists of his head being shaved slick except for a two-inch circle on the top center of it, where a braided ponytail stands up like the wick of a candle.

"I've got piercings you haven't seen," Quentin boasts.

"Please, spare me the details," Libby says. "That's exactly my point, you have several pounds of metal hanging on you. You'll sound so many alarms at the airport they might decide shooting you is easier than a body search."

He doesn't argue further, which surprises her. It's unheard of for him to give up so easily, but with the day of departure drawing nearer, she doesn't have time to worry about it, now. She continues through the greenhouse to her office, where she finds an email from the Global Federation of Botanists confirming her airline and hotel reservations.

As she begins to read it, Quentin burst in without knocking. She starts to rebuke him for the intrusion, but before she can he blurts out, "Percy needs you in the lab, right away."

"Then, why doesn't he call me? It's much quicker than sending you to get me."

"Hey, how would I know? Nobody around here tells me anything. Someone said to get Libby, so I did."

She rises from her desk, shoos him out of the office ahead of her, and then locks the door before heading over to the lab. The second she's out of sight, Quentin uses a spare key he swiped earlier to enter her office.

Seeing the email from GFB on the screen, he has an idea and types out a reply which reads:

There seems to be an oversight with regard to the airline and room reservations. There is no mention of a ticket or hotel accommodation for my assistant, Quentin Maddox, who will be traveling with me. Please correct this error ASAP. Thanks, Doctor Libby Corcoran.

6

He hits send and leaves the office through the other door to avoid running into Libby.

Libby is simmering over Quentin's practical joke, if that's what it was, as she reenters her office. This is the final straw. As soon as she gets back from the symposium she is going to have it out with him, once and for all. It's over, no more free ride, no more feeling sorry for him, this is goodbye, adios, sayonara, get lost and don't come back. In fact, if he pulls another stunt like this before she leaves, she'll have him thrown into the wood chipper, and then use his shredded body as fertilizer.

"Why have you let him stay around for this long?" Libby asks aloud.

It's a mystery she puzzles over often, and can come up with only one explanation. She's intrigued by how his mind works. He's like a rare plant species she studies to determine how it responds to a particular type of manure or the absence of light. And, if she's totally honest with herself there's a certain quality about him she envies—his complete indifference toward structure, his disregard for rules or guidance of any kind. How nice it would be to forget about all her responsibilities, her business and clients, her schedule and commitments, even if only for a few hours.

Settling into her chair facing the computer screen once again, she rereads and prints the page of airline and hotel information, then quickly scans the other emails in her inbox. Seeing nothing that needs an immediate response she moves on to her daily planner looking for holes in it, fifteen minutes here or there to use preparing for the trip. She has to pack—no first she has to make a packing list, otherwise there's no way she'll get there with everything she needs.

Not far away, Quentin is going over his own list, and the first item on it is to intercept the email reply from the botany people, the one confirming an airline ticket and room reservation for him. The GFB is located in Amsterdam, according to the letterhead on the email, so their office is probably closed for the day. The very earliest they can respond will be noon tomorrow their time, which is four a.m. here. All he has to do is check Libby's email before she gets to her office in the morning, copy the information and delete it before she gets wind of what he's done.

# ~2~

Since coming to Taos, Quentin spends most nights in his sleeping bag on the floor of a grow light enclosure. Libby had several of these units custom-made to use for exotic plant experiments. They're climate-controlled, with timers for the lights, ventilation and irrigation systems. Occasionally, he's awakened by a sprinkler or grow light coming on, and sometimes the smell of fertilizer makes him nauseous, but other than that they make for a warm, comfortable place to bed down for the night. Besides, he doesn't have a lot of options these days.

It wasn't always that way. You wouldn't suspect it from looking at him now, but Quentin was born into a wealthy family. As the only child of a self-made multi-millionaire he grew up pampered and spoiled rotten. If left up to his mother, he'd still be in Bel Air, living like an Arab prince, partying with his rich friends, carrying two credit cards with unlimited balances, driving around in his Maserati convertible—the one he got for his seventeenth birthday—and living a life most people can only dream about. But his father, William, stepped in to put a stop to it.

The maid, Rosalina, rouses Quentin at two in the afternoon, from where he lies sleeping on the pool table in the rec room, and says his dad wishes to have a father-and-son chat in the study. It's a real man's room, with oak-paneled walls, the scent of tobacco and leather, a crystal decanter on the bar full of twenty-year-old bourbon whiskey and a stone fireplace with an antique mantle imported from Spain.

As Quentin enters the study, William is standing with his hands behind his back, looking out the window at a garden where hibiscus, oleander and gladiolas are blooming. He's dressed in English riding apparel, because he just returned from the equestrian center. The odor of horse sweat and saddle leather still lingers. Quentin takes a cigar from a gold-plated humidor.

"Put that back! That's a sixty-dollar Arturo Fuente," William tells him. Quentin puts it in his pocket and plops into a leather recliner, draping a leg over the arm.

"What did you want to talk to me about?"

"You're twenty-two, and after four years at UCLA, you have less than ten credit hours. You stay out all night, sleep all day, refuse to clean up after yourself and cover your body in graffiti. As far as I can tell you have no interest in a career or any ambition whatsoever."

"That's not true," Quentin argues. "There are a lot of things I can do."

"Will any of those things earn money?"

"What difference does that make? You've got more money than we can spend in a lifetime."

Quentin's attitude and ignorance of the value of a dollar comes as no surprise to William Maddox. Anything and everything he asks for is given to him on a silver platter. He never had the chance to learn to be self-sufficient and for that, William has only himself to blame. Fortunately, Quentin is young. There's still time to turn his life around.

"I'm cutting you off, starting right now. You're going to have to learn to take care of yourself. I've cancelled your credit cards and closed your checking account at the bank."

"You can't do that!" Quentin shouts. "Those are mine, not yours."

William won't budge, so Quentin appeals to his mother, Julia, to intervene.

"Quentin darling, your father only wants what's best for you, and so do I. In time, you'll come to understand, and someday, you'll thank us for this."

"Don't count on it," Quentin says.

They give their son ten thousand dollars and kick him out of the house. He packs a suitcase, throws it in the Maserati and leaves, but doesn't go far. The Los Angeles area is all he knows. Sure, he's visited other places, but all his friends and the things he likes to do are here, in the place where he's lived his entire life. So, he checks into a hotel, parties with his buddies, blows through the cash in a week, and then calls his father.

"I'm down to my last ten bucks."

"I strongly advise you to get a job," William tells his son, and hangs up. A few days later, after borrowing from friends and accumulating debt with a drug dealer or two, he calls his mother, only to have her hang up on him, too.

As the pressure from creditors escalates, he decides it might be best to leave town until things cool off, so he drives to Las Vegas, fully intending to lay low for a while. He knows how poker is played and understands the basics of blackjack. It seems like as good a way as any to make some spending money. Who knows? Maybe he'll have a winning streak and make enough to pay his debts in Los Angeles, so he can go home. He's fortunate, and meets a really nice guy who loans him some money to get started. All he asks for in return is to hold on to the title of the Maserati until the loan and interest are repaid. It takes Quentin only three days to lose the money he's borrowed and the Maserati.

With no money, car, or friends to turn to, Quentin has to beg, borrow and steal to survive, but it isn't as hard to do as he thought it might be. In fact, he soon finds he has a talent for panhandling. From Las Vegas he hitches a ride to Salt Lake City, then to Phoenix, and Denver after that. He does okay, most places, but after toughing it out through one winter in Denver, he decides to head someplace warmer. While traveling south he comes upon LBC Botanical Research—Libby's place. And the rest, as they say, is history.

Quentin wakes with a start, as the grow light directly overhead comes on. He checks his watch to see it's six a.m., time to get going. No one comes to work before seven, not even Libby. As he moves through the darkness between the enclosure where he slept and Libby's office, he sees lights on at her house. She's already up, so he needs to work quickly. Inside her office he leaves the lights off and feels with his hands for the computer monitor switch. It should provide sufficient illumination for his purposes.

"Bingo," he says aloud, upon finding the email reply in Libby's inbox. It reads:

Enclosed are the confirmation numbers for airline tickets and hotel accommodations for your assistant, Quentin Maddox. Because the arrangements were made so close to departure, I was unable to get two seats together, except on the final leg of the flights. However, I was able to book rooms for you and Mr. Maddox at the same hotel.

Quentin scribbles the confirmation numbers onto a piece of paper, and then deletes the email so Libby won't see it. If all goes well, he'll be on the plane between Doha and Mahé before Libby finds out what he's done, which will be too late to do anything about it. She'll be mad at first, of course, but once they arrive on the island, and the ocean breeze, warm air and fragrant tropical flowers have beguiled her, she'll get over it.

# ~3~

With three stops and a layover at each, the flight to Mahé from Albuquerque will take an exhausting thirty hours, not counting the two-hour drive from Taos to the airport in Albuquerque. By the time she arrives and gets checked in at the hotel, she'll be so jet-lagged she'll probably end up sleeping until she's scheduled to give her presentation. There will be no opportunity to shop for anything she forgot to bring. In fact, it might get a bit hectic in Mahé, especially if things go as she hopes they will with Gunter.

With that in mind, she decides to drive to Albuquerque on Tuesday, the day before her flight departs and stay overnight, so she can have her hair done, find a sexy evening dress, perfume with a scent men can't resist, and maybe some lingerie with thong panties and a sheer bra, just in case things go that far. God, she hopes things go that far. That's one thing Quentin got right, she could do with some quality one-on-one time with a special man.

Tuesday morning Libby makes a final inspection tour of her facility to go over things with her people before leaving for Albuquerque. She's wearing denim jeans, sneakers and a white lab coat, which is her normal work attire. Her long auburn hair is pulled back into a ponytail and fastened with a rubber band. Horn rimmed glasses, too big for her face, rest on the tip of her nose as she speaks to Umberto.

"Do you have any questions about anything before I go?" she asks.

Umberto is in charge of maintaining the mechanical systems of the facility—irrigation, automated solar screens, grow light timers, greenhouse ventilation and humidity controllers. He's a large Latino man with a thick head of salt and pepper hair, broad shoulders and an even broader tummy. Libby finds him on a ladder inspecting a ventilation fan. She cranes her neck to look up at him. Out of respect for his boss, he climbs down to her level.

"No, ma'am, don't worry about anything here. It will be fine," he answers obediently. He's arguably her most dependable and trustworthy employee. Terms like punctual, hard-working, earnest and loyal are used to describe him, but telling Libby not to worry is like telling a swallow not to fly south in the winter. It's what she does.

"If you have any problems, anything at all, you can call me on my cell phone. Because of the time difference, I may not pick up, but you can leave a message and I'll get back to you as soon as I can. If something breaks, remember we have an account at the hardware store in town. You can send Quentin to pick it up, if you like."

"Yes, ma'am, I remember. But, if I need something, I'll have Jesse, Gina, Lucille and Diego. I would rather send one of them. That way, I know it will be the right part, and they'll be back in an hour."

"Fine, whatever you feel is best. Where is Quentin, by the way? I haven't seen him anywhere this morning." Umberto just shrugs in response.

From there she stops in to talk with her lab staff. Dozens of studies are in progress around the clock. As she enters, Percy is looking at something through a microscope and doesn't hear her come in. Libby looks over his shoulder at the specimen he's examining. It's a brown spot on a leaf from an almond tree. The grove where the leaf came from is infested with something and in danger of losing hundreds of valuable trees, unless Libby's company can find the source of the problem, and a means of treating it.

"How's it coming?" she asks.

"I'm making progress. I've been able to eliminate a couple of possibilities. It's not a fungus, and it's not from a pesticide."

"Well, keep at it. We've got to figure it out before things get much worse."

"So, the big day has finally arrived. I'll bet you're anxious to get away from this place, and have some me time."

"You have no idea. If anything urgent comes up you can reach me by phone, but if it's not something needing my immediate attention, send me an email."

"Will do, but I don't foresee anything we can't handle for a week. You just relax and have a great vacation."

"Thanks, Percy. I plan to. Where are the others?"

"Beth went to town to overnight the report to Colton Farms."

"But I haven't reviewed it, yet," Libby reminds him.

"We know you have a lot on your plate, and the report seems pretty straightforward, so she thought it'd be okay to send it out."

Though it bothers Libby, she knows it's not something she can afford to be distracted by, now.

"I'm sure it will be alright, but it's not the way we do things, here. What about Scott, where's he?"

"I believe he's uploading the video of that new hybrid rose blooming to YouTube."

"Great, I'm anxious to see how many views it will generate. Have you seen Quentin?"

"Not since early this morning, and I count myself lucky he hasn't been around pestering me or abusing the lab equipment. The other day, I saw him pick his nose and put the booger on a glass slide, so he could look at it under a microscope."

"Yuck. Thanks for sharing that with me. The image of Quentin picking his nose is now burned into my memory. It will be what comes to mind each time I see him from now on." *All the more reason to get rid of him*, she thinks to herself.

"Can I ask you something?" Percy says, and then continues before she can answer. "Why do you keep him around? As far as I can tell he never does anything productive. I've never understood why you don't fire him."

"I haven't fired him because he's not an employee, at least not officially. He showed up one day looking for a handout. I felt sorry for him, so I let him do a few odd jobs in exchange for a meal. I thought he'd be gone by the end of the day, but he asked if he could work a few more days to earn traveling money and I said he could. A few days later he asked to stay a little longer, and a little longer turned into four months."

"Are you and he…, I mean, I know you work long hours, and probably don't have much time for dating, so I was wondering if that's why you keep Quentin around?" It is a full minute before Libby realizes what he's getting at.

"What! You think Quentin and I are lovers, is that what you're asking?" she snaps, angrily. "Not that it's any of your business, but heavens no, we're not. How could you even think that, have you taken a good look at him?"

"I'm sorry, you're right, it's ridiculous. I don't know what I was thinking."

"You're damn right it's ridiculous," she replies, then she has to chuckle at the pure absurdity of the idea of Quentin and her as a couple.

Percy lets out a sigh of relief. During the year he's worked at the lab, Libby hasn't revealed much about her social life, if she has one. Naturally, he's curious. She's young, successful, single and unattached, as far as he can tell. There's no question she's an attractive woman, or could be with a little effort.

"Maybe, when you get back, we could have dinner together, some evening? Do you like Mexican food? There's a new place north of town. It would give us a chance to get to know one another outside of work."

13

She's dumbstruck by the suggestion and slow to respond. Not that the idea is that far-fetched. Percy is thirty-one, a couple of years older than her, and nice-looking in a geekish sort of way, but not at all her type. Alright, she doesn't really have a type, but if she did, he wouldn't be it.

"I'm sorry, Percy, I don't socialize with my employees." It sounds arrogant, even to her. She tries again. "I didn't mean for that to sound so uppity, I just think it's important for me to keep my business and personal life separate."

"Oh, I see." For an uncomfortable moment they don't speak, then sensing Libby is eager to leave he says, "Well, I better get back to the almond tree leaf. Have a great trip."

"Thanks, Percy. I'll see you in a week." *That was awkward*, she thinks as she's leaving. On the way to her office, she passes through the flower greenhouse, figuring Quentin might be napping behind the azalea beds. She'd be just as happy not to see him, but his disappearance is puzzling her. Typically, he would be in the lab or one of the greenhouses getting in the way and making a nuisance of himself. She brushes it off and continues on to her office, glancing at her watch as she does. There's just enough time to check her email once more before leaving for Albuquerque.

The first one she sees in her inbox is from her mother. The message is short. It reads:

Call me before you leave town, it's very important. Diane

"It's always very important, isn't it, Diane?" Libby mutters.

Between her thirteenth and fourteenth birthdays Libby grew four inches. She could have passed for nineteen, which made it awkward for her mother to pass herself off as twenty-three. That's when her mother instructed Libby to call her Diane, instead of Mom. "So no one gets the wrong idea," was the way she put it.

As much as she hates to, she punches in her mother's phone number. Conversations with Diane are rarely brief. Usually the woman will spew an unintelligible and uninterrupted stream of babble that can go on for an hour. Her mother picks up immediately, as if she's been holding the phone in her hand, begging for it to ring.

"Liberty, I'm so glad you called. I've just received the most distressing news. You have to cancel your trip."

"Why, what's wrong, now?" Libby calmly replies.

"I woke up this morning with the strangest feeling, like the time I had a premonition something was going to happen to your Uncle Lloyd, and that same evening he was involved in an automobile accident."

"First of all Diane, he wasn't my uncle, he was one of several men you were seeing at the time. And as I recall, he had a substance abuse problem and wrecked his car regularly."

"Liberty, shut up and listen to me. As I was saying, I have a bad feeling, and because I know you're leaving tomorrow, and that you'll be flying and traveling to foreign countries, I scheduled an emergency appointment with Lucinda."

"Diane, please don't tell me you're suggesting I cancel my vacation because of something that phony psychic saw on a tarot card."

"There's nothing phony about Lucinda, she's a proven clairvoyant. Besides, this has nothing to do with tarot cards, everyone knows those can't be trusted. This is based on your astrological path. She mapped out your natal chart. I gave her all the pertinent information—your date, place and time of birth, everything. Tomorrow is the absolute worst day for you to travel anywhere. I want you to promise me, you'll cancel your trip."

Libby can feel her head begin to throb, and knows it will only get worse the longer she speaks to her mother.

"I really have to go, now. I've got so much to do, what with cancelling my flight and hotel reservations, not to mention letting the GFB know I won't be speaking at their symposium due to the fact my mother says I shouldn't travel just now, because the stars are misaligned."

"I hate it when you take that tone with me, Liberty. Lucinda's predictions are not to be taken lightly. Mark my words, you'll be sorry you didn't listen."

"Believe me, I'm already sorry, just not for the reason you think. Did you want to say something like 'Have a great trip, Libby!', before I hang up?"

"You are without a doubt the most stubborn person in the world, Liberty Belle, but I love you in spite of it. Please be careful."

"I will, and I love you too, Diane. Bye now."

The next email is from Jessica Rawlins, Libby's agent and the person responsible for booking her TV appearances, speaking engagements and endorsement deals. It starts out wishing Libby a safe trip and requesting she email her when she gets to Mahé. The rest of it is a reminder of everything scheduled for the three months following her return. It pretty much guarantees she won't get another day off in the foreseeable future.

# ~4~

Libby's first thought upon walking into the Chipper Clipper Hair Salon in downtown Albuquerque is turn around and leave. The stylist beckoning her toward the swivel chair, Tonya, looks as if her own hair is cut with a lawnmower and set afire afterward. But, the woman's hair she just finished cutting looks sensational.

"I could recommend a good conditioner for you," says Tonya, as she begins snipping away at Libby's hair. "We carry it in the thirty-three-ounce size, which will probably last two months or more. Your auburn hair is beautiful, except for the split ends, and you've got quite a few. That's what's making your hair so frizzy."

"Do you have it in a travel size?" Libby asks. "I'm leaving on a trip in a few hours."

"You are, how nice! Where are you going?" Normally, the question would strike Libby as too personal coming from someone she's just met, but this is different. There's a bond which seems to form instantaneously between a girl and her hairstylist. Much like the one formed between a drunk and a bartender. Only ten minutes into the haircut, and Libby already knows Tonya is thirty-four, divorced from her second husband, has two kids, ages six and eight, and has been seeing a guy named Henry for the last three months. It seems only fair that she reciprocates. Besides, she has a few hours to kill before she has to leave for the airport.

"I'm speaking at the Global Federation of Botanists' annual symposium," Libby confides, to which Tonya scrunches her face like she's bitten into a lemon, but doesn't reply. "It's not as bad as it sounds, it's taking place on the island of Mahé."

"Hey, at least you're going to Hawaii. How bad could it be?" Libby doesn't bother correcting her. "My mother went there with her boyfriend and had a great time. They went kayaking in the ocean, saw whales and took a bus tour where they saw a volcano. Have you ever been there?"

"No, I haven't."

Actually, Libby has visited Hawaii twice, but she's not interested in talking about it. Her thoughts are on an entirely different island on the other side of the world and in another ocean, at the moment.

"Are you going alone, or will you be taking your husband or boyfriend with you?"

"I'm not married, and yes, I'll be traveling by myself."

In a low, conspiratorial voice Tonya says, "My mother said, she's never seen so many good-looking guys in one place—all tanned and walking around in swimsuits. It shouldn't be hard to hook up with someone, if a girl is so inclined."

"As a matter of fact, I'm meeting someone there. He's Austrian."

"From Down Under is he? I love the way those guys talk." Attempting an Australian accent she says, "G'day mate, g'won, throw another shrimp on the barbie."

Once again, Libby doesn't correct Tonya, instead she replies, "Yes, there's something about a guy with a foreign accent. It makes them seem mysterious."

"And, don't forget sexy."

"Yes, there's that, too," Libby agrees. "Speaking of—do you know of someplace around here where I can find intimate apparel?"

"You mean sexy lingerie, like Victoria's Secret kind of things? Yeah, there's a shop a couple of blocks away, called Allure. Their stuff is a little pricey, but it's top-of-the-line."

~~~

Following the directions Tonya gives her, Libby finds Allure a block off the main street in a small nondescript building reminiscent of a speakeasy during the days of prohibition. There's no window display featuring lingerie or signage mentioning intimate apparel, only the name of the place in unlit letters above the door. A bell jingles as she enters. A young woman wearing denim short shorts and a sheer lace top greets her.

"Hi, I'm Bridgett, welcome to Allure. Can I help you find something?"

"I'm not sure of exactly what I'm looking for, yet," Libby tells her. The girl looks her over, which makes Libby uneasy. She's always been self-conscious when it comes to her body. Not that it's a bad-looking body, but she's thin without much in the way of curves in the right places. A body type often referred to as a beanpole.

"Is this for a special occasion, like a surprise for your husband or a big date?"

17

"Kind of. I'm going on a trip, and meeting a man there."

"I see. You want to be prepared, just in case this guy you're meeting gets lucky." Libby feels herself blushing. "Don't be embarrassed, there's nothing wrong with wanting to make a good first impression. I've found the better I look, the better I feel, and the better the overall experience is as a result."

*Easy for you to say*, Libby thinks. The girl looks to be twenty, with long naturally blonde hair and the body of a Sports Illustrated swimsuit model.

"Let me show you our Silk and Sassy line of lingerie."

She leads Libby over to a display of lacy garments. Samples of the items hang on headless mannequins. Bridgett picks out a few items and points to a room.

"See what you think of these. The dressing room is right over there."

The dressing room is not much larger than a 1970s-era phone booth with a louvered door, the bottom of which is level with the middle of Libby's thighs and the top is just high enough to conceal her nipples if she crouches down slightly. She and Bridgett seem to be the only ones in the store, so she shucks her clothes and pulls on a pair of panties.

Bridgett peeks over the top of the door to ask, "What do you think?"

Her sudden appearance catches Libby off guard and she instinctively crosses her arms over her breasts. Bridgett gives her a perfunctory once-over in the same manner a tailor examines a suit.

"These are really nice," Libby manages to say.

"Try on the bra that goes with them. Here, I'll help. It's a little tricky to fasten, at first." Bridgett steps inside the small enclosure, takes the bra and wraps it around Libby from behind.

"You'll have to move your hands."

Libby lets her hands drop to her sides. Bridgett places the cups over her breasts, fastens the straps in back, smooths the wrinkles and adjusts the underwire to provide maximum cleavage.

"Don't you love the way it feels? It's like wearing nothing at all."

Indeed, Libby is thinking, it's exactly like being naked. She admires herself in the mirror while Bridgett stands behind her. It makes her boobs look bigger, like she has implants. She can't wait to see what Gunter will think.

"It's a very sensual outfit. I like it a lot." She reaches to unfasten the bra.

"I've got it," Bridgett says.

She removes the bra, brushing Libby's nipples with her fingers as she does, and then helps her slip out of the panties. The whole experience is surreal to Libby, a girl dressing and then undressing her in lingerie. It's an alien sensation.

"Try this on."

Bridgett holds up a black lace babydoll set with a sheer flyaway top and G-string bottom. Libby balances herself with a hand on Bridgett's shoulder while Bridgett slips the G-string bottom on one leg at a time. Then, she pulls the top over Libby's arms and fastens the hook in front.

"Wow!" is all Libby can say, after a glance at her image in the mirror.

"You look stunning," Bridgett tells her. She steps aside so Libby can turn and admire herself from every angle.

"It doesn't cover much, but I guess that's the idea."

"Exactly," Bridgett agrees. "One look at you in this, and the guy will be so hot to trot it will be over before he can get his pants off." They share a giggle at the thought of it. "The flyaway top comes undone with a simple flick of your fingers, like this." Bridgett demonstrates the maneuver, unhooking the babydoll top in less than a second, letting it fall open and leaving Libby fully exposed in front, except for the silver dollar-sized patch of fabric covering her crotch.

"If that doesn't get his motor started, he's brain-dead. In fact, I'm having trouble keeping my hands off you."

She squeezes Libby's butt cheek, and then gives her a lascivious wink to prove it. All of a sudden, Libby is feeling claustrophobic inside the small room with Bridgett so close.

"I think there's been a misunderstanding. I mean, don't take this the wrong way, but I prefer men."

"I like men too, just not every day," Bridgett says. "Have you ever been intimate with a woman?"

"No, I'm a traditional sort of girl. I never venture far from the straight and narrow path. It's just who I am."

"Aren't you curious about what you're missing?"

Bridgett takes hold of her sheer lace top at the waist and pulls it off over her head, letting her long blonde hair fall across her shoulders and firm breasts. She moves even closer, pressing against Libby, putting a hand on Libby's neck and pulling their faces together. Libby attempts to push her away, but Bridgett holds firm.

"Knock it off," Libby demands.

Bridgett acts as if she doesn't mean it. She pushes Libby against the wall of the small room. Libby pushes back, knocking Bridgett through the louvered door where she trips and falls to the floor.

"Why'd you do that?!" Bridgett yells at Libby.

19

"Because you wouldn't stop. I'm not into women, I told you that."

"I didn't think you were serious. I guess I read you wrong. I'm sorry. Okay? Hey, it's no big deal."

It is a big deal, Libby wants to say. She puts her street clothes back on. When she comes out of the dressing room, Bridgett has redressed herself and is behind the counter. She doesn't make eye contact as Libby approaches.

"I've got to get to the airport. My flight leaves in a couple of hours. I'll take these," Libby says, as she places the lingerie sets on the counter.

"How would you like to pay for these?" Bridgett asks, in a strictly business manner.

"I'll use my Visa, if that's okay."

"That's fine. Would you like to add your name to our email list? We have special sales every week."

"Sure," Libby replies. Bridgett gestures to a notepad and pen on the counter.

"I hope those items have the desired effect. Stop in again when you're in the area."

# ~5~

The trip to Mahé comes together so quickly, Quentin doesn't remember until two days before that he needs his passport, which is at his parents' house in Los Angeles. Ever since they threw him out, his father hasn't spoken to him and the few conversations he's had with his mother have been brief.

She asks, "How are you? Where are you? Do you have a job?"

He answers, "I'm fine. I'm in Las Vegas, or Phoenix, or Denver. I've applied for several jobs. I expect to get one, soon. That's why I'm calling. Can you wire me some money to get by on until my first paycheck?"

At that point she hangs up. So when he calls about his passport he uses a different strategy.

"I'm sorry I haven't called sooner, but I've been real busy with my new job. I'm assistant to the head of a botanical research company."

"That's wonderful, Quentin, your father will be so glad to hear you've got a good job."

"It gets better. The day after tomorrow I'm going to an island in the Indian Ocean. My boss is speaking at a botany symposium and I'll go along to help."

"A tropical island, that sounds exciting."

"Yeah, I'm looking forward to it, but there's a problem. My boss sprung this on me at the last minute, and there's not enough time to get a new passport. I'm not sure how it will affect my job if I'm not able to go because I don't have a passport. I might get fired."

"Well Quentin, you have a passport, here. It's in the drawer with your birth certificate and other personal papers. I could overnight it to you, so you don't get in trouble with your boss."

"Wow! That would be great. I never thought of that. Mom, you're a lifesaver."

"Give me the address there, and I'll send it out immediately."

It arrives by special courier the next morning.

~~~

Quentin leaves Taos a few hours ahead of Libby, wearing jeans, sneakers, a Grateful Dead T-shirt and a knit cap, carrying his travel luggage—a plastic bag containing a change of clothes, a toothbrush and a comb. He walks three miles before catching his first ride on State Road 68.

"Where're you heading?" asks the driver, through the rolled down window of the rust heap of a truck that pulls to the side of the road where Quentin stands with his hand up and thumb pointing southwest. Attached to the rear bumper is a livestock trailer with two goats in it.

"To the Albuquerque airport."

He has a sad story prepared, one that involves his grandmother on death's doorstep and his urgent need to see her one last time, but it isn't necessary. The driver squints at Quentin between the top rim of sunglasses and the crumpled brim of a straw cowboy hat for a moment, and then tells him to hop in.

It isn't until he climbs into the passenger seat and the truck is rolling down the highway, he realizes it's a woman offering him the lift. Her hair is tucked under the hat and her figure is mostly concealed by the flannel shirt and overalls she wears. She could be anywhere from forty to sixty, for all he can tell. He sees bits of chewing tobacco stuck between her teeth when she smiles.

"I'm Daisy."

"Quentin. I really appreciate the ride, Daisy. I was beginning to think I might have to walk all the way to Albuquerque."

"Yeah, some folks are kinda shy about picking up hitchhikers, especially with all the tattoos and rings through your nose, and stuff. It don't bother me none, though. In fact, I sorta like it."

She gives him another tobacco stained grin, and lets her eyes linger a moment longer than necessary. The tires crunch on gravel as the truck veers onto the shoulder. She quickly gets it righted and glances in the rear view mirror to check on the goats.

"I hope I didn't scare my goats, too badly. One of them is due to have kids in another week or so."

"Which one?" Quentin asks, as he turns to look at them.

"The female, of course." He studies the two goats, but can't distinguish which is which. Daisy is amused by this. "The one without a pecker."

"I can't see anything that looks like a pecker from this angle."

"You can't?" Daisy says with mock surprise. "Well, I see something that looks like one."

She drops her gaze to his crotch, and gives him a wink. Then, she reaches between her thighs, and Quentin tells himself to look straight ahead through the windshield, and nowhere else.

"Wanna taste?" she asks next.

Hell no, I don't, he starts to say. Then she raises the pint-size bottle of Kentucky bourbon she's been holding between her legs.

"Uh, no thanks. Are you sure that's a good idea? I mean, you don't want to scare the goats, do you?" She glances in the mirror at the goats, and then back at the bottle.

"Oh, I guess you're probably right."

She replaces the bourbon between her legs, and he starts to relax a bit. The roads between Taos and Albuquerque are steep, winding, narrow and challenging enough without the driver being inebriated. They travel in silence for the next few minutes, then she asks, "You think you can you drive this old truck?"

"Sure, if it has a gas pedal and wheels, I can drive it."

She pulls to the side of the road and they switch places. After a few miles, she's convinced Quentin can handle the truck, so she takes a healthy swig of bourbon, followed by two more. He's hoping she'll nod off, but in his peripheral vision he can see her looking him over, and it's making him really nervous. She slides over a little closer to him.

"I better pay attention to my driving," he says to her.

"That's right, keep your eyes on the road ahead."

She raises a sleeve of his T-shirt, pulls his collar down and tugs at his shirttail, examining his tattoos and piercings.

"Don't fidget around so much, Daisy ain't gonna hurt you. As near as I can tell, you must have every part of your anatomy tattooed or punctured."

"Pretty much," Quentin says, matter-of-factly.

"My ex had a bunch of tattoos. He was a biker, a mean son of a bitch, too, always going around wearing leather with chains dangling down. He had a tattoo of a bullet on his dick that swelled up and looked like a rocket ship when he got a hard-on. Let's see what Mr. Snakey looks like." She unzips his pants and fishes it out.

"Whoa!" he cries. "We're going to have a wreck if you don't cut it out."

"Just relax, and watch the road."

"This is a really bad idea."

"Aw, you're not going to deny Daisy a little fun, are you, after I was nice enough to give you a ride? Or would you rather walk from here?"

He tries thinking about something other than Daisy's hand stroking him, hoping she'll lose interest in a minute, but his indifference only makes her more determined than ever. She stays with it, but can't get a response.

"It's a stubborn little thing, isn't it? That's alright, I'm not giving up, yet. You just need a little visual stimulation."

Daisy unbuttons her flannel shirt and pulls it open. In a panic he stomps on the brake, causing the goat trailer to fishtail. Daisy is thrown onto the floor. Without bothering to check for other cars, he grabs his bag and jumps out before the truck comes to a full stop. By the time Daisy picks herself up, Quentin is out of sight, crouching behind a rock outcropping, praying Daisy will just drive away and leave him be. After a minute, he hears the truck engine rev and peeks over the rock to see it disappear down the highway. He gives it another ten minutes, just to be sure she doesn't return, and then takes up a position on the road shoulder with his thumb out, once again.

It's midafternoon when he jumps from Daisy's truck, traffic is sparse and drivers willing to give a ride to someone who looks like Quentin are few and far between. By dark he's made it only about halfway to his destination. He spends the night at a truck stop, south of Santa Fe, drinking coffee and contemplating his situation while he watches the big semis come and go. The airport is about an hour away, there's a dozen or more trucks parked outside while their drivers catch a few hours of sleep. As dawn nears they'll start pulling out and all he needs to do is get a ride with one of them to Albuquerque. How hard can it be?

# ~6~

Libby is jogging through the concourse toward the gate as fast as her long legs will carry her. This is so unlike her to be running late. Her plan was to come to Albuquerque a day early, check into a hotel, get a full eight hours of sleep, then have her hair done and do a little shopping the next morning before arriving at the airport two hours before the plane departs. Everything was going great, right on schedule with an hour to spare when things began to go awry.

After leaving Allure, she stops at a signal light a block away. Her mind is drifting back to the incident at Allure when a horn sounds to let her know the light has changed to green. She decides to stop for a coffee and try to get her head on straight before dealing with the crowd at the airport. The service is slower than expected. Before she knows it thirty minutes have passed and she's racing to make it there on time.

The announcement comes over the loudspeaker as she approaches the security checkpoint. Her flight will begin boarding in ten minutes. Fortunately, the checkpoint line is relatively short and moving quickly. She grabs a tray, kicks off her shoes, removes her watch and jewelry, throws everything along with her carry-on and purse onto the conveyor belt, and steps through the scanner. As she retrieves her things at the other end, a TSA officer says to her, "Please step over here, ma'am."

"My plane is about to begin boarding," Libby says, but the officer doesn't reply. While he runs a wand over her, another officer goes through her carry-on and purse. "Is all this really necessary? I'm going to miss my flight."

"I'm sorry for the inconvenience, ma'am. With your cooperation it won't take long."

The officer going through her carry-on finds the sack of lingerie from Allure and holds up the babydoll set at arm's length.

"Nice," he says. "I got my wife something like this from Victoria's Secret, but she never wears it." He brings it closer to his face and sniffs.

"Did you actually just smell my underwear?" Libby says, loud enough to be heard by everyone around.

She hears snickering coming from somewhere behind her, and the officer holding the babydoll is turning red. He shoves the lingerie back into the sack, not bothering to fold it neatly, closes the carry-on and hands it to Libby.

"Have a safe trip, ma'am," he says, to which Libby responds by snatching her things from him and hurrying away without stopping to put on her shoes or jewelry. The departure gate is at the far end of the concourse, and she gets there as the last of the passengers are boarding.

The Global Federation of Botanists paid for economy fare tickets, but Libby decided to upgrade to business class. She rarely indulges in such extravagance, but her business is doing very well, and she may not get another vacation like this for years. She takes her seat in the front cabin of the Boeing 737 as the curtain is drawn between her and the economy class passengers. Within minutes the plane is in the air and bound for Dallas-Ft. Worth International Airport. The seat beside her is unoccupied, she accepts champagne from the flight attendant, dons a set of earbuds and settles into the cushy recliner, as the jet soars into the clouds.

From the rear of the plane, Quentin peeks out from behind a magazine as the curtain is drawn between Libby and the filled to capacity economy cabin. So far, so good. She has no idea he's on the plane. Each step of the way will be a little trickier than the one before. At the same time, the farther away from New Mexico they get, the less likely it is she'll do anything crazy, like try to have him thrown off the plane. There's nothing to do now, except sit back and relax.

He's wearing surfer shorts, high top sneakers, a Pink Floyd T-shirt and a bandana headband. He passed through the checkpoint with his trash bag carry-on thirty minutes before Libby, and without as much as a second glance from the TSA officers. Once they reach cruising altitude, the beverage cart comes up the aisle.

"Would you care for a beverage?" the flight attendant asks Quentin.

He's sitting in the center seat between a grandmotherly-looking woman on one side against the window, and a large man in a business suit on the other side.

"What do you have?" he replies. She points to cans and bottles lined up on the cart. He studies the selection long enough for the woman to become impatient and start to move on. "I'll have a Coke."

"Almonds or peanuts?" she asks, next. When he doesn't reply immediately, she tosses a bag of peanuts on the tray beside his soda and turns away before he can protest. He's never been fond of peanuts. Almonds on the other hand, he could eat by the pound. Glancing at his seatmates, he sees the suit has polished off two packages of almonds and is licking the salt from his hand. Grandmother hasn't touched her almonds or orange juice.

"Are you going to eat your almonds?" Quentin asks her. She pivots her head to look at him.

"I'm planning to, but not yet. I'd like to save them a while longer."

"I'll trade you my peanuts. There are more peanuts to a package, than almonds. I'm allergic to peanuts, otherwise I'd eat them."

"That's nice of you to offer, but I really don't like peanuts."

"I'll take them then," the suit says, and snatches them away. Quentin eyes the peanuts mournfully, as they disappear down the suit's gullet and the crumpled empty package hits the tray beside the others. *What a waste, he doesn't even bother to chew*, Quentin notices.

On this initial leg of the trip in the Boeing 737, business and first class are the same. When Libby transfers to larger jets for the Dallas to London, London to Doha, and Doha to Mahé flights, the seating and service in business class are a slight step below first class. So, Libby is making the most of it. As the plane passes over Amarillo, she's enjoying a shrimp salad with her second glass of champagne. One flight attendant, a thirtyish African-American woman named Colleen, is looking after the six passengers seated in the cabin.

"I've seen you before," Colleen says to Libby. "Do you fly this route often?"

"Not often enough that you'd remember me."

"I never forget a face," Colleen insists. "Names sometimes, but never faces. I can't place where I've seen you, though."

A man seated across from Libby has been eavesdropping. "She's the plant doctor. Here, look," he says, thrusting a magazine toward Colleen.

It's opened to a page where Libby's face is pictured next to bottles of herbal diet supplements. The caption below it reads, recommended by Doctor Liberty Belle Corcoran, world-famous botanist.

"Now I remember," Colleen says. "I've seen you on TV." The other passengers seated nearby turn to look at Libby who's embarrassed by the attention.

"What can I take for arthritis?" one of them asks. "I have problems with my hands swelling, especially in the mornings, when I first get up."

"Turmeric can help, one thousand milligrams daily is the recommended dosage."

"What about for constipation?" asks one.

"Or psoriasis?" asks another.

27

The dispensing of free advice annoys her. She would rather pass the time in the air with a glass of champagne and a romance novel, but she answers their questions, nonetheless. She even signs autographs for a few. By the time they touch down in Dallas she has her sunglasses on hoping no one else will recognize her.

Quentin is one of the last ones off the plane. He peeks around the edge of the jet bridge before stepping into the terminal. Libby is nowhere in sight, and the chance of her spotting him in this sea of people scurrying to and from their gate is practically nil. The next flight leaves in two hours and from another terminal a mile away. Plenty of time to pick up some extra cash, because the thirty dollars he has on him will only stretch so far. He hails a passerby wearing a Lakers jersey with number twenty-four on it.

"Excuse me sir, can you spare some change so I can get something to eat? My flight's been delayed and I'm completely tapped out until I get back to L.A. Anything at all would help."

The guy is good for a dollar. Twenty minutes later, Quentin has enough for a meal at McDonald's.

# ~7~

Libby is among the first to board the flight from Dallas to London. Quentin watches from behind a column as she disappears through the door leading onto the plane. He's in the last group of people to get on and knows from the row number on his boarding pass he'll be in the rear of the plane again, which means he'll pass by Libby. There's no way to disguise himself. He doesn't have a hat and dark glasses and can't put a bag over his head. He hides behind the people slowly threading their way between the bodies and luggage in the aisle, peeking around them now and again, until he sees Libby. She's on the opposite side of the jet, halfway through the second cabin. She's busy adjusting her seat and doesn't see him pass by.

As the Boeing 777 lifts off an hour after sunset heading east toward the Atlantic Ocean, Libby is familiarizing herself with the luxurious surroundings. Each business class passenger has their own private semi-enclosed area with an entertainment system, fully reclining seating, personal lighting, ventilation, and a console with controls for those things, as well as a USB port and audio inputs. There's a self-serve bar with complimentary snacks and beverages exclusively for business class, so when they reach cruising altitude and the seat belt sign goes dark, Libby helps herself to a scone and glass of Chablis. She watches a movie with the sound muted while she enjoys her snack.

Near one a.m. on the east coast of the United States, the Boeing 777 starts across the Atlantic Ocean. A few of the passengers around Libby are lying down with their eyes shut and a blanket over them, attempting to sleep, but she's still on Taos time and wide awake. On the screen is an action movie starring Bruce Willis. The sound is muted, but Libby is not really watching it, anyway. Instead, she glances at it occasionally while catching up on emails, and seeing what some of her colleagues are saying on Facebook and Twitter. The stimulation from the movie and her iPad help pass the time on the long flight. She can't imagine what it must be like for the passengers in the economy section.

However, Quentin doesn't have to imagine what it's like, he's experiencing it firsthand. He's in the middle of a row of five seats. The only good thing about the location is he doesn't have far to go to the restroom, once he crawls over the two people on either side of him. The two on his left are a mother and her ten-year-old daughter. The two on his right are the father and seven-year-old son from the same family. The family wants to sit as close together as possible, but no one wants the middle seat. In fact, no one in their right mind would willingly sit in the middle of a five-seat row on a nine-hour transatlantic flight.

"What's that?" the ten-year-old girl asks Quentin, shortly after takeoff. She points at something on his neck.

"It's a tattoo," he answers.

"Duh, I know that. What's it a tattoo of?"

"It's a phoenix."

"You mean like in Arizona?"

"No, like a mythological bird."

"It doesn't look like a bird. I'd ask for my money back, if I were you."

"Veronica, don't bother the man," the mother says, without taking her eyes from the paperback she's reading. Veronica sticks her tongue out at Quentin. He ignores her, which makes her that much more determined to get a reaction from him.

"Veronica's sticking her tongue out!" her brother calls to the mother. The father is pretending to be asleep. "Why do you have that big hole in your ear?" the boy asks Quentin.

"Gavin, don't bother the man," the mother says. Veronica sticks her tongue out at Gavin. Gavin returns the gesture, and then starts a game of tag with his sister.

He slaps her on the arm and says, "You're it."

"No, I'm not, because I'm not playing with you," she responds.

"Okay, then you're it," he says to Quentin, and slaps him on the arm.

"Gavin, I told you not to bother the man. Now, switch places with your sister. You can sit over here by me where I can keep an eye on you."

Veronica moves in front of Quentin as Gavin walks across his lap to get to the other seat. The kids seem to be dipping from a bottomless reservoir of energy, and continue to pester Quentin the entire flight. By the time the Boeing 777 lands at Heathrow Airport, he's wishing he never left Taos.

The layover in London is three hours. Libby leisurely makes her way to the Qatar Airlines departure gate for Doha, stopping only for a bottled water en route. It's her first time at Heathrow Airport, and she's fascinated by the people and their wide variety of attire. They represent cultures, religions and political factions from every region of the world. Reaching the gate, she settles into a chair and checks her email using her iPad while she waits for boarding to begin. She's not surprised to find nothing in her inbox, since it's only four a.m. in Taos. Besides, no news is good news when she's halfway around the world and unable to do anything other than fret over any dilemma back home.

Quentin is having trouble keeping his eyes open, but he doesn't dare sit down and try to rest, for fear of dozing off and missing the boarding call. He spends the first hour between flights attempting to bum change from people, but finally gives up because he can't find anyone who speaks English.

"You wouldn't think it'd be that hard to find an English-speaking person in England," he mumbles to himself.

Arriving at the departure gate a few minutes before boarding begins, he sees immediately that he won't have to worry about Libby spotting him among the crowd of people waiting. A glance out the window at the plane explains it. It's an Airbus A380, one of those double-decker things that carries about a thousand people, must weigh a million tons when fully loaded, and defies all laws of gravity.

When they call the business class passengers, he catches a glimpse of Libby as she enters the jet bridge. The economy class passengers enter the plane through a different door than the business and first class passengers. It's then he realizes he'll be on the lower deck while Libby is on the deck above, and there's no chance she'll spot him before they reach Doha. He's relieved to know he can relax, and maybe get some sleep before the final leg of the trip.

The long line of people moves at a crawl down the aisle of the main deck. It's thirty minutes from when Quentin steps onto the Airbus until it's ready for takeoff. He has a window seat in row seventy-seven. It's luxurious compared to the previous flight—slightly roomier with his own personal entertainment system and no noisy kids next to him. An hour into the flight he's had a snack, a soda and he's snoozing comfortably.

On the deck above him, Libby has found her way to the cocktail lounge along with what appears to be half the others from business class. It has the ambience of a sports bar with a ten-to-one ratio of men to women. A few people are lined up in front of the bartender, waiting to select from an array of liquors, champagnes, beer and wine. Most seats are occupied, so several are standing holding their drink, while conversing with a fellow passenger. As the bartender is pouring Libby a glass of champagne, she sees a woman get up to leave. The man sitting next to her looks at Libby and gestures to the vacated seat beside him.

She hesitates, remembering something her mother once said about talking to strange men in bars—or was it laundromats—probably both knowing Diane. She takes a moment to size him up—Middle Eastern, judging from his skin tone and features, wearing Italian-looking slacks and shirt, with the top button undone and the sleeves rolled up to expose the gold chain around his neck, and expensive watch on his wrist.

"Thank you," she says, seating herself next to the man.

"I'm Mahdi. Is this your first time on an Airbus A380?"

"I'm Doctor Liberty Corcoran. And yes, this is the first time I've flown on a jet this size."

"You're a doctor?"

He looks her up and down from head to toe. She's wearing khaki pants, flats and a cardigan sweater buttoned to the neck.

"You don't look like a doctor."

"A doctor of botany." He seems confused by that, so Libby explains further, "Plants are my only patients."

"Ah, I see. Trees and flowers."

He sounds condescending and Libby understands why the woman who'd been sitting there had left her seat so abruptly. She sips from her champagne glass and tries to ignore him, but he's not easily dissuaded.

"Where are you from? You look Mediterranean, maybe Italian or Spanish, but the accent's different."

She lets out a long, deliberate sigh, which can't be interpreted as anything other than disinterest. She might as well have thrown a stick and yelled, "Fetch!" It requires all his willpower to keep from panting.

"I'm from the United States," she says, after a beat.

"An American! I've been there many times on business—New York, Miami, Houston—all over."

"What is it you do?"

"I'm in the oil business. I buy and sell equipment to oil refineries. My company sends me to many different countries, and whenever possible I fly on an Airbus like this one."

"Sort of an office in the sky for you."

"Exactly, I can arrange meetings, message my company and place orders, all from the comfort of my business class seat. And, when I'm not working I can come to the lounge and have a drink. What a life, eh?"

"It wouldn't be my choice of lifestyles, but to each his own, I guess."

As a child she spent more time living out of a suitcase than she cares to remember, due to her mother's predilection for moving from their rented apartment in the middle of the night without giving notice to the landlord.

The idea of a mobile office, even on a luxury airliner, holds no appeal for her.

"Do you have a family?"

From his smug expression she can see he mistakenly thinks her curiosity is more about him than his family.

He leans closer and says confidentially, "I always travel alone."

It's at that very moment the captain announces they are entering turbulent airspace. She doesn't know whether to be relieved to have an excuse to return to her seat or feel trepidation for the bumpy ride ahead.

"I'm going back to my seat," she tells Mahdi. "It was nice meeting you."

"There's no need to leave. This bench has seat belts. Here, I'll help you," Mahdi offers, but Libby is already standing and moving away before he can buckle her in.

# ~8~

It's a little after midnight local time when Libby steps off the Airbus A380 into the arrival terminal in Doha, Qatar. It seems deserted in comparison to the airports in Dallas and London, there's not the typical throng of people hustling between planes, and most of the shops and eateries are closed. The layover is only a couple of hours, so she goes straight to the departure gate for the final leg of the trip to wait.

Quentin deplanes twenty minutes later knowing Libby has a head start on him, and he probably won't see her again until the next plane begins boarding. What then? So far, he's been lucky, she has no inkling he's here in Doha and about to fly with her to Mahé. He spends the layover trying to come up with a plan, a way to defuse Libby's anger, something to tell her which sounds so logical she can't help but shrug and say, "Oh well, what's done is done," and that will be that.

As boarding for business class begins, he's crouched behind a trash container watching as Libby goes through the jet bridge. Then he realizes, regardless of what the email said, he won't be sitting next to her on the flight. There's still a chance he could sneak past her unnoticed. The next thing he realizes is there are only about a fourth as many people on this flight as the one before. He picks a spot in line behind a young couple who are walking onto the aircraft hand in hand, like newlyweds. Libby is sitting in the second row as he enters. She locks eyes on him before he can duck behind the couple, and comes out of her seat so quickly she smacks her head against the carry-on storage.

"Quentin! What the hell are you doing here?"

At the sound of her shouting, the flight crew as well as most passengers are on full alert. A flight attendant steps between them.

"Please sit back down," she says to Libby.

"He's not supposed to be on this plane!"

"You'll have to calm down and take your seat, or leave the plane," the flight attendant warns.

"Libby, I can explain," Quentin starts.

The flight attendant repeats her warning to him.

"Right now, you'll have to go to your seat or leave the plane. We are preparing for departure in three minutes."

They separate and take their respective seats before things escalate further. An hour after takeoff, Libby composes herself and finds Quentin sitting next to a window in a row of three seats. She beckons him to her with one finger and walks to the rear of the plane. He slides past his seatmates and follows.

"Alright," she says, in an eerily calm voice, "explain yourself. What are you doing here?"

"I came to help you."

"I told you I didn't need or want your help. I also told you I couldn't afford to bring you along. The airfare is three thousand dollars. Where did you get the money?"

"The botany people were willing to pay the cost of airfare and a room for your assistant, so I figured as long as it didn't cost you anything, why not come along and help."

"You're not telling me everything. The Global Federation of Botanists doesn't know who you are. Are you trying to tell me they contacted you and offered to pay your expenses to be my assistant?"

"Not exactly. I contacted them and offered my services on your behalf. They said okay, and here I am."

"I still don't feel like I'm getting the whole story, here."

"Look Libby, I know you've been looking forward to this trip, and I promise I won't do anything to spoil it for you. I'll stay out of your way and won't interfere with your plans. You won't hear, see or even sense my presence. Okay?"

She thinks about it for a minute, then says, "No."

"Ah Libby, please."

"No," she repeats. "You're not going to lounge around on the beach while I work. Not after lying to the GFB about being my assistant." She leans in close to be sure he hears every word without raising her voice. "From now until we get back to Albuquerque, you're on call twenty-four seven. Whenever and whatever I need done, you'll do it with no questions asked, whether it's carrying my purse or fetching me a cup of coffee. Am I making myself perfectly clear?"

"Yeah, I guess so," he replies.

"No, not yeah, I guess so. When I give you a command, you say, yes ma'am, nothing more."

"Got it," he says. She glares at him sternly until he says, "I mean, yes ma'am."

"That's better. Keep saying it over and over in your head, until it becomes second nature. Now, go back to your seat and behave yourself. After we land, go directly to baggage claim, so you can handle my luggage."

"Yes, ma'am," he replies, before returning to his seat.

The flight attendant who had stopped the argument earlier sees Libby return to her seat and asks, "Is everything alright?"

"Yes," Libby replies. "I'm sorry I got upset before, but everything is fine, now."

"Good, I'm glad to hear it. Can I get you a glass of champagne?"

"Thank you. That sounds wonderful."

The rest of the flight goes smoothly. She has a second glass of champagne and a meal of almond-encrusted cod with a vegetable medley, and then sleeps for two hours. When the pilot announces they will be landing in ten minutes, she brings her seatback into the upright position to take in the view out the window as the aircraft approaches the landing strip.

The Seychelles Archipelago consists of one hundred fifteen islands, most of which are uninhabited. Mahé is the largest and most populated of them all. As the Airbus A319 drops lower she can see the nearby islands, coral reefs, white sand beaches, clear blue water, and mountains covered with tropical vegetation. *It's absolutely gorgeous*, she thinks.

The passengers deplane down steps onto the tarmac. Libby goes directly to the baggage claim area, not waiting for Quentin. He gets there a few minutes later as the first luggage is coming off the plane. He's smiling broadly.

"This place is really something. Did you see all the people partying on the beach?"

An airport baggage handler approaches, but Libby waves him off.

"Thanks, but my boy will carry my luggage." She points to two big suitcases. "Those two are mine, grab them and we'll find the shuttle going to my hotel."

"Our hotel," Quentin corrects her. "The botany people booked me into the same place."

She scrunches her face in disgust.

"You're kidding, right?"

"Sorry."

"Not as sorry as I am. Oh well, let's find the shuttle. I'll worry about the rest once we get to the hotel."

At the curb in front of the airport Libby spots a shuttle van with the name of the hotel on its side.

"That's it. The Constance Ephelia. Hurry up."

She starts toward it leaving him struggling with the bags.

"I'm Doctor Liberty Corcoran, I'm staying at the Constance," she tells the shuttle driver.

He glances at a list of names on a page.

"Yes, ma'am. Three others on this plane are staying there. It shouldn't be long before we leave. And, you sir?"

Libby speaks up. "He's my assistant, Quentin Maddox."

The driver glances again at the list.

"Yes, I see him here. I didn't realize you were together."

"We're not together," Libby corrects. "Not by any stretch of the imagination. He works for me."

She looks pointedly at Quentin before adding, "For now."

# ~9~

Their rooms aren't ready when the shuttle van delivers them to the hotel, so they spend a couple of hours sitting by the pool enjoying food and drinks compliments of the management. The entire time, Quentin eyes the white sand beach and clear blue water, only a stone's throw away from where they sit.

"Wouldn't you rather be on the beach, checking out the guys and dipping your feet in the ocean, instead of sitting by the pool?" he asks Libby.

"Actually I would, but I'm not going to do that until my room is ready, and I can unpack my swimsuit, sunscreen lotion and a paperback."

"Well, since you don't need me for the moment, I'm going to go take a closer look."

He stands up.

"Sit down. You don't go anywhere without my permission, and I haven't given it."

"Come on, Libby. How long are you going to stay mad at me? I said I was sorry, what more do you want?"

"What I want is for you to not be here in Mahé, and it's already too late to change that. As to how long I'll remain mad at you—maybe forever."

"You're overreacting, it's no big deal. My being here isn't costing you a penny. If I'd been able to sneak onto the last flight without you seeing me, you wouldn't even know I was here, and we wouldn't be having this conversation."

"And that would make everything A-OK because no one's the wiser to your thievery? Do you have a conscience, and even if you don't, have you considered the possible blowback from what you've done?"

"You know, I used to think you were a really nice person, but I can see now that I was wrong about that. You can be a real bitch when you want to be."

Quentin knows he's made a mistake the second the "B" word leaves his lips, but it's too late to retract it, and besides, it's about time somebody put Libby in her place. Their voices rise incrementally with each exchange until the people nearby are watching them nervously. Libby notices. She smiles and chuckles as if what is transpiring between Quentin and her is nothing more than playful bantering. She lowers her voice to just above a whisper.

"Perhaps, you're right, maybe I am making too much out of this. Maybe it's unrealistic of me to expect someone like yourself to possess, or even understand qualities such as honesty, loyalty or gratitude. So, you go ahead, Quentin. Go frolic on the beach, enjoy yourself, have a great time at someone else's expense and don't give it another thought."

Her words don't seem to elicit any feelings of guilt from Quentin. He rises to leave.

"Alright, I guess I'll see you around."

Then he walks past the pool, down the steps to the beach and disappears from sight.

"Good riddance," Libby mutters.

"Doctor Corcoran," says a hotel staff person, as she approaches Libby. "Your room is ready. If you'll come with me, I'll take you there."

She leads Libby a short distance to a hillside villa overlooking the beach, and along the way explains the services and amenities offered by the resort. Massage and facial treatments at the spa. Twenty-four-hour room service. Free Wi-Fi connection. Shuttles to shopping centers and the ferry dock. Casual and formal dining within the hotel. Everything she would need to make her stay on Mahé a truly five-star experience.

"I am Lani. If you need anything, anything at all, the entire hotel staff is at your service," she tells Libby, before leaving.

Libby takes a tour of the villa where she'll be living for the next four days. It has a lanai sitting area with table and chairs. A bathroom with a clawfoot tub and vessel sink. A king-size poster bed. It's bathed in natural light, and she absolutely loves it. She unpacks her suitcases, hangs the evening dresses, puts her shorts, shirts and undergarments in drawers, and gets into her swimsuit. A glance in the mirror makes her grimace. Her body is in good shape and the bikini fits well, but her skin is white enough to blind pilots of low-flying aircraft. Thirty minutes in the sun would give it some much needed color, she decides.

Fifteen minutes later, she's lying on a towel draped over a wooden chaise lounge, on the private beach adjacent to the hotel with SPF 30 sunscreen lotion slathered all over her body. She's brought along her iPad, cell phone and a paperback romance novel, but she's already chiding herself for it. Everywhere she looks people are laughing and having fun without any thoughts of checking for emails or phone calls from home or work. Instead they're snorkeling, kayaking, paragliding and windsurfing. Dozens of people, mostly young couples are simply enjoying themselves and living in the moment. She exhales a long sigh.

"That's it" she says aloud. "I'm not spending another minute in this tropical paradise thinking about anything that has any connection with business."

She covers the iPad, cell phone and paperback with a towel, and sets off to explore what the resort has to offer. A short distance away, a dark-skinned young man wearing only swim trunks, sunglasses and a broad smile sits in a beach chair under an umbrella. He's surrounded by a variety of water sports equipment available for rent. She takes a minute to look over the windsurfing boards, kayaks and pedal boats.

"Hello, m'lady. I'm Shawn. What would ya like ta do? How abouda pedal boat?"

"I don't think so."

They look like they're designed for kids, and not for someone with long legs like hers.

"Have ya ever snorkeled?" She scrunches her face slightly and shakes her head to show she's not interested, but Shawn persists. "Snorkeling in Mahé is like nowhere else in the world. There's much ta see, and the water is crystal clear."

"I'm not an experienced swimmer. How deep is the water here?"

"Not deep. Ya can go out fifty meters and it's not much over ya head. Ya really don't have ta swim. Ya just float on the surface and kick ya feet ta move forward."

Libby looks out over the water to where she gauges fifty meters to be. Several others are in the water, even beyond that. It doesn't seem so far, and the ocean is inviting.

"Okay," Libby says, feeling excited and a bit nervous at the same time.

Shawn gives her a full face snorkel fitted with a valve, a pair of swim fins and instruction on how to use them. She follows his instructions, floating parallel to the shoreline in waist-high water until she feels confident enough to venture out where it's deeper. The farther out she goes the more interesting the underwater sights become. There are fish of every shape and color, sea turtles, coral reefs and an eel with spots like a leopard. She's so fascinated by it all she loses track of how long she's been in the water, other people nearby and the distance from the shore.

From the beach, Quentin has been watching her. He's an avid surfer and a strong swimmer. He worked as a lifeguard in Malibu for a couple of summers, and during that time developed a feel for which people to keep an eye on. At the moment, he's sensing that Libby is out of her element. She's been slowly moving farther from shore and separating herself from other snorkelers.

"Okay if I take one of these two-person kayaks?" he asks Shawn.

"Sure mon. Take ya pick."

He selects one, puts it in the water and starts paddling out. Meanwhile, Libby is getting the hang of holding her breath to stay under longer. It gives her a chance to get a closer look at the coral and seagrasses along the ocean floor. She's been underwater for forty seconds and is about to surface when a large ray comes out of the darkness, and glides past within two feet of her.

Startled by it, she screams into her mask, expelling the air from her lungs, then sucks in the carbon dioxide she's just exhaled, along with a small amount of salt water that had collected in her mask. In a panic she kicks for the surface, pulling her mask off as she does. She tries to take a breath before her head is fully out of the water and gets more salt water in her mouth.

She's coughing and flailing with the snorkel mask in one hand, trying to stay afloat and taking in more water each time she inhales. She feels herself growing weaker and starting to lose consciousness. The battle is being lost and she knows it. As her vision starts to blur and she nears the point of surrender, a hand reaches out to pluck her from the water. The next thing she remembers, is lying on her back on the beach with someone's mouth pressed against hers. *Gunter,* she thinks, *he saved me.*

She reaches to wrap her arms around him, but they're pushed away and his face pulls back. *It's not Gunter, it's..., it's..., Quentin!?* She starts to scream, but gags and retches, instead. He grabs her by the arm and rolls her over as she heaves up the salt water she's swallowed.

"You're going to be okay. Just let it all out," Quentin tells her, while he pats her back.

Then, she hears people cheering and applauding. Apparently, a crowd has gathered to watch him carry her onto the beach and revive her. And with mouth to mouth resuscitation, no less.

"You're lucky I came along when I did, Libby."

"Funny, I don't feel so lucky, right now," she manages to reply.

"You'll feel better, soon. You just need a few minutes to catch your breath. Here, I'll get you out of the sun." He prepares to lift her into his arms, but she stops him.

"That's alright, I can walk. Help me to my feet." He pulls her to a standing position, and then brushes sand from her backside with his hand. "Stop doing that. I'll take it from here."

"You sure? You want me to get you anything before I go?"

"Mouthwash," she mutters, under her breath.

"What's that?"

"I said, no, I'm fine."

He turns to leave, then stops to say, "You know, most people would be thankful for having their life saved."

"Yes, most people probably would."

# ~10~

Libby isn't accustomed to staying at five-star resort hotels, not that she can't easily afford to, it's just that it goes against her upbringing. Diane, her hippie wannabe mother, would see it as a pompous extravagance which only the most arrogant of people indulge in. But Diane isn't here. Libby is, and Libby plans to take full advantage of the services offered.

After the snorkeling mishap and a little too much time in the sun, she arranges for a spa esthetician to come to her villa, thinking a skin treatment and massage will help. A knock sounds on the door, followed by a woman's voice.

"Doctor Corcoran, I am Riya from spa services."

"Yes, please come in."

Riya sets up a deluxe massage table, and has Libby undress and lie down.

"You have a slight sunburn." Riya states, pressing her fingers lightly on Libby's back. "This is not too bad. A massage might irritate it, though. I would recommend a body scrub where we exfoliate the skin with pearl powder and caviar honey. Then we will rehydrate and oxygenate to leave your skin feeling soft as a baby's behind."

As she's applying the lotion, the phone rings. "I'll get that for you," Riya says to Libby. "Miss Corcoran's villa," she answers, then listens, and after a moment says, "who should I say is calling?" She covers the mouthpiece before telling Libby, "He says his name is Gunter Schneider. Would you like to speak to him?"

"Yes, I'll talk to him." She eagerly snatches the phone from Riya. "Hi, Gunter. Welcome to Mahé. Did you just get in?"

"I arrived two hours ago. Have you enjoyed zee first day here?"

"How could anyone not love it here? White sand beaches, clear blue ocean, lush tropical landscape, everything is so beautiful."

"Yes it is. I'm looking forward to the next few days."

"You and me, both."

"Would you like to have dinner with me zis evening? I can come to your hotel."

"Crap," Libby mutters.

"What is zat?"

"I can't tonight, Gunter." It isn't that she doesn't want to see him, just not after such a stressful day. "I'm so exhausted from the long flight, I don't think I could keep my eyes open during dinner. How about tomorrow night?"

"Of course, Libby. I will see you, zen."

"So," Riya says, after the call. "We have to get you feeling better, so you can spend time with this special man. Don't worry. After your treatment and a night of rest, you'll feel brand new."

~~~

Thanks to the spa therapy, Libby sleeps soundly and wakes feeling rejuvenated. Her eyes have barely opened when a knock sounds.

"Yes."

"Libby, it's me, Quentin. I just came to check on you."

"Just a minute." She wraps a kimono around her, then opens the door. Quentin is dressed in the same shorts he was wearing the day before and a Black Sabbath T-shirt. In each hand he holds a mug of steaming coffee. She feels a pang of guilt over the way she treated him the previous day.

"I didn't wake you did I?"

"No, I was up. Come in."

"You want some coffee?"

"Yes, thanks. Where'd you get it?"

"At the restaurant, here. Did you know they've got five places to eat in this hotel?"

"Yes, I read it somewhere."

They sit on the lanai to drink the coffee. The sun rose over the horizon thirty minutes before and the temperature is in the mid-seventies.

"It's good of you to stop by and check on me. I was rude to you yesterday, especially after you rescued me."

"Don't worry about it. I know you're still upset with me because I sort of conned the botany people into paying for my airfare and room."

"Well, as it turns out, it's fortunate for me that you did, so I'm willing to forgive you if you'll forgive me."

"Consider it done."

"I guess I won't try snorkeling again, or any other water sports, for that matter."

"There's a lot to do out of the water."

"Yes, I'm sure I'll find ways to occupy my time."

"What about the guy you're supposed to have dinner with, is that still on?"

"What guy?"

"The guy you were so excited about talking to on the phone, last week."

She forgot about Quentin eavesdropping on her when Gunter called from Austria.

"Oh, him," she says, as if Gunter is nothing special. "I spoke with him last night. We might have dinner together later, if I'm feeling up to it."

"If you want my advice…," Quentin begins.

"I don't, thank you just the same," Libby interjects.

He continues anyway.

"Playing hard to get doesn't always work well. There are plenty of hot women on the island who are looking to party. I met three chicks in the short period I spent on the beach, yesterday, and they were all ready, willing and able, if you know what I mean."

"Did you not hear me say I don't want your advice? And that goes double when it comes to dating, romance and matters of the heart."

"I'm just trying to help."

"That kind of help, I don't need. However, there is a way you could be of assistance to me. I have to give a presentation to the GFB today at two, and then again tomorrow morning at ten. I could use your help carrying my satchel and passing out leaflets. Could you do that for me?"

"Sure, count on me. Where do you want me to be, and when?"

"Meet me here at eleven. That should give us plenty of time to prepare."

~~~

The location where Libby is giving her presentation to the assembled members of the Global Federation of Botanists is Mission Lodge in Morne Seychellois National Park. It's the site of an old mission school which overlooks the ocean, more than two thousand feet above sea level. There's nothing there but the ruins of the original buildings, a small pavilion to provide shelter for tourists during a storm, and a large variety of trees and tropical vegetation, an idyllic gathering place for a group of botanists.

Libby and Quentin board a shuttle bus along with several GFB members to make the twenty-minute ride from the hotel up the narrow and winding San Soucis Road. Because of the outdoor venue and rugged terrain, Libby dresses comfortably in shorts, a white short-sleeve top and sneakers. When they reach their destination she's greeted by a stout middle-aged woman wearing a bright yellow pantsuit with big pink and green flowers imprinted on it.

"Hello Doctor Corcoran. I'm Dolores Preston with the Global Federation of Botanists. It's an honor to have you here and a pleasure to meet you."

"Please, call me Libby. I'm delighted to be here. But then, who wouldn't be. The island is beautiful and Mission Lodge seems like the perfect location for my presentation."

"Let me show you where you'll be speaking," Dolores says, gesturing for Libby to follow her. "Over here is a sloped clearing shaped like a natural amphitheater. Since we're without electricity, I thought it would work well."

"This will be fine. I'll set up at the bottom of the hill where the ground levels out."

"We have folding tables and chairs stacked over there, if you need them. It's thirty minutes until you're scheduled to begin, just let me know if you need anything else."

"Take two tables and two chairs down there," Libby says to Quentin. He follows her instructions without hesitating or questioning, like an obedient servant.

"There's a cooler of bottled water by the stack of tables. I'll grab one for you, in case your throat gets dry in the middle of your presentation."

"Good thinking, Quentin. I've been going over my notes, preoccupied with the speech and forgot all about that."

Libby scans the faces of the people gathering around, expecting to see Gunter Schneider among them. It's been two years since they've seen one another, and a person's appearance can change significantly in that period. Naturally, he'll be curious to see what she looks like now, and she feels the same about him.

"Hello, Libby."

She freezes at the sound of his voice behind her.

"Gunter, how nice to see you."

"Are you feeling better, today?"

"Actually, I am. As a matter of fact, I'm feeling up to dinner tonight. After lying in bed for most of the afternoon yesterday and all last night, I'd love a night out."

"Wonderful. I will meet you in zee lobby of your hotel at seven thirty, if zat is okay."

"That's perfect."

"Well, I should go and let you get ready for your program. I'll see you tonight."

She watches him walk away until he disappears in the crowd, and then turns her attention to the opening lines of her presentation. Quentin returns with a bottled water and sets it on the table near where Libby will stand to address the audience.

"Is that guy you were talking to the one you've got a date with?"

"That's the guy."

"He's sort of dorky-looking, don't you think?"

"No, I don't. As a matter of fact, I think he's anything but dorky-looking. You're just saying that to get under my skin."

"Yeah, you're right, I am. Actually, he's not so bad-looking, if you're into guys with a lot of hair, big teeth and no tats."

"It so happens that is the sort of guy I'm into, but this is not something I want to discuss with you. You wouldn't understand and besides, we need to begin the presentation."

# ~11~

Dolores gets the botany group's attention with a whistle, and then introduces Libby.

"Good afternoon, everyone. We're very fortunate to have as our guest speaker a woman who is the author of several articles published in the Journal of Botany, a frequent guest on television and radio shows, and a recognized expert in the field of plant breeding and genetics. Please welcome Doctor Liberty Belle Corcoran."

"Thank you," Libby says, as the smattering of applause fades. "Only a few short years ago, career opportunities for college graduates with a degree in botany were relatively few. With the growing global population, comes increased industrial production and development. Never before has there been a bigger need to understand the living relationship between plants and people. There are plants that feed us, plants that heal us, plants that improve our environment and plants that provide us with shelter. As botanists, we are in entrusted with protecting this invaluable resource, while maximizing the benefits."

Libby reads from a page, occasionally looking up to make eye contact with someone in the audience, only to find each time she has their interest, which pleases her. As much money as the GFB has spent to have her appear, she hopes they feel she's worth it. The next time she looks up from her page, she sees Gunter. She pauses, loses her place and it takes a second to restart. Gunter is standing next to a woman—a young and very attractive Scandinavian-looking woman. He's standing right next to her, too close, Libby feels. She shakes the thought from her mind and concentrates on her presentation. It lasts for another hour and as she's wrapping up, she sees Gunter and his lady friend have left.

"I saw that guy you like walking that way with a girl," Quentin says, after Libby finishes.

"Probably a colleague of his."

"Yeah, probably," Quentin says, without much conviction. "Still, she's pretty hot. You want me to go spy on them? They might be off in the forest getting it on, right now."

"I seriously doubt that. Gunter is not that sort of man."

"Libby, every guy is that sort of man. Did you see her hooters?"

"As usual, you don't know what you're talking about. Do me a favor and go see when the bus is leaving. I'm anxious to go back to the hotel."

"I asked the driver earlier. He said around four, another twenty minutes." Then, in a whisper, he says, "There are a couple of old guys looking at you and heading this way."

She turns to see two men, possibly in their seventies, short in height and slight in build, using walking canes to slowly make their way toward her.

"Doctor Corcoran," one of them says when he's close enough to be heard. We want to tell you how much we enjoyed your presentation. I am Winston Cheung of Hong Kong, and this is my brother Edgar."

Their facial features, speech and mannerisms hint at a mix of Asian and European parentage. Winston she guesses to be the older of the two. His countenance is serene. There's little movement of his eyes or hands as he speaks. Edgar's demeanor is quite the opposite. His eyes dance behind thick spectacles, his head bobs continually, and he gestures nervously as he speaks.

"What you said about the number of known phytochemicals there are, and how many undiscovered ones might still be out there somewhere, I found that fascinating."

"Yes, fascinating," Winston agrees. "To think there are plants that can be used to treat or cure ailments such as AIDS, cancer or leukemia, and all we need to do is find them."

"Are you biochemists?" Libby asks.

"Until I retired five years ago, I taught botany at the university level," Edgar says.

"And I am primarily an herbalist," Winston says. "Plants and their uses have been a lifelong passion for both of us, as it was for our parents before they died."

"As a teacher, the depth of your family's knowledge must have been an invaluable resource for you," she says to Edgar.

"Yes, indeed it was."

Most other times she would be happy, even eager to talk shop with Edgar and Winston. They probably have hundreds of interesting stories to recount, but the midafternoon heat is causing discomfort and she's still a little jet-lagged, so she excuses herself.

"It was nice meeting both of you. Our bus is taking us back to the hotel in a minute, but maybe we'll speak again before the end of the symposium."

Winston's disappointment is evident as he says, "Yes, we would enjoy that."

On the ride back to the hotel Quentin asks, "Do you need me to do anything for you, tonight? If you do I can stick around."

"I'll be fine, but thanks anyway. Are you going somewhere? Not that it's any of my business, I'm just curious."

"A girl I met yesterday told me about a beach party that's supposed to be happening tonight. I thought I'd go check it out."

"Oh, I see."

"You don't mind, do you?"

"No, but stay out of trouble. You're in a foreign country and unfamiliar with their laws."

"You sound like my mother."

"Well, you are my responsibility to some extent. You're masquerading as an employee of mine, so whatever you do reflects on me and my business."

"Don't worry, I'll behave."

~~~

Early that evening in her villa, Libby takes a bath, applies lotion to her skin, French braids her hair, dabs perfume on her neck, between her breasts and on her upper thighs. She slips into her new sexy lingerie and evening dress, then admires herself in the mirror. Imitating Gunter, she says to her image, "Libby, you look vonderful."

It's a few minutes after seven and she's a little anxious over the date with Gunter. She considers going to the hotel bar for a drink to settle her nerves, but decides against it. Instead, she steps out onto the lanai to calm herself with the sound of the sea and aroma of tropical flowers. There's a light breeze and soft music playing somewhere in the distance. Footfalls, accompanied by the click-clack sound of walking canes on the pathway in front of the villa draw her attention to two men coming her way.

"Doctor Corcoran," Winston Cheung says. "We are sorry to disturb you."

"What are you doing here?" she asks, unable to hide her trepidation over their sudden appearance. The hillside around her is covered with trees and shrubbery. The setting sun coming through them cast shadows on the villa. It's an intimate setting, but at the moment it seems too secluded and she feels vulnerable.

"Please do not be alarmed. We mean you no harm," Edgar says. "We have something important to discuss with you. Something I am sure will interest you. We could not tell you earlier today because we did not want to be overheard. I think you will understand the need for secrecy once we have explained."

"How did you know where I was staying and which room I was in?"

"We learned that the tour bus brought you here, so we walked around the hotel hoping to bump into you, and that is when we spotted you here," Winston tells her. Edgar is bobbing his head up and down as his brother speaks, as if to corroborate his story.

Libby considers running inside and locking the door, then calling for hotel security.

Winston tries to allay her fears. "If we could have a few minutes of your time, we would like to tell you about a discovery I made thirty years ago. A discovery that potentially could change our lives, and yours as well."

Libby is curious, but the alarm bells are still sounding in her head. "I've made plans for this evening, I was just about to leave."

"You see, Winston. I told you Doctor Corcoran would most likely be too busy to see us. We have wasted our time and hers," Edgar chides his brother. Then, to Libby he says, "We are sorry to have bothered you. Please, forgive us."

Winston isn't willing to stop there. "Perhaps, we can arrange a time to meet with you tomorrow."

"I have a presentation at ten tomorrow morning. I'm not sure of my plans after that."

"Edgar and I are planning to attend your presentation. Afterward, we will adjust our schedule to accommodate yours in order to speak with you. You can let us know what you decide after your presentation, tomorrow."

They leave as quietly and inconspicuously as they came, melding into the landscape. Libby is so preoccupied by the conversation with the Cheung brothers, she doesn't arrive at the hotel lobby until seven forty-five.

"I'm sorry I'm late," she tells Gunter.

He kisses her cheek, and then while holding her at arm's length, looks her over from top to bottom.

"It was worth zee wait."

# ~12~

Success has not come easily for Libby. Her impressive botanical research business is the product of hard work, discipline and sacrifice. She wasn't born into a family with money, influence and connections. She didn't win the lottery, inherit a million bucks from a rich uncle or marry the son of a Fortune 500 CEO. Instead, she's devoted herself to her career and her studies, completely disregarding her need and desire for social interaction—especially the sort she's indulging in tonight. That's why she wants to put her career completely out of her mind, and drink in every moment of this special evening.

"Zee food here is excellent I think, considering where we are—a small remote island," Gunter says.

Every comment he makes is designed to impress Libby and it's working. She's hanging on his every word.

"Yes, it's delicious," she replies. "And, the wine you selected will go perfectly with the lobster."

He spent twenty minutes going through the process of choosing a vintage, examining the cork, swishing the amber liquid around in his mouth, rejecting the first two bottles and settling on the third. He insists on removing the lobster from its shell himself.

"It is a necessary part of zee whole experience."

After the waiter brings the lobster to the table, along with two bibs and the tools to crack the shell, Gunter says to Libby, "Let me help you with zat."

He rises from his seat, steps behind her and fastens the bib straps while she holds her hair away from her neck. His fingers brush lightly across her bare shoulders as his hands come away, giving her goose bumps and a tingle of excitement. They finish the lobster and wine, then order chocolate mousse and a double expresso for dessert. All the while Gunter is lavishing praise on Libby—her work, her fine mind, her lovely evening dress and beautiful hair. She's buzzing from the wine, caffeine and chocolate, and completely under the spell of this beguiling Austrian.

The bill arrives and Libby sneaks a peek at the amount—five hundred dollars and change. She offers to split it, but he insists on paying. Now, there's an implicit obligation to spread her legs to repay his kindness—not that she wouldn't love to do just that—but something her mother once told her is echoing in the hollows of her mind.

*"Never give in too quickly. It sets a precedent, and from then on, the man will always want it quick and easy. They'll take pleasure for themselves and give nothing in return."*

It's one of the few things her mother ever said she feels is true.

"Why don't we go to your room and have a nightcap," Gunter suggests.

"I'm not ready to go to my room, yet. I'm feeling a little wired. Let's go for a walk on the beach."

"Zat's a wonderful idea. I will get two cognacs to take with us."

"While you do that, I'm going to step into the ladies room."

At the sink in the restroom, Libby checks herself in the mirror. She feels the anxiety building, her face is flush and sweat is beading on her forehead. She dabs at the moisture with a tissue while taking several deep breaths to slow her heart rate. It's always this way. The closer she gets to a man, the more hindered she becomes by feelings of inadequacy.

Gunter smiles as she approaches. He's holding two plastic cups. "I would prefer to drink cognac from a glass, but zee plastic is better should we drop it on zee beach."

He hands one of the cups to Libby, then places his free hand on the small of her back and guides her through the restaurant, down the steps to the beach below. Sandwiched between tropical foliage and water, lit only by the stars and moon, it's an incredibly private and intimate setting. There's not another person in sight and no sound other than the waves lapping the shoreline. The beach is pockmarked by boulders, some as big as a Volkswagen. Libby stops to lean over a waist-high chunk of rock, sip cognac and gaze out at the ocean.

"It's so beautiful."

"Yes, you are," Gunter replies, and wraps his arms around her waist from behind. His touch causes her to shiver. "Are you cold?"

"A little," she confides, "but your hands are warm."

He moves them slowly across her tummy and abdomen, stroking and caressing while kissing her neck and shoulders.               "Mm," she purrs.

He slides his hands up to her breasts, gently squeezing while nipping at her ear.

"Mm-hmm," she purrs, a little louder.

"Bend over and put your elbows on zee rock," he instructs.

53

"Why?" she asks, though she already knows what he has in mind.

"You will see."

He puts a hand on her back and gently coaxes her into position.

"Uh…, I'm not sure about this, Gunter. Maybe we should wait until we're in my villa."

"I don't think I can wait another minute, Libby."

He raises her dress and grabs her panties, intent on ripping them away.

"Wait. Those are brand new. Don't tear them."

"Okay, zen. I will take them off."

She doesn't resist. This isn't how she saw the evening going, but it is a beautiful setting. Despite her discomfort with the risk of someone walking by while they're doing it, this will be a moment to remember. She hears his trouser zipper sliding open and braces herself.

"Don't move, don't turn around and don't turn your head to look at me," comes a voice from somewhere behind them.

Libby flinches, but doesn't turn her head. She's more startled than scared. Still bent over with her elbows on the rock, she cautiously sneaks a look between her legs to see two pairs of legs beyond hers. One pair has trousers pulled down to the knees, the other pair belongs to the voice. A hand reaches into the pocket of Gunter's trousers and comes away with his wallet.

"Hey!" Libby shouts.

Gunter presses a firm hand to her back. "He has a gun."

"Give me the watch," the thief says to Gunter, who offers no resistance. The thief pockets it, and then says to Libby, "Now you. Your purse and watch."

She hesitates. The thief presses the gun harder against Gunter's back.

"Please, Libby. He will shoot us if we don't obey."

She hands over the purse and watch without altering her position, which by now is feeling very awkward.

"Now, lie down in the sand, right there."

The thief points the gun at a spot. Gunter complies, moving away from Libby and dropping down on his stomach. Libby starts to raise her head, but the thief stops her.

"No, you stay where you are. If either of you turns to look at me, I will shoot you."

Libby feels a hand roughly touch her ass, and then slide down and up the inside of her thigh. The thought of what he is about to do makes her nauseous.

"Please, don't," she begs.

"Shut up," the thief says, and jabs the gun in Libby's ribs.

The feel of the gun against her side is so overwhelming it overrides any thought of resistance. At that moment, she knows without a doubt, she'll do anything he asks in order to save her life. She tries not to think about the pain, trauma or disease that will follow, hoping only that it will be swift. For the second time in a matter of a few minutes, she hears a zipper being pulled open and knows the rape is about to begin.

For some unknown reason the thief appears to hesitate, maybe having second thoughts. Suddenly, the gun drops from his hand, striking the boulder beside Libby and falling to the ground. An instant later, the thief himself is on the ground along with it. She sees him lying on the beach next to the boulder, not moving, not even breathing as far as she can tell. She risks a glance behind her and sees a figure slink into the bushes. Gunter is still lying face down in the sand with his trousers down around his knees, unaware of what's happening.

"Gunter, get up. Something happened to him. He's just lying there, not moving."

Gunter cranes his neck to see that Libby is right, the thief is crumpled on the ground like someone threw his switch and he collapsed in a heap. He rises and pulls up his trousers. Libby shakes sand from her panties and redresses herself. They kneel beside the man, seeing his face for the first time. He's a dark-skinned man in his late teens or early twenties with short curly hair and stubble on his chin. Gunter places the back of his hand to the man's neck.

"I do not feel anything."

"I think I saw someone in the bushes right after he fell."

She doesn't say she's reasonably certain of who it was. The size, shape and slow deliberate movements were those of Winston Cheung, she's almost positive of it.

"Should we notify the police or EMS?"

"I think it is too late for zee EMS, and if we go to zee police, we might be detained for several weeks. We might have to get an attorney. There are no witnesses to what happened, except for zee person in zee bushes."

Libby looks to where she last saw the man she believes to be Winston Cheung. In the dim light he could be standing in the dense vegetation, and she wouldn't be able see him there. She wants to be certain there's nothing to be done for the thief before deciding to skulk away, as if they are the perpetrators and not the victims.

Careful to leave no fingerprints on the corpse, Gunter retrieves his wallet, her purse and the watches from the man's pocket.

"He doesn't seem to be breathing at all. I don't understand what happened to him." Then, she notices what appears to be a feather on the side of his neck. She points to it and asks Gunter, "What do you make of that?"

"I don't know, some kind of jewelry, maybe. We better leave here, now. Somebody might see us if we stay any longer."

"Alright," Libby reluctantly agrees.

She leans closer to have a final look, and that's when she understands that it's not a feather. It's the tail end of a small dart. *A poisonous dart?* It's one possible explanation.

# ~13~

After the incident on the beach, Gunter and Libby take a circuitous route back to her villa, avoiding the bar and restaurant area where they might be seen. He decides to stay there for the remainder of the night.

"If anyone asks," he says, meaning the police, "We will tell zem we came straight to zee room after dinner."

For her part, Libby isn't overly bothered by the incident. She's always possessed the ability to emotionally detach herself from a traumatic experience. It's a discipline developed during a childhood of acting as a counterbalance to her mother's capricious nature. Gunter, on the other hand, is visibly shaken. He doesn't understand how Libby can remain so calm.

"You don't appear to be zat bothered by it."

"I'll probably feel differently about it tomorrow. It happened so quickly, I'm still trying to process it. Let's try to sleep. I have a presentation to do tomorrow morning at ten."

Gunter leaves at first light and takes a taxi back to his hotel. Intending to rest for only a few minutes more, Libby falls back asleep and is still dozing when someone knocks on the door. She sits up in bed and calls out, "Who is it?"

"It's me, Quentin."

Feeling a tad hungover as she rises from bed, she puts on her kimono and goes to the door, not bothering to check the time. Quentin is dressed in the same clothes he was wearing the day before, and looking as if he slept in them. Libby takes notice of his empty hands.

"It's not a good idea to wake me if you're not bringing me coffee."

"You're just getting up? I thought you wanted to leave here at nine."

"I do. What time is it?"

"It's five minutes before nine, and I don't think you want to go looking like that."

"Oh, crap. I overslept. Come back in twenty minutes. I'll be ready, then."

They miss the shuttle bus, and have to grab a taxi. Both sit in the back seat. Quentin doesn't say anything, but he's smirking at her as if he's privy to a private joke. Libby does her best to ignore him, but it's really starting to bug her.

"What is it?" she snaps.

"Nice perfume—a little strong for my taste, but it smells great."

"I didn't have time to shower. If it bothers you, roll the window down. Or better still, keep away from me."

"I didn't say it bothered me. It's just not like you—sleeping in, smelling like a brothel. Does this mean what I think it does? Your date went well and you got…,"

"Don't go there, Quentin. I'm your boss, not your buddy. It's inappropriate for you to speak so informally to me."

"Well, whoop-de-do. Excuse me, boss." He feigns offense, crossing his arms and leaning as far away as the small car will allow for the rest of the ride.

*Let him pout,* she tells herself. With all that's happened she can't be concerned with his bruised feelings.

The presentation is being given in a conference room at the Four Seasons Resort, the same place where Gunter is staying. The group is smaller than the one she addressed the day before, no more than fifty people are in attendance. She scans the attendees for Gunter as she speaks. Winston and Edgar Cheung are sitting in the front row listening attentively, even though the presentation is the same as the day before. Each time she makes eye contact with Winston, she tries to discern from his manner if it was him who came to her aid, twelve hours earlier, but he's unreadable.

After the presentation, several people come up to the lectern to introduce themselves and have a few words with Libby. The Cheung brothers remain in their seats during this time. Winston waits calmly for the last person to leave. Edgar fidgets impatiently. When she's finally alone, they rise and amble over with the help of their walking canes.

"It's good to see you both, again," she tells them. She wants to know if it was Winston she saw last night, but is unsure of how to ask, so she takes an indirect approach. "I trust you had a pleasant evening after we parted yesterday?"

Edgar is equally vague as he answers, "Yes, we had a delicious dinner and quiet stroll on the beach, afterward." *Did he just implicate himself?*

Winston interrupts her thoughts saying, "As we mentioned before, we are very anxious to discuss an important matter with you. Perhaps, we could do so now."

Although the two men seem harmless on the surface, their cryptic behavior troubles Libby, but at the same time, if they are the ones who thwarted the robbery and rape, she's indebted to them.

"I had sort of a rough night, as you may realize." She pauses to read their reaction, but once again, there is none. "I was planning to go back to my room and rest this afternoon."

"Come now, Doctor Corcoran," Winston says. "Your time in Seychelles is limited, and there is much to see here. Especially for a botany professional like yourself."

Then, Edgar adds, "We have arranged for a local guide to give us a private tour. We would be honored to have you join us. As I am sure you are aware, there are several endemic plant species in Seychelles. It would be sad if someone like yourself who has devoted her life to the study of such plants was to miss an opportunity such as this."

She's aware of the impressive biodiversity the area offers, and had hoped to see a large portion of it on this trip."I was planning to do some botanical sightseeing while I'm here. It's generous of you to invite me along, and I accept your offer."

"Splendid!" Winston says. "We will pick you up at your hotel at two."

"Those are the same two who talked to you after the presentation, yesterday. What'd they want now?" Quentin asks, after they leave.

"There's something they want to discuss with me. They've invited me to take a tour of the island with them."

"Do you want me to come along, in case one of them tries something?"

"Good of you to offer, but I can take care of myself. In fact, this was the last presentation I have to give, which means my vacation has officially begun. I shouldn't need you again for the remainder of this trip, but if something comes up, I'll leave a message for you at the hotel."

"Cool! That gives me a day and a half to party with my amigos."

"Enjoy yourself, but stay out of trouble until we depart on Monday."

"You do the same, boss." Then, he wraps her in a hug, which takes Libby by surprise. "Thanks for not staying mad at me. You're being really cool about this whole thing."

"Alright, Quentin." She squirms out of his embrace. "I'm not comfortable with too much PDA. A handshake will suffice."

"It's your vacation, boss. You've got to loosen up and start living."

"I'll work on it. Now, go have fun and I'll see you later."

She watches him leave, then picks up a courtesy phone.

"Would you put me through to Mr. Gunter Schneider, please," she says to the operator. It rings four times before he picks up.

"Hello?"

"Hi, Gunter. It's me, Libby. I'm downstairs in the lobby. I just finished my presentation and thought you might like to join me for lunch."

There's a pause before he answers.

"I'm not feeling well. It must have been something I ate last night."

She waits a beat, hoping he'll suggest they get together later, but he doesn't.

"Well, some other time, then."

"Yes, some other time would be better."

Being dismissed so unceremoniously by Gunter stings more than she cares to admit.

"If you're feeling better later, call me," she says, but Gunter has already disconnected.

~~~

Back in her villa, Libby changes into shorts, a short-sleeve shirt and hiking shoes, before meeting the Cheung brothers. They're standing in the hotel portico leaning on their walking canes next to a car and driver. Libby gets in the back seat with Winston. Edgar sits beside the driver.

"This is Marc," Winston says, indicating the driver. "He will be showing us some of the interesting botanical treasures the island has to offer. Marc, please take us to see a jellyfish tree."

They leave the hotel heading northwest and go a few miles to where Marc pulls off the road. They follow him into the thick foliage, down a narrow trail until they come to the medusagyne tree. Sometimes it's referred to as a medusa tree, because its flower resembles the head of Medusa from Greek mythology, but more often it's called the jellyfish tree due to the jellyfish-like shape of the dehisced fruit. Winston nods to Marc, who then walks back to the car, leaving the three of them alone.

"We have a proposition to present to you," Winston says, after Marc is gone. "And a request to make as well. The request is that you not discuss what we tell you with anyone else, without our permission."

"Alright," Libby says. Winston and Edgar look at her expectantly, obviously wanting something more, so she adds, "You have my word."

"When I was a young man," Winston begins, "I traveled all over the world, from the jungles of Borneo, to the Sinharaja Forest in Sri Lanka, the Brazilian Amazon and many other fascinating places. I was a treasure hunter, but not the kind who looks for gold or precious gemstones. My quest was of a different sort."

Edgar cuts in to say, "Winston, this young lady does not want to listen to you ramble on about the past. Get to the point."

"I was about to, when you interrupted me. Now where was I?"

"I think you were going to tell me about a treasure you found," Libby says.

"Yes, that is exactly what I was going to tell you. It was on an excursion into West Papua, Indonesia when I came upon it. Are you familiar with West Papua?"

"No, I can't say that I am."

"It is the west side of the island of New Guinea. I won't bore you with a detailed history of the island, but people have inhabited New Guinea for fifty thousand years. The western half of the island, was incorporated into Indonesia in the 1960s, something the indigenous people of West Papua vehemently opposed.

"I went there in 1986 with a group of research scientists. Besides me, there was an entomologist, a herpetologist and a geologist. We obtained permits from the Indonesian government to study and collect samples in the mountainous central part of West Papua, an area which has not been widely explored, even today."

Winston pauses, momentarily lost in the memory of his experiences from thirty years before. Libby senses he's about to reveal something of great significance, so she waits patiently. Edgar clears his throat to bring Winston back to the present.

"Sorry," Winston says. "It was a huge success in that we photographed and identified more than fifty species of plants, reptiles and insects which were unknown of before then."

"And one of those is the treasure you want to tell me about?" Libby asks.

"No, not one of those," Edgar says. "Tell her about the berry, Winston."

"I am, Edgar. It is important that I explain the circumstances that put it in my possession. It is information she will need in order to evaluate the risk involved with the search."

"The search for what?" Libby inquires.

"For the plant the berry comes from," Edgar says.

# ~14~

Next, Marc takes them to the northern tip of the island to see another endangered species of plant growing on a rocky outcrop atop a hill overlooking the ocean. Libby is torn between the beautiful view and interesting pitcher plants. The Seychelles pitcher plant is a low-growing tubular-shaped plant with the unique ability to catch and digest insects and small reptiles.

Winston continues from where he left off earlier. His narration of the research expedition into West Papua in 1986 sounds like a National Geographic documentary. For six weeks the scientists and their guides trekked through jungles, forded rivers and climbed mountains, encountering every imaginable obstacle along the way. Fascinated, but wanting to keep that part to herself, Libby listens solicitously with a neutral expression affixed to her face.

"It was near the end of our expedition. Our party was descending the northernmost slope of the Snow Mountains. A Dutch explorer named them that because of the glacier ice caps. There is not much ice left, today. Most of it melted years ago, but it would not have mattered to us anyway, because we did not climb higher than eight thousand feet."

For the third time, Edgar interrupts to say, "Winston, you are rambling again."

"It's alright," Libby says. "Actually, I find his description of the terrain helpful. And what they experienced is quite interesting." In the short period she's known the Cheungs she's learned the bantering is a ubiquitous part of any conversation the two are involved in. It annoyed her at first, but now she finds it mildly amusing.

"Thank you, Doctor Corcoran," Winston says. "My brother has many fine qualities, but patience is not one of them."

Edgar responds with a monosyllabic grunt. Winston continues.

"Our intention was to travel by Jeep back to Jayapura, once we reached the prearranged rendezvous point in the valley below. It would take another day to get there. We walked in single file along a narrow trail with a native guide in front and another at the rear. The guide in front motioned for us to stop. There was a boy sitting on a rock under the shade of a tree, several yards ahead. There were so many different tribes and as many different languages spoken. We had trouble communicating with the indigenous people and it was difficult to know who was hostile or not, so we just stood there as our guide tried to determine if the boy was by himself.

"After a few minutes, he stood and held out one hand, palm up. With the other hand he gestured, indicating he wanted to trade what he held in his hand for something we had. Our guide motioned for him to come closer. In his hand was the berry. He spoke the word, Chamala. It was very odd in shape and texture, but I would not know how unusual it was until many months later. I traded cigarettes and chewing gum for it.

"Using primitive sign language, I tried to ascertain what kind of bush the berry grew on and where it could be found, but I failed to get any helpful information from him. I did not examine the berry then, we were in a hurry to get to the rendezvous point. I put it with the other samples I had collected, and did not get around to looking at it again until several months later. Here are photographs taken in 1987."

He takes a group of pictures from his pocket for Libby to see. The first is of the berry next to a coin. It is round, but not perfectly so, and pale in color, almost translucent.

"Was it preserved in a sealed container prior to this picture being taken?" Libby asks.

"It was kept in a plastic bag and in a closed box where it was not exposed to light from the time I acquired it until it was photographed."

"It looks almost clear. Was it that way when you got it or did the color fade afterward?"

"The color did not change noticeably during that period. The finer details of the outer layer, or skin if you will, are not visible in the photograph. Under a microscope the molecular structure resembles crystals intricately linked together in the shape of a sphere."

"I don't suppose you brought the berry with you?"

The expression on his face changes abruptly. Winston glances away at something beyond the horizon as he answers, "I sent it to a dear and trusted friend, Bussaba Meesang. She was a pharmacognosist, and I wanted to get her opinion on it."

"What did she tell you?"

"Three months after receiving it, she died suddenly. The berry was never located in her home nor returned to me."

"She was murdered, and the berry was stolen," Edgar gruffly interjects.

"That is strictly conjecture, Edgar. We have no proof of it."

63

"You think she was murdered over a berry? That's pretty far-fetched, don't you think? Regardless of how unusual it might be, it's hardly worth killing for. How did she die?"

"She drowned in her own bathtub," Winston answers. "The police thought she might have fallen and hit her head as she was getting into the tub."

"I doubt they looked into it very thoroughly, but they did not know what we know," Edgar adds.

"And, what is that?"

"I received a letter from her, dated three days before her death. Enclosed with it was a copy of her lab notes pertaining to the berry. She stated in the letter that she wanted me to have a copy for safekeeping."

"Rather ominous, would you not agree?" Edgar says.

"That doesn't strike me as unusual. Written notes often get misplaced, or if she kept her lab records on a computer there's always a possibility of accidentally deleting them. It seems reasonable to send a backup copy to a colleague. There must have been something in those notes that has held your interest for all these years. Otherwise, we wouldn't be sitting here talking about a berry you no longer possess."

"Yes, there is. Bussaba was a fine and dedicated scientist, but her methods would be considered unorthodox by most others in her field of studies. As a matter of practice, she often incorporated lab animals in her experiments. She believed the reaction of a bird, frog, mouse or fish would alert her to certain aspects of a plant's phytochemistry. Properties she might otherwise overlook."

"That's an interesting approach, though I can't say I've ever used that method."

"Tell her about the mice, Winston," Edgar coaxes.

"I was about to do just that. She wrote of an experiment involving six mice. A sample was taken from the berry, and mixed with water and rice to form a paste. Amounts varying from fifty to one hundred milligrams were fed once daily to each of the six mice. The results are documented in her notes, and although the study was incomplete it noted accelerated body and hair growth, as well as evidence of increased sensory perception."

Even the most experienced researchers are tempted at times to believe they've made a great discovery before all testing is finished. Libby is guilty of jumping to a conclusion herself on more than one occasion. Edgar and Winston are eyeing her expectantly, hoping she understands the significance of Bussaba Meesang's observations.

"A plant that could be used to augment growth or enhance the senses would certainly have potential, but it doesn't sound like the lab notes provide you with proof of anything. However, I think I see where this is leading. You have a theory about this berry and you'd like me to help prove or disprove it. My first question is why me?"

"Because you are uniquely qualified. You have the knowledge, youth and incentive necessary in order to be successful. Edgar and I are old. We lack the physical capabilities to initiate a search of this magnitude."

There was that word again—"search".

"I'm not clear on what you're proposing. When you say 'search', are you talking about searching through books and journals for the plant that produces the berry?"

The brothers glance at one another, then at Libby.

"I am sorry. I thought you understood. We would like you to lead an expedition into West Papua to find the source of the berry."

"You're kidding, right? I know nothing about West Papua or that part of the world, for that matter. I wouldn't know where to start. It's mind-boggling to even consider it."

"This could be the greatest botanical discovery of all time. Ask yourself this Doctor Corcoran. How will you feel if the discovery is made by someone else?"

"It's a shot in the dark, and a long shot at that," Libby says.

"If I may," Edgar says. "I would like to give you something else to consider. West Papua, like Seychelles is rich in biodiversity. Their ecosystems once supported thousands of species of plant and animal life, but many of those are extinct or endangered, mostly due to human encroachment. Indonesia's population is expanding rapidly, and moving farther into West Papua. We may have only a brief window of opportunity to find the plant, before it is gone forever."

Everyone has a soft spot. Edgar touched upon Libby's.

"You make a good argument. I'll give your proposal due consideration. That's all I can promise for now."

"Thank you, Doctor Corcoran. That is all we ask."

# ~15~

The Constance Ephelia where Libby is staying is on the west side of the island, and shaded from the early morning sun by Morne Seychellois, the highest mountain there. At seven a.m. the light is dim as she leaves her villa carrying a cup of coffee, intent on strolling the beach to begin the last full day of her stay in Mahé. It's the same beach where Gunter and she were robbed—or nearly robbed, to be accurate. Strangely enough, nothing has been reported about the thief's body being found. Certainly the authorities would have been around to ask questions by now. That is, unless the body was disposed of before being discovered the next morning.

The tour around the island with the Cheung brothers ended without Libby finding out if Winston was the one she'd seen retreating into the bushes—the one who killed the thief and spared her from being raped. Something he said as he was leaving leads her to believe the brothers might have followed Gunter and her to the beach that night.

"I saw you speaking with Gunter Schneider, yesterday." Her first thought was that he'd seen them at dinner, but then he explains, "Before your presentation at Mission Lodge."

"Yes, I met him two years ago, in Bora Bora. Do you know Gunter?"

"Yes, we've known him for a while." His tone turns bitter, suggesting there's an unpleasant history between Gunter and himself. Then, he adds, "You would be well advised to exercise caution around him. He's not all he appears to be." He leaves before elaborating further, leaving Libby wondering what the comment is meant to infer.

The spot where the attempted robbery took place is difficult to pinpoint. They had a lot to drink with dinner. She stops at each boulder she passes that is as close in size and proximity from the water as the one she was leaning over when the thief appeared. After examining a few, she lays her hands on one which feels oddly familiar. She tries to recall exactly where the person she thought was Winston disappeared into the bushes. There are no telltale markings in the sand around the boulder, but when she takes a closer look at the bushes, she finds leaves have been trampled where someone stepped from the beach into the foliage.

Often when Libby is deeply immersed in studying a project she talks aloud to herself, engaging her right brain in conversation with the left.

"Alright Libby, what do you know, and what is merely speculation?" asks the left brain.

"I'm certain this is where Gunter and I were robbed. I speculate the thief came alone. He chanced upon us and acted on impulse, seizing an opportunity to get some quick cash," answers the right.

"What about the person or persons who intervened? Was it a coincidence—a Good Samaritan who happened by at the right time?"

"No. It's more likely the person who came to our aid was following the thief, Gunter or me."

"What was the feathered dart-like thing in his neck?"

"It makes sense it was a projectile laced with a fast-acting poison, either hurled or shot from some type of gun or bow, but I didn't see it well enough to be certain. There are plants which produce poisonous substances, I've studied several of them. That would support the theory it was Winston."

She returns to the spot where they left the thief lying to look again for clues. There are no definitive footprints, or marks where a body was dragged away.

"Can you be sure the man was dead?"

"No, I can't be sure. In fact, that might be the missing piece of the puzzle. There are plants which produce toxins that paralyze. The proper dosage will slow a person's metabolism to where their pulse and breathing is barely perceptible. It's entirely possible the man got up and walked away later that evening."

Libby proceeds farther down the beach heading away from the hotel, searching for tracks or other clues that might confirm her suspicions. She's covered only a hundred yards when she spots a couple squatting beside something lying near the water's edge. They're dressed as if out for an early morning jog, and the thing they've found is the size of a human body, but mostly hidden from Libby by the couple. *Could it be the thief,* she wonders? She hastens her stride.

The couple is gesturing at it while calmly conversing in a foreign language Libby can't identify. The man says something that sounds like, "Doober gloken flob muffin," and then points to his own head. The woman with him nods as if she agrees. Libby steps past the couple for a better look. It's the body of a man lying on his back, completely nude except for a pair of white BVD briefs pulled over his head. A thin layer of sand covers most of his skin.

"Glickel speet poobid arft," the woman says to Libby, as she points at the body. Seeing Libby doesn't understand, she mimics a person smoking a joint and then starts to laugh. The man thinks it's hilarious.

Libby gives them a reproachful look. "How can you be so callous?"

The couple interprets the look, if not the words. They pantomime an explanation which Libby construes to mean she's misunderstood. She looks again at the body to see his chest slowly rise and fall. As her eyes venture farther south, she notices something else rising. The guy is getting an erection, which she's fairly certain doesn't happen to dead men.

"He's alive!" Libby declares. The couple nod their heads, eagerly. The woman imitates a person smoking again.

"He's stoned," Libby says. More vigorous nodding from the couple.

"Boutin glaggel," the woman says. Libby doesn't attempt to translate that one.

The three of them stand there a moment longer, unsure of what to do next. Libby feels the need to do something, so she kneels beside the man, and is about to shake him when she notices a tattoo on his arm. It's vaguely familiar. She brushes the sand away from it to confirm her worst fear.

"Quentin!" she screams. There's no response. She tries again. "Quentin! Wake up you idiot!" His head raises an inch, and then plops back down. She takes the underwear off of his head. He's beyond comatose.

With the couple's help, she gets him to his feet. They walk him out into the ocean until the water is up to their knees and let him drop.

He comes up coughing, sputtering and shouts, "Help! Man overboard!"

"Look around, stupid. Your hands are touching bottom and the shore is a few feet away."

He spits out a mouthful of salt water, rubs his eyes with his knuckles and blinks several times before saying, "Hey boss. Where are we?"

Seeing they're no longer needed, the couple leaves Quentin in Libby's hands and continue on their way. Libby hears the woman say, "Nooker souda wach dein," to the man, as they jog away.

"Who are they?" Quentin asks.

"They're the ones who found you passed out on the beach, lying buck naked, except for a pair of tidy-whities over your head. What do you have to say for yourself?"

"They don't belong to me, I don't wear briefs."

"That's not what I mean, and you know it. I told you to behave yourself. You could have gotten thrown in jail. What would you have done, then?"

"I guess I would have called you, not that it matters, because I wasn't thrown in jail."

"Not yet, anyway. Stay right where you are until I get back, and keep your private parts underwater and out of sight. I don't know whether or not there's a law against public nudity, but let's not take a chance."

She goes to grab a towel from the hotel. While she's gone Quentin tries to piece together the events of the night before. He's still sitting in the water where she left him when she returns. She holds the towel at arm's length while diverting her eyes.

"Wrap this around you and go straight to your room. Everyone will think you're coming back from a swim. I'd suggest you don't stray far from the hotel until we leave tomorrow."

"Heck boss, it's my last day here and there's a ton of stuff I haven't seen, yet."

"I know how you feel, there's a lot I'd like to do while I'm here, but bailing your ass out of trouble isn't anywhere on my list."

With the towel around his waist, he says, "Alright, my Johnson is covered. You can stop looking up at the sky, now. Besides, you must have seen everything before you shoved me into the ocean, unless you did it with your eyes shut."

"Believe me when I say, I wish they had been. The memory of you lying there will haunt me for years to come. Now, go get cleaned up and put some clothes on."

He begins walking toward the hotel, then stops and turns back to face her. "It's starting to come back to me, now—what happened last night, I mean."

"I am not in the least interested in hearing about your amazing adventure, Quentin. Not now, and not later, thank you very much."

"Your boyfriend was there."

"What? Who was there?"

"You know. That German guy."

"He's Austrian."

"Whatever. He was there at the party."

"What party, and where?"

"Oh, so now you're interested. Tell you what, I'll make a deal with you. Take me on a ferry ride and I'll tell you a few things you don't know about your German friend."

"What am I, your big sister? The last thing I want to do today is babysit you."

"Suit yourself. I just thought you might enjoy a boat ride to the islands of Praslin and La Digue. Doesn't that sound better than hanging out here? And along the way, I'll tell you about your German friend and his Swedish lady friend."

# ~16~

Libby and Quentin sit side by side with a view of Praslin and La Digue off the bow of the high speed catamaran. The sky overhead is cloudless and the water is crystal clear. Dolphins and flying fish swim along the port side, attempting to keep pace with the ferry boat. Libby takes pictures to show the folks at home.

"I can't believe how calm the water is here," Quentin remarks. "On the coast of California where I grew up there are always big waves. Even a boat this size would be bouncing up and down so hard we'd have to hang on to our seats to keep from falling overboard."

"I didn't realize you were from California."

"There's a lot you don't know about me."

"Let's face it. There's a lot we don't know about each other, and it's probably better if we keep it that way."

Libby has been planning an excursion to Praslin since before leaving Taos. There's a species of palm tree growing there she'd like to see. When Quentin suggests a ferry ride, she lets him believe he coerced her into it. They meet in the hotel lobby to take a taxi to the ferry terminal. He shows up shirtless and barefoot.

"I'd really prefer you wear a shirt and shoes," Libby says.

"Sorry, this is all I've got left."

So, she buys him a pair of sandals and a T-shirt at the wharf, before they board the ferry. He insists on a sleeveless one with "MAHÉ" printed on it.

"It shows off my ink. Chicks dig ink."

"Trust me. Not all chicks."

Once the ferry is underway, Libby asks, "Are you going to tell me about Gunter, or was that just a ruse to get a boat ride?"

"You sure you don't want to wait until we get back to the hotel? It might bum you out."

"Yes, it might. But, if Gunter wants to see me tonight, it might also be something I'd like to know beforehand."

"Alright then, here goes. After your presentation at the Four Seasons, I figured as long as I was there I should check out the talent on the beach,

71

just to see if it's any better there than at our hotel. So, I'm strolling along taking it all in. I've got my shirt off, soaking up some rays, just chillin' and giving all the girls a good look. You remember that blonde we saw at your first presentation, the one your buddy Hans took up with?"

"His name is Gunter, but yes, I remember the woman."

"Her name is Ines, she's Swedish. She was there on the beach looking really hot in this tiny bikini. There were two other Swedish girls with her—not as hot as her, but not too shabby either. Ines was with this older dude who looked like some kind of Arab sheikh. He was watching Ines pretty closely, but the other girls were getting friendly with some of the guys on the beach. One of them was hot for me."

"Really," Libby says, dubiously.

"I told you. Chicks dig body art. Anyway, I go over to talk to her. Her name is Ebba. We hit it off, but before long she has to leave to go somewhere with Ines and the others. She tells me there's a party going on that night and asks if I'd like to go. I tell her I do, and she says to meet her at that same place around six."

"So, it was a beach party, there at the Four Seasons?"

"No, as it turns out, it was on this big fancy yacht the sheikh owns. Ebba picked me and some other people up at the resort. We all got into this inflatable boat, right there on the beach and rode out to the yacht. It cruised around the island while we partied. It was so cool." Quentin seems to drift off momentarily.

Libby prompts him to continue. "What does that have to do with Gunter?"

"Oh, I almost forgot. He was one of the people who rode with me in the inflatable."

"Did he recognize you? Did you talk to him at all?"

"I can't say if he recognized me, but we didn't talk."

Libby thinks back to the conversation with Gunter when she called his room after the presentation that day. He was tired and not feeling well, which is understandable given the events of the night before. It doesn't make sense he recovered enough in a few hours to go to a party. Still, that in and of itself doesn't make Gunter a bad person.

"So far you haven't told me anything I should be concerned over. Gunter went to a party without me, so what? It's not like he's obligated to me."

"I don't think you'd be so quick to say it's no big deal if you'd seen what went on at that party. It was crazy wild. There was grass, cocaine, all kinds of pills, and drugs I've never heard of being passed around. The Swedish girls were popping pills and washing them down with whiskey. After a while, they got naked and Ebba tells everyone to do the same, because we're going to have an orgy."

"Stop right there, I don't want to hear any more." She puts her hands to her ears in case Quentin persists with a graphic description of what happened after that.

"So, there we are. Everyone's naked, except for the sheikh."

"I don't believe a word of it. You take a kind of perverse pleasure in saying things that shock and disgust me. I'm convinced that's the real reason for your tattoos and piercings. It pleases you to see people scrunch up their faces in disbelief when they look at you."

The rebuke has no discernable effect on him.

"There's something more you need to hear. You can choose to believe it, or not, I don't care. But I wouldn't feel right about keeping it from you."

"Just give me the PG version of events. Spare me any details involving drugs, nudity or sex."

"It's going to mean leaving some stuff out, but I'll try. So, Ines and the sheikh leave the party just as things are heating up. I take it they went to his private quarters. He's the kind of guy who doesn't mind watching, but doesn't want to participate, if you catch my meaning."

"Yes, I understand what that implies."

"Anyway, it wasn't ten minutes until Ines comes back, but without the sheikh. She was acting weird."

"Sounds like the pot calling the kettle black."

"Huh?"

"Nothing, go on."

"She was sitting on a stool at the bar by herself, having a drink and watching the others. Hans goes over to talk to her. He's joking around with her, rubbing up against her and trying to get something going, but she acts like she's not interested."

"Slut," Libby mutters.

"Which one?"

"Both of them."

"Hans keeps working on her, but she's not having any of it. Then, I see him slip something into her drink while she's not looking. He hangs around making small talk while Ines finishes her drink. She gets up to pour another, but then she stumbles and looks like she's going to pass out. He catches her as she starts to fall and carries her outside. No one seems to notice, but me."

"Did they come back in?"

73

"Not right away. I got curious, and thought you'd want to know, so I poked my head out to see what they were doing."

"What'd you see?"

"She was bent over the railing like she was throwing up. He was behind her, holding onto her waist and, uh, you know." He thrust his pelvis forward a few times to demonstrate. "This might be one of those details you didn't want to hear about."

"Okay, I get the picture. There's no need to say more." She spends a minute processing the story. "I appreciate you telling me about it. It's not easy to listen to, but it's best that I know the truth."

"I kind of thought you'd feel that way. I'm sorry if it bums you out though."

"That's okay. There is one thing I'm still curious about, though. How did you end up on the beach close to the Constance Ephelia?"

"I wish I knew. I must have passed out at some point, but that's always the way it is. The best parties are the ones you don't remember being at." It's an attempt at humor, which Libby seems badly in need of, but it falls short. "Come on, boss. Snap out of your funk. It's the last day in paradise. What would you like to see on Praslin Island? There are supposed to be some really cool beaches, and a place where they've got these monster-size tortoises."

"I have something else in mind. Let's find a coco de mer palm tree. I'd like to see one growing in its native environment."

"That doesn't sound like much fun, but if that's what you want to do, we will."

"I've had it on my list of things to do ever since I started planning this trip. It only grows two places in the world. Here on Praslin Island and on Curieuse Island, which is something like ten miles away. It produces the biggest nut of any plant in the world, sort of a double coconut that resembles a woman's pelvis on one side and her buttocks on the opposite side."

"Wicked," says Quentin. "I'd like to see one of those, myself."

At the ferry dock in Praslin Libby finds a man offering guided tours of the island by car.

"I'm interested in seeing a coco de mer palm growing—preferably one with fruit." She lets the words linger and percolate for a moment, but he doesn't seem to understand. So she resorts to sign language, holding her hands apart in the approximate size and shape of the nut, and then places her hands on her hips to indicate what it looks like. A wide grin spreads across his face.

"I think he's getting the wrong idea," Quentin says.

"Sexy nut," the man blurts out. "You wanna sexy nut?"

"Yes, that's right," Libby says. "Take us to see one."

"Dis way," he says, gesturing to his car.

They load into a small car with no doors and start down the road. They've gone less than a half mile from the ferry dock when he stops at a gift shop and gets out.

"No, we don't want to shop," Libby tries to explain. "We want to see the coco de mer."

"Yah, it here," he tells her, and points toward the gift shop.

"We might as well go in," Quentin says. "Maybe the store owner can translate for us."

Fortunately, the gift shop owner speaks excellent English. Libby explains what she wants.

"It may be difficult to find a nice specimen growing on a tree. The fruit takes about seven years to mature, and we've had problems with poachers recently. However, if you're interested in owning one of the nuts, we sell them here."

"Can I see one?" Quentin asks.

"Certainly, step over here." Two large nuts are displayed in a glass case. "These two are as big as they typically grow, and I'm not sure when I'll get more in like these. Supply and demand has driven the price way up."

"What's the price on that one?" Libby says, pointing to the larger of the two.

"Fifteen thousand rupees, that's roughly one thousand one hundred U.S. dollars. And, we can ship to anywhere in the world."

"A thousand bucks for a big coconut! Are you serious?" Quentin exclaims.

"A thousand one hundred to be precise. And yes, I'm perfectly serious."

Libby's attention is transfixed on the nut. Quentin is staring at her, waiting for her to come out of her trance and tell this guy off.

Instead, she says, "Do you accept Visa?"

After completing the transaction, Mano shows them some of the coco de mer palms growing on the island and then drops them back at the ferry dock. Quentin is still shell-shocked and they're almost back to Mahé before he breaks his silence.

"I can't believe you paid over a thousand bucks for that thing."

"That's because to you it's just a big coconut. You don't understand. It's the fruit of a tree that grows only one place in the world. It's an endangered species because it could be wiped out by disease or a weather phenomenon and disappear completely at any time. It's entirely possible something like that could happen this year, or next year. The coco de mer is living on borrowed time. Owning a coco de mer nut is like owning a living dinosaur."

# ~17~

The grand finale of the Global Federation of Botanists' symposium is a gala dinner held at the Berjaya Resort, overlooking Beau Vallon Bay. All members and guest speakers such as Libby are invited to attend. It's the pinnacle event of the week and few, if any, of the invitees decline. Showing up for the symposium and skipping the dinner, would be the equivalent of spending New Year's Eve in Times Square, and leaving before the ball drops.

Formal attire is suggested, but not required. Libby goes all out, and is nothing short of absolutely stunning decked out in a black off-the-shoulder evening gown, with her hair styled in a French braid updo. Her breasts spill out of the strapless push-up bra she's wearing, tantalizing the men as she passes by. Strappy high heel sandals which boosts her seventy inches of height an additional three inches provide the finishing touch.

Earlier that day, she purchased a semi-dressy shirt and slacks for Quentin, so he could come along with her. It's the only way to be sure he doesn't get himself in trouble on the night before they leave. As much as she hates to admit it, she's grown fond of him—not in a romantic, or even sisterly sense. It's more like the way one might feel about an injured bird they find and care for, hoping one day it will be healthy enough to fly away. The years of studying plants has given her a unique perspective on life. All living things have their place and a significant contribution to make to our planet's evolution, even if it's not always immediately evident.

"Boss, I hope I'm not out of line by saying this, but you look really hot," Quentin tells her, when they arrive.

"Thank you. You look..., well, uh..., not as bad as you usually do."

"Thanks, it's been a while since I've worn slacks."

The hotel has combined a large meeting room with the restaurant and outside eating area in order to accommodate the GFB event. A man is checking invitations at the door before granting entrance. He gives Quentin a long hard look.

"He's with me," Libby says. He glances at her, letting his eyes wander down a bit.

"You're sure?" he asks.

"Yes, I'm sure."

He scans something on a laptop computer and says, "You're assigned to table H, seats nine and ten. The tables and seats are marked. Would you like someone to show you to your seats?"

"Thank you, no. I'm sure we can find them."

"Enjoy your evening."

There are already a few hundred people there, mostly standing with a drink in their hand while chatting with others. A few couples are dancing to music provided by a live band. Every head in the place turns as Libby walks past. Her head is swiveling from side to side, trying to spot Gunter in the crowd. In spite of the warnings from Quentin and Winston Cheung, she still wants to talk with him. She's willing to give him the benefit of the doubt and an opportunity to exonerate himself in her eyes.

"Can I say something?" Quentin asks. She stops walking and turns to face him, knowing from his tone of voice what's coming.

"I'd really rather you didn't." Either he doesn't hear her or chooses to ignore it.

"You're like this super smart, great-looking lady. You could be with almost any guy here. Don't waste your time with Hans. Trust me, he's not worthy of you."

"Why is it you feel compelled to advise me on something you know absolutely nothing about? Especially after I've asked you not to, repeatedly."

"I know something about love, and getting dumped on. It hasn't always been smooth sailing for me in that department. I've had my heart broken."

"I didn't realize that."

"I'm serious. I may look like a stone-cold chick magnet, but deep down I'm just a regular guy with real feelings."

"No, I meant I didn't know you had a heart."

"And I didn't know you had a sense of humor."

His gaze focuses on something behind her. Thinking it must be Gunter, she whirls around, but is disappointed to see it's only Winston and Edgar Cheung approaching.

"Doctor Corcoran. You are looking splendid. Did you enjoy your excursion on the ferry, this afternoon?" Winston inquires.

"I wish you wouldn't sneak up on me like that," Libby tells them.

"It was not our intention to alarm you. We saw you scanning the room as if looking for someone, and I thought, or rather, I hoped it might be Winston and me."

Libby isn't buying it. She says to Quentin, "Would you mind getting me a glass of champagne from the open bar, over there?" She points across the room, then adds, "Take your time." When he's out of earshot, she turns her attention to the Cheung brothers.

"Have you two been following me? You seem to know more about my activities than one would glean from casual observation."

Her words come out a little harsher than intended, but she's getting tired of the cat-and-mouse game.

"We are concerned for your safety. That is the only reason we have surveilled your movements," Winston explains.

"So, it was you on the beach that night," Libby says, too loudly. It draws a curious glance from a couple passing by, and Winston waits a moment before replying.

"Edgar and I have enemies. It is possible your association with us could place you in jeopardy. It is only prudent to take steps to see no harm comes to you."

"First of all, I'm no more associated with you, than most other people on this island. I'd never met or heard of you before this week. And second, even if that wasn't the case, it doesn't mean your enemies are mine. I'm not inclined to take sides in a dispute that doesn't directly involve me."

"Edgar and I may have unwittingly involved you. You see, we are somewhat naive in our knowledge of computers and the internet. We have viewed many articles about you online, and mentioned your name in email correspondence without realizing that information could be remotely accessed by a third party."

Compared to the Cheung brothers Libby is a computer genius. She immediately understands the implications of what they're saying. Quentin returns with the champagne, and hands the glass to Libby. She downs it in one gulp, hands the glass back to him and says, "Get me another, please." Again, she glances around the room in search of Gunter.

"If you are hoping to see Gunter Schneider, I should inform you he departed Mahé earlier today on an Emirates Airlines flight to Dubai."

Libby is struck with a pang of sorrow. She doesn't doubt what Winston is saying. He's obviously keeping tabs on Gunter, as well as her.

"How do you know that? Or maybe I should ask, why do you?"

"As I said, we have enemies. One of them is a pharmaceutical company based in Thailand. Gunter Schneider has a working relationship with them."

"Did you have something to do with his decision to leave so abruptly?"

"No. While I confess his sudden departure is convenient for us, we had no part in it. Mr. Schneider's reason for leaving may have been influenced by his actions at a party he attended on a yacht belonging to Ali Saad Al-Bishi. I believe your assistant, Quentin Maddox was there."

Libby doesn't bother to confirm Quentin's presence at the party, it isn't necessary. It's beginning to seem like everyone saw through Gunter, but her.

She quietly asks, "Did you kill the thief? And what did you do with his body?"

"It is best if certain things are not openly discussed, but I can assure you that Edgar and I have not killed anyone."

Libby continues to eye them warily.

Edgar says, "I cannot blame you for being suspicious of our motives. I acknowledge we have been secretive. In our defense, we have not told you everything, because you have not yet committed to becoming a partner in our venture."

"It was only yesterday you explained about the search. I haven't had a chance to consider it."

"I know it seems unreasonable for us to expect you to decide so quickly, but Winston and I are not young. When we die, key pieces of information will die with us, unless we share the information with someone like yourself, beforehand."

Quentin returns with Libby's second glass of champagne. Edgar pauses, expecting Libby to dismiss Quentin, once again, but she's anxious to join the festivities and be done with the dreary conversation. She takes a sip of champagne, and then casually asks, "When are you planning to begin the search you mentioned?"

"As soon as possible," Winston answers, without hesitating.

"Call me on my personal number, one week from today. It was good meeting you both. I hope you have a safe trip home."

"Thank you," Winston says. Without another word, he and Edgar merge into the crowd.

"What are they searching for?" Quentin asks, after they've gone.

"The same thing we're all searching for—happiness." She gulps down the second glass of champagne.

"I'll get you another," Quentin offers.

"Not yet," she tells him. "I'm probably going to regret asking this, but do you dance?"

"You mean, with you?"

"No, with yourself," she says sarcastically. "Of course with me. Why else would I ask?"

80

"Well, I dance, but I don't know if we can dance together. It might look kind of weird."

"You know what? Tonight, I feel like being a little weird."

# ~18~

Libby's botanical research facility is located on a lightly traveled two-lane blacktop road. It climbs, winds and descends through the Miranda Canyon like a snake chasing its tail through a picket fence. A one-mile jog down and back from her place provides Libby with a more than ample cardiovascular workout. It's something she stopped doing a few months before, telling herself it wasn't necessary given her age, excellent health and nutritional diet. Thirty plus hours of sitting on planes and in airports during the trip home convinced her otherwise.

She's on the final leg of her run, with one hundred yards up a steep grade remaining between her and the house, which sits on a level piece of ground at the top of the hill. She breaks into a sprint, lengthening her stride and imagines a ribbon across the finish line, just ahead. Raising her arms high, she can almost feel the ribbon snap as she steps onto her driveway and slows to a walk, continuing to pace back and forth until her pulse returns to normal.

Her adobe-style house is a single level with three bedrooms, two baths and a detached two-car garage. From the outside, it looks modest and unimposing, blending seamlessly into the high desert topography. Surrounding the entrance is a courtyard with a cactus garden, a rustic wood bench, Native American pottery and a wall-mounted thermometer made of clay, which at the moment shows the temperature is forty-five degrees. Even in June, the nights are chilly here. In spite of it, Libby's shirt is drenched in sweat. A towel waits on the rustic wood bench beside the front door, so she can dry herself before going inside.

In stark contrast to the exterior, the interior of Libby's home is decorated in an elegant high-tech style. It's luxurious, pampering and self-indulgent. It is Libby's fortress, her sanctuary, her shelter, and a place she rarely shares with anyone else. She sleeps alone in a king-size bed atop a comfort controlled mattress, amid throw pillows and stuffed animals. She prepares gourmet dinners for one in her chef-style kitchen. She has an entertainment center with a 70-inch flat screen TV and a state-of-the-art stereo system she seldom turns on. There's a sunken whirlpool tub in the master bathroom which has never seen water. Once upon a time, it bothered her. She felt lonely and wished for someone to share it with. Not any longer. She's come to accept the solo lifestyle as her fate. Two hundred feet behind the house is the sprawling complex of greenhouses, offices and laboratories which make up her botanical research facility. The place where she sometimes spends twelve to fourteen hours a day.

She drapes the towel over her shoulder and unlocks the front door. The clock in the entry says six fifty-five, which means she's back from her morning run five minutes ahead of schedule. After a bite to eat and a quick shower, she'll be in her office by eight. The timer on the coffee maker is set for six forty-five. She smells the aroma of freshly brewed Kenyan coffee coming from the kitchen, and hears a chocolate-filled croissant calling her name. She bought it at the bakery in town the day before, as a reward for sticking to her running routine, and as incentive to sprint the final one hundred yards. She crosses the dining room heading toward the kitchen, but stops short of it.

"What the hell are you doing in my house?!!" she shouts at Quentin, who is sitting in her breakfast nook with a mug of coffee and the remains of the chocolate-filled croissant on the table in front of him. He holds up a finger asking her to wait while he finishes chewing.

"I didn't have any coffee, so I came to borrow a cup from you."

"I can't begin to list all the rules you've broken by being here."

"Come on, boss. You know me. You know I'm not going to steal anything. So what, if I helped myself to a cup of coffee. I mean, what's the big deal?"

"What's the big deal?! The big deal is this. You broke into my home and invaded my privacy, which is a major big deal all by itself. Then, you sit at my breakfast table with your dirty bare feet in the chair next to you, as if you own the place. I could forgive you for helping yourself to the coffee—hell, I would have given you a cup, if you'd come to the door like a normal person, knocked, waited for me to answer it, and then asked politely. But the one thing that absolutely drops the bar to a new record low for you—which I wouldn't have believed possible before now. The thing that is hands down the worst. The thing that really has me steamed is this: You ate my fricking croissant! I swear to God, if I had a gun I'd shoot you."

"Wow! I've never heard you use the word 'fricking' before. All of a sudden, I'm seeing you in a whole new light, and I think I like it. You keep too much bottled up inside. Every now and again, you've got to let it out, or else you'll go crazy."

83

"I'm about to show you me going crazy if you're not out of here in three seconds. One—,"

"Alright, I'm going."

"Two—,"

"I'm almost finished with my coffee."

"Take it with you. I'll get the cup back, later. Three! Now go!"

She shoves him out the back door and throws the deadbolt once he's gone. Then, she pours herself a cup of coffee and starts rummaging through the cupboards for something to eat that doesn't need to be cooked. She finds a rice cake. It's dry and tasteless. She takes one bite and tosses the rest away. Her heart was set on having a croissant, and there's nothing in the house to serve as a substitute.

"Damn him," she mutters. "I might as well get ready for work."

When they returned from the botany symposium, ten days earlier, Libby officially hired Quentin as a full-time employee. A decision she questions every day. During the time in Mahé she had a chance to see a different side of him, not that it ever threatened to overshadow or cancel out his less desirable qualities, just that she saw potential there, and thought with a little guidance and encouragement he could make something of himself. His job title is night watchman, though he's made a point of letting her know he doesn't like to be called that.

"Nobody calls them that anymore, not since the last century. It makes me feel like I'm eighty years old. How about we say I'm the head of nocturnal security?"

"I don't care what you call yourself, as long as you perform the duties of a night watchman."

"I'll need a gun. I'm thinking a Heckler and Koch machine gun."

"I am strictly forbidding you from bringing a gun onto my property. You don't need one."

"What am I supposed to do if I catch someone trying to break into a building, ask them nicely to please not do that?"

"Don't worry, you're plenty scary enough without a gun."

He gets a modest salary and lives on-site in a small circa 1960 travel trailer. Initially, Libby considered giving Quentin a job as a janitor, but that would introduce another set of problems. He'd be underfoot all day, pestering her other employees and preventing them from doing their work. That's when she came up with the idea for a night watchman. A position where he works nights and sleeps during the day will keep him out of everyone's way.

Libby's stomach is rumbling as she opens the door to her office at eight, but she puts it out of her mind, along with the earlier encounter with Quentin, and gets down to business. A few emails came in overnight. She scans through them, and replies where necessary. There's an email from Gunter Schneider which came in three days ago. It's become a part of her routine each morning since to reread the email, as if she missed something when she read it the day before.

Hello Libby, I am sorry I left Mahé without saying goodbye. I received a call saying my mother had become ill and was in the hospital, so I left on the next plane departing Mahé. Thankfully, my mother is getting better and will fully recover soon. I will be coming to the United States in the near future, though the actual date has not been confirmed. Maybe I will see you then. Gunter

Though she wouldn't confess it to anyone, the arrival of the email from Gunter made her heart soar. Getting over her disappointment at his sudden departure from Mahé has been difficult. However, the timing of the email is suspect. It arrived in her inbox an hour after she received a call on her personal phone from Winston Cheung. As usual, he got right to the point.

"Doctor Corcoran, please tell me you have decided to join us."

"I wish it was that simple, Mr. Cheung. I've given your proposal a great deal of consideration, and if I had to decide this very minute, I'd have to say no. There is simply no room in my schedule for an endeavor of this magnitude." She hears him let out a long sigh.

"This is very disappointing to us."

"I'm sorry. I know I told you I'd have an answer for you when you called. I spoke with my agent after returning from the symposium, and I have speaking engagements and appearances booked well into next year. Cancelling those would mean a loss of tens of thousands of dollars."

"Doctor Corcoran, may I call you Libby? I feel as if I have known you for many years, because even though we met only recently, I have followed your accomplishments since you were a student at the University of Washington."

"Yes Winston, it's fine to call me Libby."

"Thank you, Libby. It is entirely my fault you are not aware of the importance of our project. I have failed in my efforts to convince you. My words have been insufficient. However, all is not lost if you are still undecided. There is something you need to see, with your own eyes. I will bring it to you. Only then can you fully understand."

"Bring what to me, and when?"

"Again, these things should not be talked of over the telephone.  I will see you, soon."

It seems unlikely that Gunter's email stating he is coming to the United States, sent an hour after Winston disconnected, is merely a coincidence.

# ~19~

Each passing day without a word from either Gunter or Winston is making Libby that much more anxious. Every time she leaves her house to go to work or to town, she expects to find Winston and Edgar waiting for her when she returns. As she's closing her office, preparing to go home Wednesday evening, she asks Quentin to be extra vigilant of trespassers, especially when it comes to her house.

He asks, "Why?"

She says, "Quentin, can't I ask you to do something without having to explain why?"

"Is it your ex-husband?"

"I don't have an ex-husband."

"An old boyfriend?"

"Same answer. Look, if you see anyone sneaking around here at night, shine a flashlight in their face and ask them to identify themselves."

"I don't have a flashlight. How about I say something like, 'Halt! Who goes there?'"

"I'm sure that will work just fine."

"It would help if I had a machine gun."

"No guns, Quentin. I'll buy you a flashlight. Find one online and bookmark the page for Gwen. I'll let her know I've approved the purchase."

~~~

As she steps onto her driveway at the end of her Saturday morning jog, she's blinded by a bright light and hears Quentin shout, "Halt! Who goes there?"

"Quentin, it's me. Get that light out of my eyes."

"Hi boss. Yeah, I knew it was you. I'm just practicing with my new flashlight. What do you think, pretty cool, eh?"

"Well, it is bright."

"It's a four thousand lumen tactical flashlight, like cops use. If someone attacks me, I can use it like a club. Here, feel how heavy it is."

"That's alright. I'll take your word for it."

"Watch this." He shines it in the sky, moving it in an arc. "It looks like a searchlight."

"I'm glad you're having fun with it. Just don't let the bad guys sneak past you while you're playing with your new toy."

"Don't worry. Nobody is getting past me."

"Good to hear. I'm going inside. Do you want coffee to take with you?"

"Thanks boss, but my shift ends in an hour and I don't plan on staying up much past that. Coffee will just keep me awake."

It does ease her concerns over possible intruders to know Quentin is taking his job more seriously, though with him it's hard to say how long that will last. Libby goes inside to eat and shower before work. She'll be the only one at the research facility, either today or tomorrow. She looks forward to weekends for that reason. The company phone is answered by the service, her personal phone is turned off. She locks the doors so no one can disturb her, and works as long or as little as she likes.

She's in the office at eight going over this week's entries into the laboratory log book. Notes are taken by the lab techs on every study performed, and those notes are compiled into a report, and all reports are recorded into the computerized log book, and every Saturday Libby reviews it. Although she's never told them in so many words, the lab staff is well aware of this practice, which eliminates the need for her to remind them late Friday to make sure their reports are filed before they leave for the weekend.

At eleven, Libby takes a break from perusing the log book and checks her email. There's one from her agent, Jessica Rawlins, reminding Libby of a TV appearance on Tuesday. She's scheduled to appear on a segment called "Rising Stars of New Mexico", featuring young successful entrepreneurs from around the state. It's hosted by Grayson Whitney, and airs on the Albuquerque NBC affiliate station. The email from Jessica reads:

Libby, you'll need to be at the station no later than 6:30 a.m. for makeup and prep. I've made a reservation for you at the downtown Sheraton for Monday night. Good luck, and give Grayson a kiss for me. Jessica

The next one is from her mother, Diane. The subject line is in all caps. It reads:

URGENT!!! OPEN IMMEDIATELY!!!

The text of email is more of the same:

88

CALL ME AS SOON AS YOU GET THIS.  NEED TO TALK TO YOU.

"You are such a drama queen, Diane," Libby mutters.  She could put it off until later, but in the meantime Diane will just get more and more worked up.  She turns on her phone and speed dials the number.  Diane picks up immediately.

"Oh Liberty!" she screams so loudly Libby has to hold the phone away from her ear.  "I'm in the car.  Hold on while I find somewhere to pull over."

Diane drops the phone and the line goes dead.  Libby knows she'll call back as soon as she's able, so she waits with phone in hand until it sounds an incoming call.

"Why'd you hang up on me?  I asked you to hold on.  Oh well, it doesn't matter, now.  Listen, I'm halfway between Reno and Las Vegas.  I've had the most horrific argument with your Uncle Claude."  Libby only vaguely remembers her mother previously mentioning someone named Claude, and she's quite certain he's no relation.

"Did things get physical, are you alright?"

"We didn't fight, not like that.  I'm not bruised and nothing is broken, but it was very traumatic, nonetheless.  He said some terrible things.  I had to get away from him, before I said or did something I'd regret later, so I jumped in the car and left."

"Good for you.  It was the right thing to do.  You have to put some space between you and him until things cool down.  Then, you can talk and calmly sort out your differences."

"We're past that.  Things went too far.  I hope I never see that man again, for as long as I live.  His name will never pass my lips, and his image is permanently erased from my memory."

*If I had a nickel for every time I've heard you say that*, Libby thinks.

"I hesitate to ask this next question, but what are you doing in Nevada?  You two didn't have one of those quickie weddings, did you?"

"Heavens no, we didn't get married, thank God.  Claude and I drove to Lake Tahoe yesterday, planning to stay until Sunday.  Everything was fine until he lost a lot of money in the casino last night.  He was in a foul mood over that when we returned to the motel, and it got worse overnight."  Libby is jotting notes in order to follow the story as Diane is speaking.

"You and Claude drove to Lake Tahoe in your car, or his car?"

"His car.  My car is in the shop.  I thought I told you that."

"So, does this mean you're in his car right now? Because, if that's the case, technically speaking, you've stolen his car and the police could be looking for you, at this very minute."

"I never thought of that."

"If you turn around now, and go back, you can say you borrowed the car because you needed a couple of hours to cool off. Then, tell Claude you've had time to think about it, and you're ready to talk things through with him."

"It's too late to go back. I'm through with Claude and all men like him. This is a new chapter in my life, starting today." Libby has a bad feeling about where this is leading. It began when Diane said she was between Reno and Las Vegas.

"Diane, a book can only have so many chapters. Your life is already a saga. You should consider settling into a more stable lifestyle."

"That's exactly what I intend to do. Now, I'm going to hang up and get back on the road. I'm a sitting duck if a highway patrolman sees me. I plan to drive all night if necessary to get there by morning."

"Wait! Don't hang up."

"I'm sorry, Liberty. I've got to go, but I'll call again when I can."

"Diane?! Mother?!" Libby pleads for a response, but Diane has disconnected. "Wonderful, my mother is coming to stay with me—my worst nightmare, times ten. What have I done to deserve this?"

By the time she finishes scanning her emails, it's twelve thirty, so she decides to break for lunch. As she reaches to switch off her computer the icon denoting incoming email flashes. She goes to her inbox, but doesn't recognize the sender. She might have deleted it right then and there, thinking it was spam, except for what is in the subject line:

Liberty was a naughty girl at Allure.

Her hands hover over the keyboard while she tries to decide, then she clicks to open the email. The short message reads:

You could be the next internet sensation, or not. It's up to you. Either way, I make money. Open the attachment to view a sample clip. Don't bother trying to reply. I'll be in touch. Bridgett

When the attachment opens, a single frame of a video appears. The image is blurry, but she recognizes her own face and that of Bridgett, the sales clerk at the lingerie shop. They are nude from the waist up. Judging

90

from the angle, the camera was mounted in the ceiling of the dressing room. In spite of what the email says, Libby types a response to Bridgett:

You won't get away with this. I can promise you that.

She hits send. Within seconds it comes back as undeliverable. One by one she thinks of her friends, employees, the men she's dated, business associates, colleagues and Diane. What will they think?

# ~20~

Libby determines the travel time from Las Vegas to Taos, adds three hours because it's Diane driving, and calculates her arrival will come no sooner than midnight. With that in mind, she decides to stick to her normal bedtime schedule, but before retiring for the night she calls Quentin.

"Yo," he answers, hoarsely.

"Were you sleeping?"

"Oh, it's you, boss. I guess I might have dozed off for a second. What's up?"

"My mother is coming to visit. There's an outside chance she'll arrive after midnight and before daylight. I wanted you to be aware of this."

"What does she look like?"

"It doesn't matter. If a woman drives up, it's probably her."

"What kind of car is she in?"

"I'm not sure. It's not hers. She stole it from her boyfriend."

"Wow! She sounds like one cool mom."

"I'm sure she'll be glad to hear you think so."

Libby goes to bed before midnight and sleeps soundly until her alarm wakes her at six. At six thirty she puts on her running clothes, intending to begin the day with a jog. She starts jogging toward the road, then stops when she sees a car in her driveway—a black, late model Lincoln. It has to belong to Claude, which means Diane is somewhere nearby.

"Diane," Libby calls, but gets no response. "Quentin," she calls, next. Still no response.

She looks toward the complex of buildings and greenhouses. It's a virtual maze to anyone unfamiliar with the layout, and there is no outside lighting on any of it. In fact, the only visible light, other than inside her home, is coming from Quentin's trailer. She presses the horn down and holds it there. After a minute the trailer door opens and Quentin emerges. He heads toward Libby with Diane following close behind.

"Liberty!" she shouts, and spreads her arms wide as if she expects Libby to come running, but Libby remains standing beside the Lincoln.

"Hi Diane," Libby calls back.

"She got here a couple of hours ago. We didn't want to wake you," Quentin says.

"How very kind of you both."

Diane is wearing tight-fitting capris, pointed toe high heels, and a tube top. She has a men's sport coat draped over her shoulders and struggles to maintain her balance. The odor of marijuana lingers on her hair and clothing. Libby looks at her disapprovingly.

"Liberty, get that scowl off your face, and stop being so judgmental. I was wired from caffeine and the long drive when I got here. Quentin picked up on it immediately, and offered me something to help me mellow out. He's very intuitive that way."

"You two have been smoking pot since you got here?"

"Not the whole time," Quentin answers.

"We just smoked one joint, that's all," Diane says. "Liberty, I have the worst case of the munchies. Do you have any jelly donuts? A couple of jelly donuts would taste really good, about now."

"I second that," Quentin says.

"Sorry, I'm fresh out of jelly donuts. How about a lightly salted rice cake?"

"Yuck! I'm not that stoned."

Seeing her mother wasted on grass, pills or booze is nothing new for Libby. A good part of her childhood was spent looking after Diane.

"Come on, let's get you inside. We'll find something for you to eat, and then maybe you'll want to get some sleep."

"I'll see you later, Diane," Quentin tells her.

"Oh wait." Diane gives him a hug and a kiss on the lips. "Thanks for the smoke," she says, and then adds, "and the other stuff, too."

"What other stuff?" Libby wants to know. Quentin makes a hasty retreat to his trailer.

"It's nothing you need to be concerned about, Liberty. Let's go inside like you suggested. It's cold out here and I want to see what you have in your refrigerator."

Libby puts an arm around Diane to steady her as they walk to the house. *Just like old times*, she muses. In spite of her vagabond lifestyle and the periods of excessive drug use, Diane looks pretty good for her age, which is a closely guarded secret in itself. Libby estimates she's forty-seven or eight, but with her terrific figure and no visible gray hair she can easily convince people she's thirty-five.

After an omelet breakfast, Diane sleeps until late afternoon. On the table in the kitchen, there's a note from Libby saying she is working, and for

Diane to make herself at home. When she walked out of the motel room in Reno, she intended to return in an hour, but the farther away she got, the farther away she wanted to be.

Her purse and cell phone were the only things she thought to grab before fleeing, so she rummages through Libby's drawers and closets for clothes to wear. Libby is taller than her, and slightly smaller in the chest and hips, but she finds a few things she can make work. She's looking herself over in the mirror when Libby walks in.

"For a single young woman who is the CEO of her own company, your wardrobe is appalling. It needs more flash and dazzle, less gray and more color, less fabric and more sizzle. Men have very short attention spans. You have only a second to turn their heads, before they pass by and keep on walking."

"I'm sorry, Diane. All of my leopard skin tights are at the dry cleaners. It's good to see you managed to find something that wasn't too terribly conservative for your taste."

"Well, I couldn't walk around naked, so I put on the first thing I found that fit. It's a shame you didn't inherit my curvy figure."

"As much as I enjoy listening to you criticize my clothes and body, why don't we sit at the kitchen table and have a serious discussion about your short-term plans, instead."

"Oh Liberty. Don't be such a drag. Why does everything have to be neat and orderly with you? Can't you just relax and go with the flow, every now and then?"

"I should remind you, it's my neat and orderly side that manages my career and business, which is doing quite well, in spite of my inability to go with the flow, blow in the wind, go along to get along, or whatever other pseudo-hippie cliché you choose."

"Oh alright, Liberty. I give up. I can see you're not going to stop hounding me until we've had this boring discussion, so let's get it over with."

They sit at the table in the breakfast nook. Before she begins, Libby pours them both a glass of Chablis.

"Maybe this will help," she says.

"It couldn't hurt," Diane agrees.

"I understand you had a long drive, you're tired and haven't had time to think about things. You're welcome to stay as long as is necessary, but I'm not comfortable with a stolen car sitting in my driveway. Have you talked to what's-his-name since leaving Reno?"

"He's called several times, but I haven't picked up. His messages say he's sorry and to please call him back. I feel bad that I took his car and left him stranded there, but I don't want to go back to face him."

"I don't know the man, but I wouldn't think he'd wait long before calling the police to report his vehicle stolen, especially considering you won't return his calls. How about if I call him? I'll tell him you were here, but you left in another car, and that I want to make arrangements to get his car back to him."

"I like that idea. That way he can't come here and try to talk me into returning. It's over between us. That much I'm sure of."

"Okay, I'll take care of it tomorrow morning. What about you? Are you going back to California or somewhere else? What about your clothes and furniture?"

"One question at a time. My clothes, and what other personal belongings I have, are at Claude's house in Mendocino. He'll probably burn them when he gets home."

"I'll see what I can work out with him when I talk to him tomorrow. Maybe, he'll agree to let a moving company pack your stuff and ship it here. If I can resolve those things with Claude, it only leaves one other matter for us to discuss. You."

"Can't I have a few days to think about what it is I want to do?" Diane massages her temples in an effort to stave off the headache beginning to form just behind her eyes. "Does it have to be decided right now?"

"No, we don't have to decide right this minute." Libby feels sorry for her mother, but Diane is the one who dug the hole she currently occupies, and Libby isn't going to let herself be dragged into it.

"We've always been able to speak freely with one another. Some harsh words have been exchanged on several occasions, and yet, here we are, still on speaking terms, still working through our differences, and still loving one another as best we can. That being said, I've built a great life for myself, all by myself, and it hasn't been easy. I'm not going to let you come in and turn it upside down. Whatever turmoil you've created in your life, you're going to have to deal with on your own. You can stay here while you decide what you want to do next, but it's only temporary."

Diane looks at Libby as if seeing her for the first time.

"When did you become so cold, Liberty? I may not have been the best mother, but I was the best I knew how to be. I was just a frightened child myself when you were born. I wasn't ready for the responsibility of being a mother." Diane turns her face to hide the tears. Libby rises slowly, goes to her mother and hugs her tightly.

"It was tough on both of us, Diane. And honestly, I don't care to dwell on what's happened in the past any more than you do."

"So, have we discussed it enough for now?"

"Yes, you're free to go."

"Good, I'm going to see if I can borrow some grass from Quentin. It will help me get centered, so I can get to work on putting my life in order."

"Good luck with that—scoring grass from Quentin, I mean. There's a spare house key hanging on a hook in the pantry. Take it with you, in case I'm asleep when you get home."

# ~21~

Although Libby gets to the TV station with time to spare, the staff treats her as if she's an hour late. They whisk her away to a room to await makeup application the moment she arrives. She soon learns that's just the way it is in the television world. Time is at a premium. Sponsors pay a thousand bucks for every second their commercial is aired. Off camera, everyone is running hither and yon like the place is on fire. That is, everyone except Grayson Whitney.

He glides into the room wearing a tailored Cambridge gray suit and a red power tie. His longish hair is swept back, a stylish growth of beard graces his handsome smiling face, and when he speaks Libby almost goes giddy.

"Good morning, Doctor Corcoran. I'm Grayson Whitney." The words ooze from his lips like maple syrup over buckwheat pancakes—soft, slow and sweet, with a bit of southern flavor to them. "Do you mind if I call you Liberty? I love the way it sounds."

*You can call me any fricking thing you want,* she thinks, but only manages to say is, "Uh, sure, Mr. Whitney, that's fine."

"Super, Liberty. Please, call me Grayson. Your people sent me a promo package, highlighting your more notable accomplishments. I'll mention those in the introduction. My assistant Jenna will escort you from here to the set and cue you when it's time to walk onstage."

"Well, it sounds like it's all taken care of. All that's left for me, is to try and not trip over my words. How hard can that be, right?"

"That's right. Nothing to be nervous about. I'll see you on the set."

It's seven thirty when the makeup artist dabs the moisture from Libby's forehead one last time before Jenna takes her to the set.

"Our next guest is known as The Plant Doctor. She's an expert in the field of plant genetics and has her own thriving botanical research business. And by the way guys, she's single. Let's welcome Doctor Liberty Belle Corcoran."

Jenna nudges Libby toward Grayson, who is standing to applaud her. She steps from behind a curtain into a small room with only Grayson and his camera crew. People watching at home get the impression the show is filmed in front of a live audience, because of the canned applause and cheering sound effects playing in the background. Before today, Libby thought so, too. She smiles and waves to the camera. It's what Jenna said to do. Grayson gestures to a chair. They sit and he begins.

"Liberty, you were born in California, went to school in Washington, and then moved to New Mexico five years ago. Have I got that right?"

"Yes, Grayson. As the saying goes, I wasn't born in New Mexico, but I got here as soon as I could." She smiles at the camera, as Grayson throws his head back and lets out a loud guffaw.

The rest of the show is more of the same, lasting only fifteen minutes. Libby is at ease in front of a camera or microphone, but not to the extent Grayson is. It's like he was born to be a talk show host—asking the right questions, laughing at the appropriate times, and turning serious when it's called for.

She can't determine if it's just part of the performance, but the entire time they're on camera, he seems to be flirting with her. Before leaving, she decides to push the issue further.

"If you find yourself in Taos some weekend, give me a call," she tells him.

His response is a generic and equivocal, "I'll do that," which she interprets to mean, *not bloody likely.*

It is still early morning when she goes from the station back to the Sheraton. After checking out, she makes one last stop in Albuquerque before heading home. The building hasn't changed since she was last there. She parks in the empty lot in front of the store and gets out. The sign with the name, Allure, is still above the door, but the door itself is locked. She looks up and down the street for possible witnesses, as she considers breaking into the building.

There are other shops nearby, parked cars where people might be and possibly cameras mounted out of sight, so she goes around to the back of the building. The rear door, which can't be seen from the side street sits ajar. The jamb is split at the strike plate. Apparently, someone else wanted a look inside. She eases the door farther open.

There's nothing to see but bare walls—no lingerie, racks, shelves, counters or cash register. Not a scrap of paper was left behind. It makes her briefly wonder whether or not she's in the right place. Discouraged and befuddled, she exits through the same rear door. As she rounds the corner of the building, heading back to the parking lot, her head is down and her mind is elsewhere. She doesn't notice the guy standing beside her SUV until she's only a few feet away. He calmly pulls what looks like a wallet from his vest pocket and flips it open to display a badge.

"Can I ask you what you're doing here?" he says.

"Who are you?"

"I'm Detective Hugh Rowden, with the Albuquerque Police Department. The business that was here is part of an investigation we're conducting."

"Have they done something wrong?" Libby asks, innocently.

"Because it's an ongoing investigation, I can't disclose the details, but it involves complaints filed against the store. Have you purchased anything from the store known as Allure?"

"Um, no. This is the first time I've been here. I heard about it from a friend, and thought I'd have a look while I was in town."

"Why were you snooping around in back of the building?"

"I was not snooping," Libby says, indignantly. "I was merely trying to determine if Allure was still in business. As you can see, there are no windows in the front of the building, and no hours of operation posted on the front door."

It is obvious from his expression he's not buying it.

"There's nothing to be embarrassed about, I mean, if you have been to the store before. Buying sexy lingerie isn't illegal. Everyone owns a few pairs of undies, right?"

"As I said, I haven't been here before today. Now, if there's nothing more, I've got a long drive back to Taos."

"Before you go, I need to see your ID."

"I've done nothing wrong," Libby protests.

"No ma'am. No one said you did." She takes her driver's license from her purse and hands it to him. "Liberty Corcoran," he reads, as he compares the license photo to her face.

"Doctor Liberty Corcoran," she corrects.

He nods once and hands the license back to her. "If you did purchase an item here, you might have noticed something which would help our investigation. Or maybe the friend you mentioned saw something." He takes a business card from a pocket and hands it to Libby. "If you or your friend think of anything, give me a call."

It's one o'clock when Libby gets home. The Lincoln is gone. After a lengthy phone conversation with Claude on Monday, she made arrangements with an auto transport company to have it picked up and delivered to him. She goes inside her house to have lunch before going to her office. Diane isn't there, which means she's probably in Quentin's trailer getting high.

While she snacks on celery stalks with peanut butter, she checks her personal email and finds a second message from Bridgett that came in two hours ago. She's been expecting it, knowing a request for money is coming. It contains text and a link to a website. The text reads:

I knew you were going to be a star the first time I laid eyes on you. Here's a link where you can see for yourself. Have $10,000 in cash ready to go. Nothing larger than twenties. I'll let you know how and when to deliver it to me. Bridgett

Then Libby clicks on the link dreading what she's about to see. It takes her to a pay-per-view pornography website. The homepage offers fifteen-second sample clips to entice people into paying via credit card for the longer videos. To view a clip you click on the title. One is named, "Lesbians in Lingerie". She clicks on it. Sure enough, it's more footage of Bridgett and her, but fortunately, their faces are blurred, so no one can recognize her.

The intention is to demonstrate to Libby what could happen if she doesn't comply with the blackmailer's demands. Never one to overreact, Libby imagines the possible ways it will play out. If she pays the money, there's no guarantee that will be the end of it. Even if she takes possession of the video, there could be multiple copies. But if she doesn't pay and the video goes public, it could cost her a lot more than ten thousand dollars.

There's bound to be a connection between the investigation Detective Rowden alluded to and the blackmailer. One possibility is there are other women being blackmailed, and one or more of them went to the police. Hence, the complaints against Allure, Detective Rowden mentioned. The best course of action for her is to string Bridgett along and give the police or one of the other victims a chance to put her out of business.

# ~22~

The email from Bridgett with delivery instructions hits Libby's inbox two days later, arriving at seven in the morning. It reads:

Put the $10,000 in a black trash bag and secure it with duct tape. Get in your SUV alone with the bag. Drive south on Highway 68, leaving Taos at 9 a.m. today. When a car behind you blinks their lights on and off three times, throw the bag with the money out the passenger side window to the side of the road. Don't stop or slow down. Continue driving south.

Bridgett had given it a lot of thought. An inconspicuous garbage bag discarded on the side of a road that's not heavily traveled, not letting her know in advance where it will happen. Libby has given it a lot of thought, too. Actually, she's thought of little else since the previous email from Bridgett. It is one of the toughest decisions she's ever made, but the one that makes the most sense, nonetheless.

Nine o'clock comes and goes. Libby stays put. At noon, while Libby is working in her office, the second email of the day from Bridgett arrives. It reads:

I really thought you were smarter than that. Oh well. As I said before, I make money either way. Enjoy your new celebrity status. Bridgett

It doesn't take long before the news is out and spreading like wildfire. Libby's agent, Jessica Rawlins uses a special software program to monitor the internet. It alerts her every time one of her clients' name is mentioned online. She's the first to call Libby.

"Libby! What have you done to me?" are her first words.

"What have I done to you? I presume you're talking about the video. All I can say is it's not what it looks like. I was set up. The video was made without my knowledge or consent."

"It doesn't matter. Appearances are everything in this business. Personally, I could care less what you do behind closed doors, or whom you do it with, for that matter. But, many of the companies whose products you endorse are owned by ultraconservative types. They're the sort of people who will cancel your contract and demand their money back at the first whiff of a scandal. I'm holding my breath and keeping my fingers crossed this doesn't get back to them."

"I'm sorry, Jessica. I don't know what to say. I guess, I let my guard down at a bad time. Maybe it won't last long, and it will be forgotten about by tomorrow."

"I think that's too much to hope for. We need to take steps to limit the damage. I don't want you to talk to anyone in the media, or anyone who might communicate with the media. And, that includes social media. I'm cancelling all personal appearances for the next two weeks. I want you to stay home and maintain a low profile. I'll monitor public reaction, and keep you posted."

Libby is doing her own monitoring of the situation by inputting her name into the Google search box. The edited fifteen-minute video of her is being offered for sale on dozens of pornographic pay-per-view websites. She reluctantly purchases the opportunity to see it for herself. This time nothing is blurred. There are plenty of clear, close-up shots of her face and other body parts. The notion of strangers, possibly thousands of them, watching the images, drooling over them and fantasizing about her as they do is making her nauseous.

She locks her office door, tells Leslie to hold all calls, and that she's not to be disturbed. She remains there until after everyone else has left to go home. By tomorrow morning at least one of her employees will know, and shortly afterward all of them will know. They'll look at her differently, probably lose respect for her. It could change everything, but there's nothing she can do other than ride out the storm.

It's almost dark when she locks up and slowly walks the one hundred yards to her house, feeling drained from the hours spent worrying. The aroma of spaghetti cooking greets her as she opens the front door. Diane is in the kitchen tending pots of noodles and sauce.

"Well, this brings back memories," Libby says. Although she never said as much, Libby grew up thinking her mother was a terrible cook. Her friends all had mothers who cooked hot meals like meatloaf and chicken casserole. Most of the time, Diane and she ate something out of a can or a box. But every once in a while, on a special occasion or when Libby was feeling blue, Diane made spaghetti.

"Gwen said you're not feeling well. I picked up a loaf of French bread along with the other stuff. Do you have any red wine? A merlot would be nice."

"As a matter of fact, I do have a bottle of merlot. Do you need help with anything?"

"No, it's just about done. The table is already set. If you'll open the wine and get out a couple of glasses for it, we'll be good to go."

Diane forks the pasta onto plates, adds a liberal helping of sauce and sets it on the table, along with a bowl of salad and a basket of bread, sliced and slathered with garlic butter. She lights a candle while Libby pours the wine, then they sit down and dig in.

"Thanks, this is a nice surprise, especially after the day I've had," Libby says.

"Do you want to talk about it?"

Libby does want to talk about it, but she's unsure about disclosing the lurid details to Diane.

"Promise me you won't jump to any false conclusions."

"I promise."

"You remember the symposium in Mahé I went to, a few weeks ago. Before I got on the plane in Albuquerque, I had my hair done and went shopping. One of the places I shopped at was a lingerie store."

"Ooh, that sounds promising."

"There's a man I met a couple of years ago. We made plans to have dinner together while we were in Mahé."

"How did that work out?"

"I'm not sure, but that's another story. Inside the lingerie store there were hidden cameras recording video of me while I tried on lingerie. Last week I received an email threatening to release the video over the internet. A few days later I received another email demanding money. Early this morning, I got an email with instructions for delivering the money. I decided I wasn't going to let myself be blackmailed. Apparently, the video was sold to several pornographic websites. It's already been viewed hundreds of times, maybe thousands by now."

"It's sick, the things people will do for money, but I doubt anyone will recognize you. The people who visit those porn sites don't care about faces."

"The thing is, the people responsible for making and selling the video linked it to me with hashtags. Whenever someone enters my name into an internet search engine, a link to the video comes up. My agent knew about the video within minutes of it going online."

"I'm sorry this has happened to you, Liberty. I know it must seem terribly unfair. You'll feel differently about it in a few days, and I'm not just saying that to placate you. We all have the capacity to overcome obstacles which at first seem overwhelming. You have unlimited internal strength to draw upon when necessary. You've always had it, since you were little. You were as tough as nails, then. I think you still are."

"I hope you're right about that, but I haven't told you everything about the video. It's more than just the nudity that I have to worry about. The sales clerk at the store is in the video, too. It's been edited to make it look like we're two lesbians having sex."

"Oh," Diane says, then shoves a forkful of pasta into her mouth and spends a minute chewing it before speaking again. "I always hoped you'd meet a man, fall in love and have kids. I know I never said as much, but I wanted you to have the things I missed out on. Just because I've never been able to keep a man for long, doesn't mean you can't."

"Diane, I am not a lesbian," Libby asserts, with a little grit in her tone. "That's why I asked you to not jump to any conclusions. The video was edited to make it look worse than it really was. I was naked because I was trying on lingerie, and Bridgett initiated things by groping me, not the other way around."

There are another few minutes of awkward silence which follows as Diane processes what she's heard. Libby knows Diane is not the prudish sort. She's been around the proverbial block and back more than a few times.

"This may not be the ideal moment to ask, but why is it you've never once spoken to me about my father. Did you think I'd be ashamed because you had me out of wedlock?"

"No, that wasn't it."

"Then what? I've always been curious about him. Don't you know who it was? Is that why you've never told me? I've always assumed that was the reason."

Diane is visibly stung by Libby's words.

"I'm sorry you've felt that way toward me for all these years. I've always known who your father is, but I thought it best you didn't."

"Why? What possible reason could there be for keeping it from me?"

"Knowing would only make you think less of me than you already do."

"Now, it's my turn to say, I'm sorry you've felt that way about me for all these years. I'm almost thirty, a mature adult by anyone's standards. I have the right to know who my father is, and you most definitely deserve to be relieved of the guilt you've been carrying around over it."

Diane thinks about it for a long while. It will be ugly and painful to talk about, and knowing the truth won't bring the closure Libby hopes it will. On the other hand, Diane can't deny she has a right to know the truth.

"It's not guilt that has kept me from telling you how I became pregnant with you. It's shame. If you're certain you want to know, then I'll tell you, but I'll warn you in advance, once the genie is out of the bottle, there's no putting it back in. You know what I'm saying?"

"Yes, I know exactly what you're saying. And yes, I'm certain I want to know."

"My father, Amos Corcoran died when I was eight. I remember him as kind and loving to my mother and me. Elisabeth, my mother, was never the same afterward."

Libby has heard this part of the story before, and each time it's told she has to wonder why Diane, after losing a father she loved, can't understand Libby's need to know more about her own father.

"Elisabeth was still young when Amos died. She began seeing other men. I remember some of them. I'm sure I didn't meet them all. Eventually, she remarried. It happened suddenly, when I was fourteen. She met a man, Duane Harvey, who swept her off her feet, but he turned out to be mean and abusive. One day, only a few months after they married, while he was at work and I was in school, Elisabeth left. I never saw or heard from her again. I was crushed. Duane said I could stay with him if I cooked and cleaned the house to earn my keep."

Libby has an eerie sensation she knows where this story is going. Diane's pain is evident. Libby almost tells her to stop, but she's held on to this secret for so long and she's so close to sharing it. She lets her finish.

"He raped me for the first time less than a week after Elisabeth left. It went on for two months, almost every night. I went to school during the day and came home to that monster every night because I didn't know what else to do. A teacher noticed the drastic change in my behavior and kept me after class to talk to me. I broke down and told her. She called the police, then and there. He went to prison and I stayed in a foster home until I was seven months pregnant with you. Then, I lived in a home for single pregnant girls like myself until you were three months old."

"My father is Duane Harvey?" Libby asks. "Do you know where he is now?"

"No, and I don't want to know. His face has haunted my dreams ever since then."

Libby rises from her seat to give her mother a hug. "You told me what I wanted to know and I can see it wasn't easy for you."

"No, it wasn't, but I am glad to finally get it off my chest."

"Thanks for telling me."

"You're welcome." Diane breaks the embrace, dabs at her eyes with a napkin, and then asks, "Do you have another bottle of merlot?"

"Coming right up."

# ~23~

Libby doesn't go jogging the next morning because it suddenly doesn't feel safe to run by herself along a dark lonely stretch of road, even one so close to home. The video going online has exposed her to a different, and possibly more dangerous element. Who knows what some people are capable of doing? Instead, she readies herself for work, determined to go in early and treat this business day like any other. It turns out to be a task easier said than done.

Two of her workers, Gwen and Lucille, call in sick. That's how the day begins. All morning she's given a wide berth as she passes the others. Scott and Percy are talking animatedly to one another as she enters the lab building, but go quiet when they see her. Umberto is unable to meet her eyes when they speak. Leslie gives one-word replies to every question Libby asks her. Finally, just before noon, she requests that all of her employees come to the lunchroom for a company meeting.

"It's apparent some or all of you have become aware of a certain video of me which was posted online yesterday. If you haven't already, please don't view it. It was edited to look like I'm involved in a lesbian romance. The person who made the video did so without my knowledge or consent for the purpose of blackmailing me. I'm sorry for the damage done to the image of this company and my own reputation. Please don't let it affect how you feel about your job and the valuable work we do here. That's all I wanted to say. It's lunchtime, so I won't keep you any longer."

No one gets up to leave immediately. They look at one another expectantly. Then, Percy breaks the silence.

"Can I say something?"

"Go ahead," Libby says, and braces for a rebuke.

"I've never had anything like this happen to me, and I'm not sure what I'd do if I was in your shoes, but it seems to me like you've handled it pretty well."

Gina, Jesse and Scott nod in agreement. The tension in the air seems to dissipate. Shortly after lunch, Leslie knocks on her office door.

"I know you said you weren't taking calls from anyone other than clients, but there's a Detective Rowden on line two. He says you know him."

"I'll talk to him." Leslie returns to the front office as Libby picks up the phone. "This is Doctor Corcoran."

Without preamble Rowden says, "You weren't completely honest with me when we spoke the other day."

"I'm not sure what you're referring to," Libby says, calmly.

"You led me to believe you never shopped at Allure."

"Did I?" She realizes Rowden's call means he's aware of the video, but she's not going to volunteer any additional information if she can avoid it.

"You're not the only one who got caught up in this. You may have information that will help catch the person responsible, which in turn would help you with your situation."

"I don't think I know anything that would help with your investigation, Detective Rowden."

"I don't know if you can help or not, but I'd like to speak with you. Can you come to the police station here in Albuquerque for an interview?

"No, I'm sorry, but it's out of the question. I'm too busy to break away from here anytime in the foreseeable future."

She tells him she has to go and disconnects. Hopefully, that's the last she'll hear from him. He may or may not have good intentions, but there's a group of reporters who spend all their time hanging out at police stations. The last thing she needs is to have her name on a police report that the newspapers get wind of.

~~~

Just when she thinks things are at their worst, the next wave strikes. Jessica Rawlins calls to tell Libby.

"I hate to be the bearer of bad news, but as your agent, it is part of my job. The Good Way Company has informed me they won't be renewing your contract when it expires next month. In the meantime, they are cancelling all advertisements using your name or face to endorse their herbal products."

"Crap," Libby mutters. "Well, at least I still have plenty of other endorsement deals."

"I'm afraid not, dear. They're deserting you left and right, like rats from a sinking ship."

"Crap, crap," Libby reiterates. "Well, at least I have plenty of speaking appearances lined up. That will make up for some of the losses." Jessica is mum. "Not those, too?"

"Yes, those too. It seems you built a client base with an ultraconservative bias. They're afraid of the potential fallout. There is one bit of good news, however. You've been asked to appear on the nationally televised Tori Hayden Show."

"Who the hell is Tori Hayden?"

"She hosts a daytime talk show, featuring couples coming face to face with their cheating spouse's lover. They're looking for more LGBTQ-oriented guests."

"No fricking way!"

"I already told them you probably wouldn't be interested."

"Is that it? Haven't any other offers or inquiries come in?"

"Not a one. Your public career is in a holding pattern. Everyone seems to be waiting for the next shoe to drop. Liberty, please tell me there are no more shoes of this sort in your closet."

"None that I know of."

"That's not very reassuring, but it will have to do. Has that police detective contacted you again?"

"No, I haven't heard a peep out of him. He seems to think that with my help they could catch the blackmailer. Do you think I should talk to him?"

"Absolutely not. The video is going to run its course whether they catch the blackmailer or not. And if she is caught, the police will want their time in the spotlight. It's our worst nightmare. Anyone who doesn't know about the video already, will surely know after the case makes the evening news in Albuquerque."

"I see what you're saying. I'm glad I didn't agree to an interview at the station."

"Me too. You made the right decision. We'll get through this. It may take a while, but I'll be with you every step of the way. Keep your chin up."

# ~24~

With everything that's happened since the video was posted online, Libby has all but forgotten about Winston Cheung saying he is coming to see her. She's reminded of it when she receives an email from Gunter. It reads:

Libby, My business trip to the United States will take me to your part of the country on Thursday, the day after tomorrow. I will come visit if that is okay with you. Gunter

She thinks about it for only a minute before replying.

Gunter, looking forward to seeing you. Come for dinner and stay the night. Libby

It's bold of her, she knows, but they were intimate with one another in Mahé, and he'll only be here for a matter of hours, so why waste time playing coy? Besides, he's an incredibly good-looking man, and she's not getting any younger.

There's still the nagging question of the connection between Gunter, Winston Cheung and the mysterious plant, however. It wouldn't be wise to let her guard down with either one of them. Ever since Mahé, there's been a pattern of one showing up after the other. Gunter appears, then leaves, and the Cheung brothers appear, or vice versa. If the pattern repeats itself, Winston Cheung will be coming soon, if he's not already here.

With Gunter's arrival scheduled for Thursday, Libby plans to speak with Diane ahead of time to ask her nicely if she wouldn't mind making herself scarce while Gunter is visiting. It's not that Diane won't understand Libby's desire to have an intimate evening alone with the attractive Austrian, it's just that she'll be unable to resist sneaking a look for herself, and her timing isn't always perfect. If their introduction is prearranged it might prevent Diane from popping in at an awkward moment.

When Libby comes home Wednesday evening, Diane is in the kitchen preparing to put a meatloaf in the oven. She's wearing an apron to keep the tomato sauce off her yoga outfit. Before Libby can broach the subject of Gunter's visit, Diane throws her a curve ball.

"I invited Quentin to dinner, tonight."

"You did what?"

"He doesn't take care of himself like he should. I thought he could do with a good home-cooked meal."

"I don't like the idea of Quentin coming here for dinner."

"He thought you'd say that. He thinks you don't like him. I explained to him that you treat everyone that way, and he shouldn't take it personally."

"I don't treat everyone the way I treat Quentin, and he should take it personally. Let's not foster any hope of he and I becoming buddies."

"Liberty, you don't know him like I do. You have to look beyond the surface, past the tattoos, nose ring and interesting hairstyle, to see the real person."

"The last thing I want to do is look beyond Quentin's surface. Anyway, I have something I want to discuss with you, and I'm not comfortable talking in front of Quentin."

"Then, we'll talk about it before he gets here. How's that?"

"Oh, alright. I'm having a friend for dinner tomorrow night."

"A friend, like a man friend?"

"Yes, he's a man."

"Hold it right there. Don't say another word. I want to put this in the oven, pour a glass of wine and get comfortable before you go any further."

It takes a few minutes to get the meatloaf baking, uncork a bottle of wine and pour a glass. Then, Diane kicks her shoes off, gets comfy on the sofa and tells Libby to go ahead. Libby sits across from her.

"As I was saying, a friend of mine from Austria is going to be in town tomorrow."

"Austria! My goodness, he's coming all this way to see you?"

"He's in the country on business and is going to be passing through this area. He emailed me about stopping by."

"What does he look like?"

"He's absolutely gorgeous. A tall, blue-eyed blonde."

"That's wonderful, Liberty. I'm so happy for you. I can't wait to meet him."

"Yes, that's what I wanted to talk to you about."

Before she can say another word, there's a knock on the door.

"That must be Quentin," Diane says. "I'll let him in." She hops up from the sofa and starts for the door.

"But I haven't finished telling you about tomorrow night."

"That's okay. It will give us something to talk about during dinner."

Which is exactly what Libby wants to avoid—discussing Gunter with Quentin listening in.

"I'm going to get out of my work clothes. I'll be back in a minute."

In her bedroom, Libby takes off her slacks and lab coat, throws them in the laundry basket, and puts on sweatpants and a T-shirt. She washes her hands and splashes water on her face, dries, and then checks her image in the mirror. A stress-induced zit is starting to form on the tip of her nose. "Great, what next?" she asks herself.

Diane and Quentin are sitting at the kitchen table talking in low voices when she comes from the bedroom. He's wearing camo coveralls and leather work boots, his go-to outfit for any occasion as of late. Diane has removed the apron. The workout tank top and leggings make her look pixyish beside Quentin. Libby knows they're talking about her. As she enters the kitchen, Diane attempts to artfully segue the conversation to another topic.

"It's important to be at ease with your asana, in order to open all channels and allow the energy to flow in and out."

"Yeah, I see what you mean," Quentin says, though his puzzled look says otherwise.

"You're not fooling anyone. If you can't say it to my face, you probably shouldn't be saying it at all," Libby tells Diane.

"We weren't talking about you," Diane lies.

"Yeah, right."

"Finish what you started to say before Quentin arrived," Diane says to Libby.

Libby looks at Diane, then at Quentin, then back at Diane.

"I'll tell you later."

"You want me to go outside for a few minutes?"

"Yes, please," Libby says, and Quentin starts to rise.

"Sit down, she's just kidding," Diane tells him.

"No, I wasn't," Libby says.

"I can never tell when she's serious or when she's kidding. Her expression is the same either way," Quentin says.

"She's tough to read that way," Diane acknowledges.

"Tell me about it. I was around her for months before I even realized she had a sense of humor."

Excluding Quentin from the conversation is more trouble than it's worth, so Libby gives up.

"Look, all I wanted to say is tomorrow when my friend arrives, I'll introduce you. Afterward, I was hoping you would excuse yourself, and maybe read a book or watch TV in your room. Would you mind doing that for me?"

"Well, of course I don't mind. Did you think I was going to hang around like a third wheel while your handsome Austrian fellow is here?"

"No, but I thought it best if we sort of synchronized our schedules, so neither of us is interrupted at an inopportune moment."

"Just give it to me in plain English."

"She talks that way because she thinks I don't understand what she's saying," Quentin explains. "Sometimes when she's talking about me to someone else with me standing right there, she spells out the words."

"Alright, here it is in the simplest of terms. I'll introduce you to my friend at six thirty, and by six forty you'll have disappeared for the rest of the evening. Clear enough?"

"Perfectly. I meet your gentleman friend at six thirty and at six forty I'm like Cinderella at the stroke of midnight. Poof, I'm gone."

"You can hang with me, if you want," Quentin offers.

"I'd love to. See, Liberty. It's all settled. Don't worry about a thing. Just enjoy tomorrow evening with your Austrian hunk."

"Did you say Austrian?" Quentin asks. "That wouldn't be Hans, now would it?"

"It's no one you know."

# ~25~

Gunter sends a text message to let Libby know he'll be arriving by private plane at the Taos Regional Airport, Thursday afternoon at five. She leaves work early to shower, fix her hair, put on makeup and change clothes. Summer is only a week away, so she selects something appropriate for the weather, an apricot spaghetti strap sundress that compliments her auburn hair and shows off her long legs. She dabs a little concealer on the tip of her nose to hide the zit which refuses to go away, applies ruby red lipstick and dons a pair of large rose-tinted sunglasses.

The airport is north of Taos on a tract of flat barren land seven thousand feet above sea level. It's not like an urban airport where there are signs pointing you to arrivals and departures, so it's confusing at first glance. She stops at the only building with cars parked out front and goes inside. A wall of windows at the rear of the building gives Libby a view of the runway. No planes are coming or going.

A young woman sits behind a counter under a sign which reads Taos Aviation. She is meticulously applying a two-tone coat of polish to her fingernails. Libby is hesitant to interrupt, and at the same time curious as to how the pink and yellow nails will look with the woman's green and orange hair. The woman glances up, giving Libby permission to speak.

"I'm Doctor Liberty Corcoran. I'm here to pick up a friend."

"I'm Cassandra. Pick one up for me while you're at it."

She's the sort of person who laughs at her own jokes. Libby gives her a minute to pull herself together.

"He's supposed to arrive by private plane at five o'clock."

"No planes have come in from anywhere in the last hour. You can wait in the pilot's lounge, if you want."

Cassandra points to a corner where there are two vending machines, four chairs and a table with magazines, newspapers and an ashtray. Libby takes a seat in one of the chairs and scans through the magazines. Behind the counter where Cassandra sits, there's a two-way radio that picks up local air-to-air and air-to-ground communications. Libby listens when voices sound, but everything said is in pilot-speak, which she understands about as well as she understands Russian.

It's almost six o'clock when she hears him announcing in his Austrian accent, "Attenschion Taos traffic. Piper eight six sierra is inbound for runway one-two."

"That's him," Libby tells Cassandra.

She watches through the rear glass wall of the building as the plane lands and taxis to an overnight tie-down area. It looks like a toy compared to the commercial jets she's used to seeing. Gunter climbs out of the cockpit, steps onto the wing and down to the tarmac. She waves at him. He waves back, smiling broadly as he comes toward her. The sleeves of his white shirt are rolled up and the collar is unbuttoned. His suit coat and tie are draped over his arm, and in his hand is an overnight bag.

"Libby," he says when he reaches her. "How wonderful to see you."

He wraps his free arm around her, pulls her close and kisses her. It's a quick kiss, lacking passion, not the hot and steamy greeting she was hoping for.

"It's great to see you too, Gunter. I was so sorry to hear about your mother."

"Thank you, zat is kind of you to say so. Mother is doing much better now, though."

"I'm glad to hear that. Come on, I'm parked right outside."

She reaches for the exit door, but Gunter beats her to it.

"Allow me," he says, and ushers Libby out like a true gentleman. It reminds her of the way he behaved at dinner in Mahé. His manners, every word, every gesture, it was all so perfect.

Libby finds it difficult to keep her eyes on the road ahead. She keeps glancing over at Gunter. As they get closer to her house, and the road is more narrow and winding, her lack of attention to it seems to be making him nervous.

"We don't have much farther to go," she reassures him.

"I have been looking forward to seeing your place."

"Well, here we are," she says, as she turns into her driveway.

He takes in the house and complex of structures beyond it. "Very nice," he comments.

"Come on in."

Because of his later than expected arrival, it's already seven. Libby has forgotten she promised Diane an introduction at six thirty, but Diane has not.

"Welcome to America," she says, as soon as he's inside, and then throws her arms around his neck to kiss him. "I'm Diane. It's so good to meet you."

"It is nice to meet you too, Diane. I'm Gunter Schneider. I did not know zat Libby has a twin sister," he schmoozes.

"Oh Liberty, this one's a keeper. No doubt about it. Come have a seat on the sofa, Gunter. Libby get this man something to drink."

Libby catches her mother's attention, then lets her eyes go from her to the door and back repeatedly, hoping she'll take the hint. She says, "Diane, don't forget about the movie you're going to see. You don't want to be late."

"What movie?" Diane asks, momentarily confused.

"The one at the movie theater in town. You're going to be late if you don't leave right now."

"Oh, that movie. That's alright. I hate sitting through the coming attractions. It won't hurt to be a few minutes late." As if that settles the matter, she turns to Gunter and asks, "What would you like to drink? You look like a bourbon sort of man, three fingers and no ice. Am I right?"

"You must have been reading my mind," Gunter says.

"Apparently, I wasn't reading your mind, because I don't have any bourbon," Libby says.

"Yes you do, Liberty. It's in the pantry. I saw it there earlier," Diane says. "Pour a little for me, too. We'll toast Gunter's first visit, here."

Libby finds the bottle in the pantry, a fifth of Old Grand-Dad Kentucky bourbon. She pours three fingers for Gunter, about a half finger for Diane, and none for herself, then carries them to the sofa where Diane is practically sitting in Gunter's lap.

Diane raises the glass and says, "Here's to Gunter's visit. May it be the first of many." Then, she upends the contents of her glass.

"Thank you," Gunter tells her. "I am overwhelmed by your hospitality."

"Don't forget about the movie," Libby reminds Diane.

"Oh, alright. I'm going."

She leans in far enough to give Gunter a look down her dress, then kisses his cheek while squeezing his thigh at the same time. Libby takes her by the arm, pulls her to the front door, takes the glass from her hand and pushes her out.

"Alone at last," she says, returning to the sofa to sit beside Gunter. "I'm sorry about Diane. She can be very trying sometimes."

"There is no apology necessary. She is very friendly."

"Yes, she's that alright. I should start dinner soon. We're having filet mignon, potatoes au gratin, and asparagus with hollandaise sauce. How does that sound?"

"Zat sounds wonderful." He puts his arms around her and pulls her closer until their faces almost touch. "What will we be having for dessert?"

"Hmm. Vat did you haf in mind?" Libby teases.

"I think we should have dessert now, and dinner later, after we have worked up an appetite."

Gunter's performance in bed is worthy of a gold medal, or at least in Libby's opinion it is. After the bandit on the beach spoiled their time together in Mahé, he probably feels he has something to prove. Libby does nothing to dissuade him from giving it his best effort.

"That was fabulous," she tells him afterward.

"You ain't seen nothing yet," he replies.

After a second go, they lie next to one another, spent but content.

"Has your appetite been sufficiently stimulated? Should I start dinner, now?" Libby asks between exhalations.

"Yes, zat sounds good. Dessert was nice. Now, we will move on to zee main course."

Libby wears her kimono with nothing underneath to dinner. Gunter sits across the table wearing only his silk boxers. They eat very slowly, taking small bites and savoring each one. For the occasion, Libby purchased two bottles of expensive French wine from a shop in town that specializes in imported beer and wine. It's red wine from the Bordeaux region, and made from a mix of cabernet sauvignon and merlot grapes. Gunter examines the label.

"Chateau Duhart-Milon. I have not heard of it, but it is very good."

"I'm glad you like it. How's your food?"

"I am sorry. I should have said so before. Everything is wonderful."

She smiles at the praise. The evening is going so well, much better than she'd anticipated. And the best part is, it's not over yet.

"Libby," Gunter says, and pauses. It's a meaningful hesitation signaling a transition in the conversation. He waits for her eyes to meet his before continuing. "It is so good to see you again, especially after leaving Mahé without saying goodbye. However, I have another reason for coming here. There is something I need to speak to you about."

His tone has turned serious, and she fears he is going to say something that will ruin their evening. She forks a bite of food into her mouth and reluctantly prompts him to go ahead.

"Okay."

117

"It concerns your involvement with Winston Cheung."

Her chin jerks up at the mention of the name. "What about him?" she says calmly.

"I know zat he is trying to enlist your help to find a special plant."

"How do you know this?"

"I have been hired as a consultant by a company with an interest in zee same plant. Winston Cheung was working for zem when he acquired zee berry."

"You know about the berry?"

"I know of zee berry, but nothing about it other zan Winston stole it from zem. The company, Khon Kaen Pharmaceutical, has been surveilling Winston's activities for several years."

"How did he steal it from them?"

"From what I understand, KKP sponsored an expedition into New Guinea, Indonesia. Everything zat was collected during zee expedition belonged to zee company. Zee berry in question was not returned to zem."

Libby knows a little about how the berry came into Winston's possession. Or at least, she has heard Winston's version of the story, but she's not ready to reveal this to Gunter.

"Are you telling me this, to warn me away? Do you think I'm in some kind of danger from Winston or this pharmaceutical company?"

"No, I don't believe you are in danger. What I think is zat you are in a unique position. Winston seems to trust you. He is prepared to divulge secrets to you. Secrets zat are very valuable to KKP. Secrets zey would be willing to pay a lot of money for. I am not trying to warn you away. I'm suggesting you play along with Winston until you have zee secrets. After zat, we can sell zem to zee highest bidder."

*We?* Libby thinks. She can't deny she's intrigued by the money. Some botanical discoveries have paid off big. Who knows what this could be worth?

"How much do you think these secrets are worth on the open market? Are we talking hundreds of dollars, thousands or tens of thousands?"

"Possibly millions, who can say for sure." He can see she's interested, but doesn't want to push too hard or too fast. "It is not something you have to decide right zis minute, just something for you to think about. You are a smart woman. You will make zee right decision when zee time comes."

"How long have you known about Winston Cheung contacting me?"

"I cannot say how long KKP has known, but me personally, I have only known for a short while."

"Did you know before Mahé?"

"Libby, I see where you are going with zat. You are wondering if I arranged to have dinner with you in Mahé just to get information about Winston. The answer is no. And if you are wondering zee same thing about me being here now, zee answer to zat is no, as well." He sets down his fork, picks up her hand and kisses it. "You are a beautiful woman and a pleasure to talk with. Zat is zee reason I am here. Zat, and zee dessert."

She feels she's not getting the truth, or not all of it, but at the same time, she likes what she's hearing and wants to believe him.

"We can have more dessert after dinner, if you like."

"I would like nothing more."

# ~26~

It could have been a scene from a movie, with Gunter in the role of leading man and Libby as his leading lady. The supporting cast includes Cassandra, minding the front counter at Taos Aviation, and Jukes Carson, sitting in the pilot's lounge. The backdrop for the scene is a wall of glass, beyond which is the airport runway where a Piper Dakota is waiting for Gunter to climb into the cockpit and fly away. At this point, the director would call for quiet on the set, and then shout into his megaphone, "Action."

Libby's eyes are brimming with tears as she says to Gunter, "Please be careful."

"Don't worry about me. I am an experienced pilot. I will be fine."

"When will I see you again?" she asks, as the first tear starts to trickle down her cheek.

"Soon, very soon, I hope." He takes her in his arms and plants his lips against hers like there's no tomorrow. It's an intense, passionate and lingering kiss.

"Get a room, already," Cassandra says. The camera pans to her at the front desk. Her nails are still pink and yellow, but her hair color has changed overnight to blue and crimson.

Then, the camera moves to Jukes in the pilot's lounge, who is a fifty-something Barney Fife look-alike. He takes a cigarette from his lips, drops it into his coffee cup, exhales a cloud of smoke and says, "Holy shit."

Gunter and Libby break from their embrace. Gunter exits the building through the glass door leading onto the tarmac with Libby clinging to his hand until the last possible second. She watches him step onto the wing of the plane, get into the pilot's seat, blow her a kiss and shut the cockpit door. She stays at the glass wall waving to Gunter, until the plane is no more than a speck on the horizon, then she turns away. Cassandra is studying her nails, thinking about adding a few sequins. Jukes is lighting another cigarette. Neither of them look up as Libby leaves the building.

"Doctor Corcoran," she hears someone call to her, as she's about to get into her SUV.

She turns to see Jukes coming toward her at a leisurely stride. He has one hand in his pocket and the other grips a burning cigarette between the index and middle fingers.

"If you'll follow me, Mr. Cheung would like to speak to you." She hesitates. "It's alright. I'm not going to hurt you, and I don't think you've got anything to worry about where those Cheung brothers are concerned. They don't look like they could fight their way out of a wet paper bag, much less harm you. They're in the last hangar down there. They asked me to come get you because they didn't want the fellow you were with to see them."

"Are you an associate of the Cheungs?"

"No ma'am. I'm just a pilot they hired to fly them here from Denver."

Now, it's beginning to make sense to Libby. Gunter had rented the plane and flown to Taos from Denver. Winston and his brother Edgar had followed him here. Jukes walks with her to the hangar, holds the door as she enters, and then returns to the pilot's lounge.

"Hello Winston, Edgar," Libby says.

The hangar is a Quonset hut structure big enough to hold a medium-sized aircraft, but at the moment it's empty. The floor is concrete. Overhead industrial florescent lights illuminate the building. Workbenches and tool boxes line the back wall. Winston and Edgar lean against the benches with their hands resting on their trademark walking canes.

"Libby, it is such a pleasure to see you again," Winston says.

"Yes indeed," Edgar agrees. "Truly a pleasure."

"I can't say I'm surprised to see you, but I didn't expect this," she spreads her arms to indicate the hangar.

"This was our pilot, Mr. Carson's idea. We expressed a desire to speak with you alone, and he arranged for the use of this building," Winston explains.

An old office chair with casters sits next to a metal desk. Edgar swivels it around and dusts it off with a handkerchief for Libby to use.

"Here, sit. We have much to show you."

Several sheets of paper and photographs are spread out on the desk. They're arranged in a particular order, Libby notices, as if telling a story. Post-its stuck to the pages explain what each stack holds. Some of the pages are handwritten notes Winston made during the expedition into West Papua. Some are notes and diagrams Bussaba Meesang made while studying the berry.

"During the expedition into West Papua in 1986, I kept a journal. These notes are excerpts from the journal in chronological order. I documented the dominant species of plants in each area we passed through, from the time we left Jayapura until we reached the farthest point of the expedition, the eight-thousand-foot level in the mountains of central West Papua. I thought the journal excerpts from the time spent at the higher elevation might be of interest to you on a personal level, since your own research facility is seven thousand feet above sea level."

"I'm sure all of this will be interesting to me in some way, but it will take days to thoroughly go over it all. Why don't you summarize it for me," Libby suggests.

"That is an excellent idea," Edgar says. "The expedition journal will be important later, but there is something here of more immediate significance." He gestures at the stack of papers marked Bussaba Meesang. "These are some of the notes she took while researching the berry sample Winston sent her. We have only recently acquired these. We believe they were stolen from her by the man who killed her, and then sold to Khon Kaen Pharmaceutical."

"How did you get them?" Libby asks.

The brothers look from one to the other before answering, "We have a person on the inside."

"Is that how you knew Gunter Schneider was coming to see me? You obviously followed him here from Denver."

"It is true we followed Mr. Schneider. I have been forthright with you regarding our suspicions of him, and his connection to KKP."

"Did Khon Kaen Pharmaceutical sponsor the 1986 expedition into West Papua?" Libby asks next. She scrutinizes his face, eyes and hands, looking for a nervous tic or twitch to indicate a forthcoming deception, but Winston remains placid.

"Yes," he admits. "They paid our expenses on the condition we share any significant find with them, which we did. Once we returned to our respective homes, and examined, analyzed and catalogued our samples, the results were given to KKP. At the time, I did not consider the berry to be significant. That was before I sent the sample to Bussaba."

"Still, once you received the preliminary report from her," Libby says. "You were aware then, it was something they would want to know about."

"If I may," Edgar interjects. "There is much we haven't told you about KKP, much you need to know, especially considering Gunter Schneider's connection with them, and your relationship with him. KKP's interest in the berry is for a different reason than ours. Please, review the information here, first."

Libby scans the documents arrayed on the desk before her. Bussaba Meesang's research notes are of particular interest. Her methods were unique. She was obviously a skilled and dedicated scientist, someone Libby would like to have known. There is a page of hand drawn diagrams of six different phytochemicals extracted from the berry sample, and notes about her difficulty in identifying them.

Two full typewritten pages are Bussaba's theory as to the possible origin of the berry. She summarizes by stating the berry is most likely the result of a naturally occurring crossbreeding of plants. Her research was done thirty years ago, and much has been learned about plant DNA since.

Libby turns her attention to the section involving Bussaba's experiments with mice. Winston has spoken of them, previously. Documents describing lab experiments are prepared with fellow scientists in mind, and written in terminology only they could appreciate, much less understand. Libby skips ahead to a summation of the results.

Six mice were fed varying amounts of the berry over a period of six weeks. At different stages of the experiment, she took one mouse at a time to dissect it. Then she examined cell samples taken from the brain, spine, muscle tissue and elsewhere. With each mouse the microglial cells taken from the brain and spine responded differently and more dramatically than all the others. They were stimulated while the others were unaffected.

"I can see why you believe this plant, if it can be found, would have great potential. I'll admit I'm intrigued. However, I'm skeptical we can locate the plant. There's an excellent chance it no longer exists. Bussaba writes that she believes it might have been the fruit of a hybrid plant, a one-time fluke of nature. If that's the case, it wouldn't have been able to reproduce. That's why I say it may already be extinct."

"We believe the plant lives," Winston says. "In fact, we believe we know the approximate location where it can be found. There is a tribe of people living in the mountains in West Papua. They are hostile to outsiders and have kept to themselves for thousands of years. The indigenous people of neighboring tribes tell stories about them. They are purported to be cannibals, and practitioners of black magic, possessing the ability to cast evil spells on their enemies. I have heard rumors about a ritual they perform involving a berry."

"How near are these people to where you acquired the berry?"

"I estimate the distance between the two places to be twenty kilometers. The boy I acquired the berry from was probably a member of the tribe. To him the berry was something of value, a precious trading commodity. The look on his face when he called it Chamala was as if he was holding a gold

123

nugget in his hand. There will be others in that area who know something of the berry. I am certain of it."

Edgar says, "Throughout our search for the berry, we have stayed a step ahead of KKP, but only a small step. This is why you must go now. We cannot allow them to find it first."

"Because you don't want them to profit from your discovery. Isn't that what you're saying?"

"No, that is not it," Edgar quickly asserts, then relents. "That is not our only reason. Winston, tell her about KKP. You know them better than I do."

"Yes, tell me why it is you've been at odds with this company for so long."

"It has not always been that way," Winston says. "The company's founder was Hanh Nguyen, who I considered a close friend. When he started his business in 1970, it was primarily a biopharmaceutical venture. Initially his focus was dietary supplements derived from plant and animal sources. He died in 1986, while we were on the expedition in West Papua. I did not learn of his passing until I returned to Hong Kong. His eldest son, Duc, took control of the company."

"I take it that's when your relationship with KKP changed," Libby says.

"Yes. Duc Nguyen wanted to take the company in a new more lucrative direction, answering the growing demand for antidepressants and antipsychotic drugs. Are you familiar with how those kinds of drugs are made?"

"Somewhat. I've studied biochemistry, but I'm no expert in pharmaceutical or chemical engineering," Libby says.

"As an herbalist," Winston says, "I have always leaned toward treating depression and schizophrenia naturally, with the seeds, leaves, roots and fruit of plants, the way it has been done for centuries. However, modern man prefers the faster-acting synthetic drugs, even if the side effects are often severe. A rift has formed between those who believe as I do and those who believe in these new synthetic drugs, and it is growing wider with time. Duc Nguyen thinks of me as someone who lives in the past, someone who is unwilling to accept change, and he sees himself as a visionary. I think of him as young and impetuous, but I will give him credit where it is due. He is shrewd and has good business instincts. He believes that in the near future antidepressant and antipsychotic drugs will come from newly discovered and hybrid plants."

"I see," Libby says. "And he believes the berry might represent one of these new discoveries he's looking for. You still haven't explained to my satisfaction why you didn't turn the berry over to KKP after the expedition, as per the original agreement with them. I'm having difficulty believing it was simply an oversight on your part."

"I will not insult your intelligence by telling you I did not think KKP would be interested in the berry. I intentionally kept it from them until I could learn more. Bussaba's death and the circumstances surrounding it changed everything."

"You think KKP had something to do with her death?"

"Yes," Edgar states, emphatically. "Duc Nguyen will stop at nothing to get what he thinks is rightfully his. He may be a shrewd businessman, but he is also ruthless and egocentric. We have no proof of his involvement in her death, but we are certain he is capable of murder."

"Our concern is that his impatience and greed will destroy the plant that produces the berry," Winston says. "If he finds it before we do, he is likely to strip it of leaves and berries or uproot it without properly preparing it to be transplanted. It could mean the extinction of the plant before the world learns of its true value."

From the very first conversations regarding this mysterious plant, Libby has felt herself being drawn in by its mystique. The preservation of endangered species of plants is something close to her heart. Winston and Edgar Cheung have chosen wisely by appealing to that sentiment. In his attempt to enlist her help, Gunter tried tempting her with the promise of monetary gains. A mistake on his part.

Winston interrupts her thoughts. "Libby, I am sorry to once again pressure you for an answer, but we are quite literally running out of time. Will you help us find and save the plant?"

"When you put that way, how can I say no?"

# ~27~

Libby's mind was made up before the latest meeting with the Cheung brothers, maybe even before Gunter came to visit. But she can't deny he played an important part in the final decision. She finds his charm and sophistication irresistible. Whatever his reasons for wanting the plant, her joining the search gives them a common purpose, and serves as a basis for staying in touch with one another.

Another contributing factor in her decision is her schedule suddenly being freed up by the stink surrounding the internet video. Even Jessica Rawlins thinks it is a good idea to leave the country for a while when Libby tells her.

"I like the sound of it. Don't you? Doctor Liberty Belle Corcoran, adventurer, scientist and explorer. Crossing oceans, risking her life in the jungle and scaling mountains in search of the lost plant. I can do a lot with that. You'll have more offers for personal appearances and endorsement deals than you can shake a stick at."

"Easy girl. You can't go public with this, yet."

"Well then, why the hell are you telling me? I'm not your fricking priest, after all. It's my job to promote you, not listen to your confidential confessions."

"I'm telling you this because I thought you'd want to know I'll be out of the country. Possibly for as long as three months, during which time I won't be available for appearances."

"There's no need to worry about that."

"All the more reason I should do this now. If all goes well, this video thing will be history, and there will be more offers than ever before, six months from now."

"I hope your wish comes true, there. Keep me posted."

~~~

Winston and Edgar Cheung came to Taos with the intention of staying until Libby was ready to leave with them for West Papua. Because of the amount of preparation and discussion necessary, it doesn't make sense for the brothers to commute between a hotel in Taos and Libby's place while they plan the trip. So, she puts them up in a spare room.

Libby, Winston, Edgar and Diane are sitting at the table in her breakfast nook at six thirty a.m. They're all in pajamas, terrycloth robes and slippers. Diane and Libby are drinking Kenyan coffee, while Winston and Edgar sip chamomile tea. In the middle of the table is a box of assorted donuts Diane picked up in town the day before.

"It is very considerate of you to provide the donuts, Diane," Winston says.

"I didn't know what you guys normally eat for breakfast, but I figured I couldn't go wrong with a variety of donuts. Go ahead, help yourself."

Edgar takes one from the box, sets it on his plate, and then Winston makes his selection.

"I hope you were comfortable enough last night," Libby says to the brothers.

Diane has been using the guest room, the only room other than Libby's with a bed. The room where Winston and Edgar are staying is normally used for storage. Libby cleared away some things and put a couple of futon mattresses on the floor for them to sleep on.

"Winston slept soundly," Edgar replies. "I know this because he snored all night. I have insomnia and lie awake most of the time, but the mattress is comfortable. It is kind of you to have us, and it will help a great deal."

Libby reaches for a chocolate frosted donut, but before she can grab it Winston says, "Libby, perhaps it would be wise to complete your exercise routine before you indulge. I believe you typically run each morning. Is that not right?"

She pauses with her hand hovering over the box of donuts. "I was planning to forego jogging while we're preparing for the expedition, so we'd have more time to go over things."

"Your conditioning is as important a factor as any other. Traversing the rugged terrain to reach your destination will test the limits of your physical endurance." Libby looks at Winston, then at her hand still hovering over the donut. He says, "I will make sure no one eats that donut while you are gone."

Libby goes for an hour-long jog, considering what Winston said about the need to be in tip-top shape as she runs. When she returns, the chocolate frosted donut is waiting for her on a plate on the kitchen table, but she's lost her desire for it. Instead she puts a carrot, spinach, wheat germ, yogurt and blueberries into the blender to make herself a healthy low-cal smoothie, and drinks it down while standing at the sink.

An hour later after she has showered and dressed, Libby sits on the couch. Winston enters the living room wearing cotton slacks and a short-sleeve linen shirt, carrying a briefcase. Edgar follows him wearing jeans and a Hawaiian shirt, bringing a small tool bag along.

"There is much to go over and time is of the essence. I think we should begin," Winston declares.

He signals to Edgar who then pulls an electronic bug detector from his tool bag, and begins sweeping the room for listening devices. Libby starts to speak, but Winston puts a finger to his lips to shush her.

Edgar moves around the room passing the antenna of the detector over anywhere a miniature digital bug could be hidden. The meter alerts him to something near the end table beside the couch. Winston makes casual conversation for the sake of anyone listening while Edgar gets down on all fours to look under the end table. He indicates to Winston that he's found one.

"It is such a lovely day. Perhaps we should go outside," Edgar suggests.

"Why don't we," Libby agrees. "Let's sit on the patio."

Edgar repeats the bug sweeping procedure around the table and chairs in the patio area before giving Winston and Libby a thumbs up. Winston then pulls notes and papers from his briefcase. He unfolds and spreads a three-foot-square map on the table.

"How did you know about the bug?" Libby asks.

"We did not know. It was a precaution," Edgar explains.

"Who would have placed it there?" she asks, although she already has a short list of suspects with Gunter Schneider at the top of it.

"Speculating as to who is responsible is one more distraction we do not have time for."

"Yes, I guess you're right. Are you going to remove it?"

"No, that would alert them to its discovery. This way we can use it to feed them false information."

"This is West Papua and the area around it," Winston says, directing her attention to the map. "Jayapura is here. I have arranged for the supplies needed for the expedition to be shipped there. Once we arrive, we will pick up the supplies and acquire the necessary travel permit. From the Sentani Airport near Jayapura we will fly with our supplies and permit to Wamena, where you will meet your guide."

Libby examines the map as Winston speaks.

"Where on the map is it where you believe the plant will be found?"

"Right about here," Winston says, pointing to a spot near the center of the province.

"This guide you mentioned. Does he come from that area, and does he know the purpose of our trip?"

"No, and no. The guide is sort of a middle man. He will hire and communicate with Dani tribesmen who are familiar with your destination and the route there."

"It looks to be no more than fifty miles from Wamena. How long do you estimate it will take to get there?"

"It is impossible to say. There are many factors to consider, not the least of which is weather. Although the monsoon season is typically during the winter months, heavy rains can come at any time, and cause landslides and wash out the roads. Besides the rain, West Papua is politically unstable at times."

"What does that mean? They're in the middle of a civil war, or something of that sort?"

"The indigenous people and the Indonesians have been at odds for more than fifty years. It is a condition the inhabitants of the island have come to accept as normal. West Papua is a place where people of differing cultures, beliefs and values have lived in close proximity for tens of thousands of years."

"I don't share your confidence that I'm the right person for this expedition."

"Libby, you are the only person for this expedition."

"How can you be so sure? I'm not a female Indiana Jones. I've never been athletically inclined. I never went camping. I'm not particularly brave and I get nauseous at the sight of blood. I'll say it again. I don't think I'm the right person for this."

"Then, I will prove I am right about you. Although there are dangers and obstacles to be aware of, each day I will show you more of what will need to be done to prepare. Within a day, maybe two, you will understand and agree that you are the one to do this."

Libby's expression is a mix of doubt and confusion. Doubt over her ability to pull it off, and confusion over why this project is so important to her. Winston pushes on in spite of her obvious discomfort.

"Here is a booklet to help you learn to speak Bahasa, the national language of Indonesia. This audio disc will help with pronunciation."

"I was never very good with foreign languages. I had a year of Latin in school and barely passed the course."

"Winston and I will help you."

"Yes," Winston says. "Kami akan membantumu."

Edgar translates for Libby's sake. "He said, we will help you. In West Papua, all businesses, the military, police and government offices are run by Indonesians. Learning to communicate directly with them is crucial. It would not be wise to depend on a translation from a third party."

Libby lets out a heavy sigh. "This is like my first day at U of W, a little overwhelming."

Winston lays his hand atop Libby's.

"Few things in life are easy for someone who expects as much of themselves as you do. Trust me and be patient. We will get through this together."

"I hope you're right about that," Libby says.

"Yes, I hope so too."

Libby hardly sleeps at all the night before they leave. But, thirty hours of the next two days will be spent sitting on planes or in airports. She can sleep then.

# ~28~

From the moment she leaves Taos to begin the long journey to West Papua, Libby feels the tug of some unknown force holding her back. Like a ghost whispering in her ear, telling her to turn around and go home, this isn't meant to be. The flight delays, nagging fatigue, extreme heat and unusually rainy weather all seem like harbingers of an impending failure. It's making her as testy as a mama bear with a newborn cub, but as the sun rises over the Baliem Valley on the morning the expedition is scheduled to begin it's a new day in every sense of the word.

"We are fortunate," Winston says, as he looks at a weather satellite view of West Papua and the surrounding area. "There are no storms in the vicinity."

The hotel in Wamena, where Winston and Edgar will stay while Libby leads the expedition, doesn't have internet access for their guests. So, the three of them are having breakfast at an internet café in the center of town. Libby is chewing on what appears to be an egg roll with a rubbery consistency, and attempting to wash it down with weak, lukewarm coffee.

"The sooner I get started the better. If the rain holds off for a couple of days, we could cover a lot of ground, maybe even make it to the search area."

Winston knows she is being overly optimistic, but why tell her so? "We will see if Mr. Dornier is ready to go when he gets here."

"It isn't his decision. You're paying for his services. He leaves when I'm ready. Where is he, anyway? I thought you told him to meet us here at nine." She glances at her watch. "It's already nine twenty."

"Let me have your watch," Edgar says. It's an inexpensive Timex she bought especially for this trip. She unfastens the wristband and gives it to him. He drops it on the floor, and then stomps on it, leaving the crystal broken and the hands askew. He gives it back to her. "Now, you are on West Papua time."

"What Edgar means is, you should not expect the people here to exhibit the same proclivity for punctuality as you."

"I don't think it's unreasonable for me to expect a person to be somewhere at a time they've agreed to, regardless of where in the world we are."

"I am only asking that you be patient with Mr. Dornier. If we have to find a replacement guide, it would only delay things further."

Libby sulks, tries again to eat the egg roll, but finally gives up and pushes it aside. Around ten o'clock by her estimate, a man comes into the café and scans the room as if looking for someone. He's a short stocky man with unkempt hair, a beard and a bulbous red nose.

"Please, tell me that's not him," Libby whispers.

"I cannot tell you it is not him, because I have never met Mr. Dornier,"

The man continues to scan the room. After a minute, his eyes find her and he lurches toward their table.

"I'm Pierre Dornier," he announces, in a gruff voice.

"Yes, Mr. Dornier. We have been expecting you. This is my brother Edgar, and this is Doctor Liberty Corcoran."

"Nice meeting you folks. So, you're wanting to go over to the other end of the valley, are you? Well, I'm the man who can show you the way. Let's get the money out of the way first off, then we can talk about when you want to go and what you'll need to bring."

"Your email reply to my inquiry quoted a price of one million rupiah per day for your services."

"What!" Libby exclaims. Edgar places his hand on her forearm to calm her.

"That is approximately seventy-five US dollars."

"Oh."

"The million is just for me. Anything else is extra. If you need porters to carry equipment and camping gear, that's another one million rupiah."

"How much of the trip can be made by Jeep?" Winston asks.

"As of right now, not much. The Trans-Papua Road Project is supposed to change that, but it won't be completed for another year, maybe longer."

Winston unfolds his map, spreads it out on the table and places his finger on a spot. "How many days will it take you to lead Doctor Corcoran to this point and back?"

Dornier uses his fingers on the map to estimate distance. His eyes seem to cross from the strain of doing the calculations in his head, while examining the map.

"There and back will take twelve days."

"She will need three porters to carry her gear."

"That would be three million rupiah a day. Which comes to…, uh, let me see…,"

"Thirty-six million rupiah," Edgar says. "Approximately twenty-seven hundred US dollars. When can you be ready to leave?"

"We can try for three days from now, or the day after that."

"We were hoping to leave sooner," Winston says.

"No way. I can't leave at the drop of a hat. I've got to reschedule my other bookings before I can leave out of here and be gone for two weeks."

Libby met the man two minutes before and already dislikes him. She can't hold back any longer.

"Given how busy you are, I think we should find someone else. Thanks for dropping by to say hello."

"Hold on, don't be so hasty. You won't find anyone of my caliber."

"That may or may not be true, but whoever we hire for this job will work on my schedule, and at my pace, not his own. If you're not willing to do that, we have no choice but to look elsewhere for someone who is."

Dornier isn't used to being spoken to like that, especially when it's a woman doing the speaking. Libby can almost see the steam coming from his nostrils, but he somehow manages to remain calm. "Alright then, what if we leave around noon, the day after tomorrow?"

"Not soon enough. I was planning to leave today, and had you gotten here at nine as you were supposed to, we might already be on our way."

He turns to Winston. "Who's running this show, you or her? She's crazy if she thinks we can go on a twelve-day excursion without a significant amount of preparation."

"You mean like packing food, medical and camping supplies?" Libby retorts. "We already have. First aid supplies, drinking water, a three-week supply of dehydrated foods, matches, a tent and sleeping bag are ready to go."

"Mr. Dornier," Winston says. "It is not a matter of who is in charge here, as much as who will be in charge on the trail. Maybe it would be best if we speak to another guide."

As much as he'd like to tell them to go to hell, the trip will net him two thousand US dollars after expenses, which is twice what he makes in the busiest month of the year. He can't afford to walk away.

"Can we compromise, maybe meet in the middle on when we leave?"

"Pierre, if you can rearrange your schedule, hire the porters and be at the Wamena Inn at eight tomorrow morning, ready to go, you've got the job. That's as flexible with our schedule as we can afford to be."

~~~

Dornier shows up on time the next morning, bringing with him three Dani tribesmen. The Dani men are tall and dressed in well-worn pants, short-sleeve shirts and sandals. Pierre Dornier is wearing cargo pants, a long-sleeve shirt and hiking boots. He looks less disheveled than the day before, but his nose is still as red as if he just came off a week-long bender.

"I'm glad to see you're here on time. I'm anxious to get started," Libby says.

"Of course I'm here on time. Pierre Dornier is a man of his word, and we can get going as soon as I'm paid."

Libby hands him a plastic bag containing eighteen million rupiah. "That's half of the amount we spoke of. The other half will be waiting for you here when we return."

"That's not how I work. I don't want to come back here to find these guys have skipped town already."

"Mr. Dornier," Winston says. "My brother and I are also men of our word. We will be here when you return, as will your payment. There may even be a bonus for you, if Doctor Corcoran is pleased with your services."

The mention of a bonus appeases him for the moment. "Alright, then. If we're going to do this, we best get started." He points at the Dani men, one at a time, and introduces them. "This is Dwe, Addis and Jali."

"Dwe, Addis and Jali," Libby repeats. "I hope I can remember those."

"It won't matter. I'll handle communicating with them. They don't understand a word of English, and only a little Bahasa."

Dornier speaks a few words of what Libby presumes is Dani, as he gestures at three extra-large backpacks containing Libby's expedition supplies. The packs are designed to carry enough cargo for an extended trek into the wilderness. They have a waterproof cover over them and weigh sixty pounds each. The tribesmen don't hesitate. They lift the packs easily onto their backs, and Dornier helps secure them in place.

"Ready, Doc?" he asks Libby.

She gives him a nod, as she adjusts her own pack. It's quite a bit smaller than the ones the porters are carrying, and much lighter. It contains water, insect repellent, trail mix and a few personal items. Dornier is carrying one for himself of a similar size to Libby's. He starts walking and Libby follows with the Dani men close behind. She glances back and waves goodbye to Winston and Edgar, who in turn give her a thumbs-up.

# ~29~

After leaving the inn, the party crosses the hanging bridge over the Baliem River. A mile farther and they come to the head of the trail that will take them across the Baliem Valley. They form a line and move in single file up the narrow trail with Addis at the front, then Dornier, Libby, Dwe and Jali. Addis takes two pieces of bamboo, one foot in length, from his waistband and begins beating them together in a steady rhythm.

"Why is he doing that?" Libby asks Dornier.

"He's letting the snakes know we're coming, so they'll get out of the way. They don't usually attack people, because we're not prey to them, but if they don't hear us coming, and we scare one, it might strike out in self-defense."

"Are there any other animals we need to be worried about?"

"Not really. They don't have dangerous ones like lions, tigers, wolves or hyenas on the island. If you're unfortunate enough to encounter a cassowary, which is unlikely, they can maim or even kill a person when provoked. Besides the snakes, the main thing to watch out for is insects. Certain types of mosquitoes, scorpions, wasps and beetles have a bite or sting that's potentially deadly. These boys," he says, meaning the porters. "Their bodies have built up an immunity from exposure to it. You and I have to be more careful, especially at night. That's when the mosquitoes like to feed."

Every couple of hours they stop to rest and drink water. Libby eats trail mix, and Dornier snacks on dried fish, while the Dani men nibble sweet potatoes and buah merah, which is Indonesian for red fruit. They pass several fruit-bearing trees and vines along the way on the first day, but Libby doesn't want to stop to examine them. She'll have another opportunity when they return by this same route.

"There's a large variety of birds on the island, if you're into that kind of thing. I take groups out on bird watching tours occasionally. They always want to see a bird of paradise. They're getting harder to find, but there are plenty of other colorful birds to see. I can point them out to you when we come across any."

"Thanks, but that's not really my thing."

Late afternoon with two or three hours of daylight left, they come to a small community of twenty or so grass thatched huts. The people are friendly. They come to welcome the strangers into their village like long-lost friends.

"We'll stop here for the night. We can set up camp in the clearing over there," Dornier says, pointing to an area one hundred meters away. "Being close to the village will give us an extra measure of safety, not that there's much to worry about. We want to have our tents up and firewood gathered well before dark."

Libby is too tired to argue, even if she wanted to. The Dani men clear a spot, gather wood and get a fire going, while Libby and Dornier put up their tents. They boil water for coffee and packages of freeze-dried macaroni and cheese.

"This stuff is not bad," Dornier says, after a bite or two.

"Anything would taste good after that hike. It looks like your men like it."

"They'll eat almost anything, as much out of curiosity as hunger."

After they finish eating the tribesmen leave the campfire to sit by themselves away from Libby and Dornier. The sun has set and it's getting cooler. Libby sips hot coffee and moves closer to the fire. Dornier finishes his coffee and pulls a flask from his backpack.

"Would you care for some of this," he asks Libby.

"What is it?"

"Canadian whiskey."

"None for me, thanks."

He pours two jiggers' worth into his cup, and puts the flask away.

"Are you sure you'll be alright in the morning?"

"Absolutely. You needn't worry about ole Pierre, here. I'll be good to go at sunup."

A short while later, Libby says goodnight and goes to her tent. She uses a flashlight to inspect for snakes, insects or other pests, and checks the mosquito netting over the tent flap before laying down. Through the opening she can still see Dornier's silhouette backlit by the fire. He's sipping from his cup and watching her prepare for sleep.

She wakes before dawn, needing to empty her bladder, but afraid to venture into the woods in the dark. The camp is quiet, except for someone snoring nearby. The campfire is out. Not even a glow from a dying ember can be seen. She can only guess at the time. It seems like another two hours before anyone stirs. By this time, there's a glow on the horizon. She douses herself with mosquito repellent, grabs the flashlight and heads to the woods.

Out of sight of the men in camp, she pulls her pants down and squats to pee. The first few drops have just hit the ground when she feels a mosquito bite her exposed ass, which she hadn't thought to spray with repellent before leaving the tent. Back in camp, Jali has the fire going and a pot of water on to boil. Dornier is not up yet.

Libby makes a breakfast of freeze-dried eggs, sausage, hash browns and coffee while they wait on Dornier to rise. She and the Dani men are done with theirs before Dornier appears. He eats his cold, which can't taste any worse than it did when it was warm.

"What happened to ole Pierre being good to go at sunup?" Libby asks.

"It's only a few minutes past. You'll find folks don't go strictly by the clock on the island."

"So I've heard."

It doesn't take long to pack up, break camp and begin the second day. A thin layer of fog covers the valley as they start out. They walk in single file once again, with Jali in front this time, rapping the bamboo sticks in time to music only he can hear. Libby's ass itches where the mosquito bit her. She manages a discreet scratch every now and again, as they walk.

"Well, what do you think about West Papua, so far?" Dornier asks Libby. It's the first thing he's said since leaving camp an hour earlier.

"It's about what I expected, but it's only the second day," she responds. "In the village where we stayed last night, I noticed some of the women were missing a part of their fingers. I was wondering why that is?"

"It's a ritual the women practice. When they lose a loved one, they amputate the end of a finger using a stone. That's how they mourn their loss."

"How odd."

"To you and me, maybe. For them it's something they've been doing for centuries. The Dani people have been here for fifty thousand years, or so I've been told, and their culture has changed more in the last fifty of those years than all the others. If it was up to the Indonesians, the Dani tribe would be extinct within a decade."

"The Indonesians aren't that bad, are they?"

"Actually, they are, but don't let yourself get sucked into it. The Indonesians outnumber the indigenous people. They own the banks, businesses and a big gold mine on the south side of the island, and they run the government. There's nothing you can do to help the native Papuans, and if you say anything to make the Indonesian government look bad, they'll deport you—or worse."

"I'm not planning to take sides in regional political issues, or any dispute between Indonesia and Papua. I don't even get involved in American politics."

"If you don't mind me saying so, you're a strange one."

"How so?"

"Most of the people I take into the valley want to see the Dani dress and act like they did two hundred years ago. You know, wearing nothing but a penis gourd and headdress, or a grass skirt. They want their picture taken with them standing next to one of the naked savages, so they can show it to their friends when they get home. You, on the other hand, don't want to stop and gawk at the natives, or take pictures. Did you even bring a camera?"

"I brought along a special camera that's designed to take high resolution close-up pictures. I use it to get highly detailed images of plant parts— leaves, stems and berries, that sort of thing."

"You're even stranger than I thought."

"I can see why you might think that. I'm a botanist. I study plants."

"I thought you were a doctor."

"I am—a plant doctor. I have a PhD in botany."

"I don't know much about plants myself, but I know there's no shortage of them here."

# ~30~

The trail runs parallel to the river along its east side. They travel northwest for three days over the rolling terrain, passing several small villages with thatched roof huts and well-tended gardens. These villagers are used to seeing outsiders coming through, even light-skinned foreigners like Libby. The children run out to greet them. The adults smile and wave.

It rains often. Some days it's a drizzle that lasts for hours, other days it comes down in buckets and lasts only a few minutes. It makes hiking up an incline difficult, and the journey that much more tiring. The moisture works its way into her clothing and shoes, causing her feet to blister.

When they stop for the night after the fourth day of the journey the mood of the Dani men changes from somber to irritable. After dinner Dwe and Jali are involved in a disagreement over something. They exchange heated words and shove one another. Addis separates them. An animated discussion between the tribesmen and Dornier follows.

Libby listens to them, as she sits by the campfire trying to dry her shoes. Dornier comes over to sit across from her. He drinks directly from his flask, then offers it to her. She declines, as he knew she would. Every night they repeat the same ritual—he drinks, offers Libby a drink, she says no.

"What was that all about?" Libby asks, referring to his discussion with the Dani men.

"There's some concern about where we're heading. We're at the northern edge of what they consider their territory. The mountains belong to many different tribes, or at least in the minds of those tribesmen they do. The mountains are broken into a hundred territories, the boundaries of which are ambiguous. It's been that way for centuries."

He takes another swig from his flask, eyeing Libby as he does. The lascivious looks he gives her are another nightly ritual, one she chooses to ignore.

"Are they worried about us trespassing on another tribe's land?" she asks. "Is that what the argument was about?"

"To be honest, I don't really know what they're arguing over. The indigenous people like the Dani don't look at property ownership the same as you and me. There are no fences or lines on a map. If a tribe is using a section of land for a garden, a hut or to hunt, then it's theirs."

"Are there still tribal battles, or is that part of the past?"

Dornier drinks from his flask, and looks off into the distance as if weighing his answer.

"There is fighting between different tribes, and within tribes at times. It starts over one man screwing another man's wife, or something trivial like that."

"In most societies, adultery and infidelity are not trivial offenses."

"Spoken like a woman whose husband cheated on her," Dornier says, with a smirk on his face she'd take pleasure in forcibly removing.

"Since I've never been married, I've never had my husband cheat on me, but if I had, I wouldn't be sharing my feelings about it with you."

"Yeah, you don't strike me as the type who shares much of anything. It must get lonely at the top, Doc."

"No more so than at the bottom, Mr. Dornier. And on that note, I think I'll say goodnight. As usual, the dinner conversation was enlightening. Let's do again, sometime soon."

On the fifth day, they leave the valley and start up the slope of a mountain. Their progress is slowed by loose rocks and dirt on the trail. By late afternoon, they are all exhausted from the effort. They stop to rest. Libby goes behind a stand of trees to relieve herself and apply more anti-itch cream to the mosquito bite that refuses to subside. In the four days since she was bitten, the thing has swollen to a whelp the size of a quarter, and is starting to worry her.

On the other side of the trees there's a pool of water formed by a spring feeding into a depression in the rock. The water is crystal clear and only a few feet deep. She hasn't bathed since leaving Wamena. The water looks so clean and inviting, she decides to stop there for the day, figuring the men won't mind.

"There's a pool of clean water on the other side of these trees," she tells Dornier. "I was thinking about camping here tonight. We could refill our water supply, and then I could bathe. Would you have any objection to that?"

"You're the boss. If that's what you want, then that's what we'll do."

After they fill all empty containers with water, while the men set up camp, Libby takes soap, shampoo, a towel and a change of clothes to the pool. It's an hour or more until nightfall. The pool is surrounded by a thick stand of trees which blocks out sound and light, giving it a peaceful, yet eerie feeling. Libby dips a hand in the pool. Fed by water coming down from the top of the mountain, it's cold, but right now she'd jump into the Arctic Ocean to rid herself of the layer of grime caked onto her skin.

She strips, steps into the water and begins scrubbing herself with soap as fast as she can. She submerges to rinse, picks up the shampoo and applies a liberal amount to her hair, massaging it in, letting the foam build. It's dripping onto her face, so she shuts her eyes while the shampoo does its job, and then submerges again to rinse it out of her hair. She raises her head out of the water, throws her hair back and opens her eyes to see three pairs of reptilian eyes staring at her from the other side of the pool.

She wants to run, but some primordial instinct from deep within is cautioning her to remain perfectly still. It's good advice, because the eyes staring at her belong to three of the biggest lizards she's ever seen outside of a sci-fi movie. There's a brief standoff, lasting no more than a minute, but it feels much longer to Libby. Then, one at a time, the lizards creep toward the pool, lower their heads to the water and drink.

Libby slowly inches backward, keeping an eye on the lizards. Her hand finds the dry bank, and she eases out of the water. The lizards don't seem disturbed by her departure. They take their time at the water's edge, drinking until satiated, and then slink away into the bramble. Libby towels off, dresses and returns to the camp. Dornier is busy setting up his tent.

"Down by the water, while I was bathing," Libby says excitedly. "Three huge lizard-like creatures came to get a drink. I've never seen anything like them." She expects him to share her enthusiasm over this astonishing sighting, but he seems unmoved by it.

"Those were monitor lizards," he replies, calmly. "Adolescents from what I could see. The adults can grow to be ten feet long. It's rare to see them around here."

"You saw them?" Libby asks, warily.

"Yeah, they came up while you were underwater rinsing off."

The thought of him sneaking a peek from behind a tree as she was undressing gives her the creeps. She can't decide whether to be embarrassed or angry at the intrusion.

"You were watching me bathe?"

"You didn't say not to," he answers, matter-of-factly, as if that makes it alright.

"Oh, I see. It's my fault, because I assumed you were a man of decent moral character. I should have known better. Is that what you're saying?"

"Look Doc, there's nothing to get upset over. You're a young, good-looking woman, and I'm a man who appreciates good-looking women. Take it as a compliment."

He gives her a smarmy smile.

"Mr. Dornier," she calmly states. "I think you take pleasure in making crass comments to women and watching them recoil in dismay. You're like the bully who intimidates others with threatening words, but when you're challenged to fight, you capitulate. I detest bullies."

"You might feel differently about ole Pierre before this is all over."

"If I do, I'll let you know, but don't hold your breath."

The Dani men listen to the exchange between Dornier and her. Afterward they joke among themselves. One says a few words while gesticulating, and the other two laugh. She can't decide which one of them is the butt of their jokes, her or Dornier. All during dinner the Dani men and Dornier sneak glances at her. This expedition has tested her resolve in every way possible, which makes succeeding that much more important. She retires to her tent immediately after dinner, and doesn't come out until daybreak.

# ~31~

On the afternoon of the sixth day they reach the spot Winston marked on the map as the place he acquired the berry. Before leaving Taos, Libby formed an impression of this region of West Papua, based on Winston Cheung's notes and information she found online. Words and pictures cannot accurately describe the densely forested land she now surveys. The plant could be growing anywhere within hundreds of square miles of unexplored territory. Finding it will be a formidable task, to say the least.

"I intend to take plant and soil samples in this area. I'll run a few simple tests, make notes, and then move a little farther up to do the same," Libby says to Dornier.

"Farther up? Up the mountain?" he asks gruffly, as if he should have been told sooner.

"Yes, farther up the mountain, meaning higher in elevation. Theoretically, different species of plants thrive at different elevations."

"How long do you think this testing will take?"

"With luck, and if all goes well, I'll finish in a few days."

"That's going to put us beyond the twelve days by the time we get back, which means you'll be owing me more money than we originally talked about."

"Winston Cheung will pay you everything you're due, no need to worry about that."

Dornier is obviously unhappy with her decision. While he sulks over it, Libby spends the day gathering plant samples taken from within a two-kilometer radius of the camp. As she analyzes them at the campsite, she feels a burning, itching sensation beginning on her face and neck. By morning her face, neck and the back of her hands are covered with a red rash—an allergic reaction to something in the forest. There's nothing in the medical supplies that will help, and she's almost out of itch cream.

They move the camp another five hundred feet up in elevation to collect more samples there. They repeat this procedure four more times, moving every day to another location. Two of those days it rains hard enough to send mud and debris tumbling down the slope of the mountain, almost taking them and their supplies with it.

Libby is disappointed with the results of the search up to this point. So far, the expedition has been a complete bust, and a total waste of time. The rash is beginning to subside, but scabs have formed in its place, and she worries it will leave scars. To make matters worse, she's felt feverish and weak the past couple of days like she's coming down with something. Her frustration with the search and weather, combined with her concern for her health has put her in a funk. It seems to be contagious. The Dani men and Dornier are just as grim.

"We can't stay out here indefinitely," Dornier tells her early one morning.

The evening before his flask had been conspicuously absent. If he's consumed his supply of Canadian whiskey, that would explain his more surly than usual disposition.

"The men have got families to get back to. I've got a business to run, and other clients that need me. If we started back today, we'd get to Wamena eighteen days after we left. That's another eighteen million rupiah on top of the eighteen you already owe me."

"Technically, you're not due any money until you get me back to Wamena in one piece, but I'm not arguing with you about the amount. You're paid by the day. More days means more money. I get that."

"You're not listening to me. It's not just the money. We left Wamena telling everyone we'd be back in twelve days. The families of the Dani men will worry, and the Cheung brothers will wonder what's happened. I'm giving you two more days, then we start back."

"You're giving me! Did I hear that correctly? You're giving me two more days! This is my expedition. That was made clear to you from the first. I say where we go and when."

"This might be your expedition, but you don't seem to have a clue about what you're doing here. If you think I'm going to sit around twiddling my thumbs forever, while you go around smelling the flowers, think again. Dwe, Addis, Jali and I are leaving here in two days."

"And what if I say no? Are you going to leave me out here?"

"If you stay, it's on you. I've given you plenty of notice."

Libby has no doubt he will make good on his threat to leave. She knows she can't stay here by herself. That gives her two days to pull off a miracle.

"Alright. I don't like it, but it seems like you've made up your mind on this. I'm not going to fight with you. Let's try to make the most of the two days. Maybe, I'll find something to make the trip worthwhile in that time.

I want to move the camp higher up the mountain, at least another one thousand feet in elevation."

"Why do you want to do that? There is less in the way of trees and plants at the higher elevations."

"I have my reasons, and I don't need to explain them to you."

"You know, I might be able to help you find whatever it is you're looking for, seeing as how I've been all over this area a thousand times. That is, if you weren't so high and mighty, and too proud to be helped by someone like me."

The quarreling has left Libby spent, and aggravated her illness. Nausea, dizziness and chills now accompany her fever. The trail leading higher is steeper than before, and so narrow and overgrown with bramble it could have been made by an animal the size of a rabbit.

"Is this trail made by an animal?" Libby asks Dornier.

He hasn't spoken to her since their argument earlier.

"No," he replies, tersely.

"No, an animal didn't make this trail. Is that what you're saying?"

"Yes."

"Come on, Mr. Dornier. Can't you try to be a little more civil? Is that asking too much?"

"This trail was made by people, and it isn't used often."

"How do you know that?"

"If it was made by an animal, there would be more scat beside the trail. Animals have used it, but the grass has been crushed by something heavier—a human."

"That's very observant of you. I'm impressed," she says, hoping the praise might help reconcile their rift.

"That's a first," he says, brushing off the compliment. "Besides the absence of animal scat, I've seen footprints. The Dani men have seen them, too."

"Footprints made from hiking boots, or sandals?"

"Bare feet, belonging to someone who never wears shoes."

"So, there's a village nearby?"

"The footprints were left by indigenous people. They came through walking uphill sometime since the last rain."

"I noticed Addis isn't using the bamboo sticks today, which I assume means there aren't snakes at this elevation. I also noticed we're traveling much slower."

"He's not using the sticks because he's trying to be as quiet as possible. He's moving slow because he's afraid. He thinks this mountain belongs to another tribe. There have been markings along the trail to indicate it."

"What sort of markings?"

"Nothing you or I would notice, but the Dani are a superstitious lot. It could be stones laid out in the shape of a five-point star or the limbs of a tree crossed in just such a manner. There are still several regions of West Papua that haven't been thoroughly explored. The people of those regions keep to themselves. Those remote tribes are the source of many a myth concerning everything from cannibalism to black magic."

"Great, that's just what I need to top off a really peachy vacation—to have a curse placed on me by a witch doctor, right before I'm eaten by a bunch of cannibals."

"Make fun of the Dani men if you want, but don't forget, they and their ancestors have been here for centuries."

She notes the changing landscape as they ascend. The species and density of plants is different the higher they go. She stops occasionally to take a closer look at the bloom or berry of a particular plant, but only spends a minute examining them, for fear of being left behind.

Ahead of her, Addis has stopped and is pointing at something, and speaking excitedly. Dwe and Jali come from the rear to see what he's pointing at, Dornier follows. All four men are speaking at once.

"What's wrong now?" Libby calls to Dornier.

"They're spooked over something. They want to turn around and go back."

"Tell them I only want to go a little farther. Tell them we'll be starting back to Wamena in two days."

Dornier conveys the message, but it does nothing to console the Dani men.

"They're adamant about not going any farther and there is nothing I can say to change their minds."

"What if we make camp here? They can stay here while I collect samples farther up."

Dornier tells them. Much discussion between them ensues. Finally they agree.

While they set up camp, Libby goes in search of samples, taking Dornier with her. The fever is getting worse.

"You'd better pace yourself. You don't look well, and you'll need to save some energy to get back to camp," Dornier advises.

"I'll worry about myself, you worry about keeping up."

With the delay due to the Dani superstitions, she proceeds carelessly, ignoring Dornier's warning to slow down. Her eyes scan the trees, shrubbery and vines for berries or blooms, and then come to rest on a bizarre scene on the trail ahead.

"What on earth is that?"

Dornier doesn't respond immediately. She turns to see he's as awestruck by the sight as she. Beside the trail, mounted on poles stuck in the ground, are what look like human heads, half their normal size.

"I've never come across anything like it in the twelve years I've been a guide here."

"Are those the heads of real people?"

"I think so. There are local myths about cannibals and head-hunters in these mountains, but I always thought that's all they were. Just stories told to scare the tourists." Libby starts to move closer. "I wouldn't do that, Doc. I'm beginning to think the Dani men might be right about this mountaintop being taboo. I say we turn around and go back to the camp."

"Oh, for Chrissake, not you too. There is always another excuse ready and waiting. If it's not the weather, or your long list of clients in dire need of your services, it's some silly superstition. Mr. Dornier, I'm tired and I'm sick, and I'm sick and tired of quarreling with you every time something doesn't meet with your approval."

"Oh yeah! Well, I've had all I want of this nonsense. We're going back to Wamena, and until we get there, you'll do what I say."

He grabs her arm and attempts to drag her back down the mountain. She struggles to free herself, finally jerking her arm away. The effort saps what little strength she has remaining. The next minute she's sprawling on the ground, feeling dizzy and nauseous. There's a tremor, like an earthquake.

"Did you feel that?" she asks Dornier, but he's not listening.

His attention is on something higher up the mountain. She's too weak to turn her head to see. Her vision is starting to blur. She feels herself slipping into unconsciousness. Then, she hears a chorus of shrill, bloodcurdling screams, and realizes they are under attack. She hasn't the strength to lift her head, much less run. The last thing she sees before everything goes dark, is Pierre Dornier fall to the ground beside her with a spear sticking in his chest.

# ~32~

It could have been anywhere from a few hours to a few days when she regains consciousness for the first time, and even then, it is only for a brief moment. She doesn't know the extent of her injuries or illness, other than her condition must be serious judging from the hallucinations. The visions are of her inside a hut surrounded by dark-skinned children with painted faces holding spears twice as tall as themselves. Then, there's this tall Caucasian man spoon-feeding her a bitter tasting broth, and girls spreading mud all over her body.

One day after being there inside the hut for an unknown period, the children help her to stand. Her legs are weak. She's naked, filthy and reeking from her own sweat and vomit. They walk her outside the hut where she sees the village for the first time, or at least the first that she recalls. There are several other huts and a few dozen villagers, none of whom are taller than three feet. That's when she realizes they're not children, but fully grown adults, a tribe of pygmies. Their fully developed genitals should have made this fact evident long before now, but she's been too out of it to put it together.

Every one of them is gawking and pointing at her, as two of the pygmies hold her arms, and parade her around the village like a prize goat at a livestock show. The little people all want to put their hands on her. They grope, squeeze, pinch and rub at her pale skin. It seems to excite them. They speak rapidly to one another, and the groping intensifies. She tries to stay calm, but the memories of the heads on poles and the spear in Dornier's chest return. It's too much to bear.

"Stop it!" she yells, as if admonishing a bunch of kids for misbehaving. They jump at the sharp sound of her voice. In a softer tone she says, "Please, don't hurt me."

Upon hearing her speak, the Caucasian man comes from somewhere to say, "I see you're American."

He's not as tall as she thought he was earlier. But then, earlier she was on her back on the ground, and he was standing next to a bunch of three-foot-tall people. He's not a bad-looking guy, although for the life of her she can't imagine why that comes to mind at this moment.

"Oh, thank God, you speak English," Libby exclaims, with great relief.

"Of course I speak English. Did you ever meet an Aussie, who didn't?"

"You're Australian?"

"I am. Daniel Jones is the name. And you are?"

"I'm Doctor Liberty Corcoran. What are you doing here?"

"I might ask you the same thing. In fact, I will. What are you doing here?"

"I asked you first."

"Oh yeah, so you did. Alrighty then. Today, I'm going to umpire a footy match."

"A what?! I don't understand. Did you say footy match? What's that?"

"Australian Rules football." Libby gives him a blank look. "You Americans call it rugby, but that's an altogether different game."

"Let me get this straight. This gang of murderous savages is going to take a break from attacking innocent passersby in order to play rugby."

"Not rugby, footy. And if I was you, I wouldn't speak unkindly of them. They don't understand a word of English, but they can read your body language. Trust me, you don't want to get them pissed."

Several of the villagers begin talking loudly and pointing at Libby as they do. "Wooni doka menjo," they chant.

"Nonyiki goopai fongo," Daniel says in response. It goes back and forth like that for a few minutes.

"What are they saying?" Libby asks.

"They're trying to decide whose team you'll be on."

"Me! I'm not playing rugby with them."

The words are barely out of her mouth when the group of pygmies begin frantically shouting, "Gitchay loop poo," repeatedly at Libby, Daniel and each other.

"Now you've done it. I tried to warn you about offending them."

"Alright, I'll play with them." She forces a smile. "How do you say, 'I was joking', in their language?"

"They don't have a word for joking, because they don't have a sense of humor."

The game of footy is played on a rocky sloping patch of ground the villagers have cleared of trees and bramble for this purpose. Rain overnight has left it muddy and slick. The villagers assemble in the middle of the field.

"I don't know the first thing about how the game is played," Libby tells Daniel.

"There's no time to give you a proper lesson. When the ball is thrown up to start the match, you grab it and pass it off to a teammate. Then, get out of the way."

"How do I know who's on my team?"

"See the markings on their bodies? Your team is red."

"Those are team markings? I thought it was war paint."

"You've been watching too many old movies about cowboys and Indians. Now get ready, it's about to begin."

The players move aside to let Libby into the center for the initial toss-up, which is where Daniel throws the ball into the air, and a player from each team jumps for it. It's obvious why she was sought after by both teams. Because of her height, she'll be the first to put hands on the ball at every toss-up.

Daniel holds the ball—a roundish gourd filled with wet moss—at arm's length. He sticks two fingers in his mouth, whistles, and simultaneously tosses the gourd into the air to signal the start of the match. At the sound of the whistle, two women from the opposing team attach themselves to Libby's legs while another jumps on her back. It doesn't stop Libby from easily snatching the gourd long before it falls within reach of the others. She quickly passes it in the direction of someone with red paint on their face. They take off running and everyone follows, knocking Libby to the ground in the process.

For most of the game she manages to stay out of the way, which is fortunate for her, given the viciousness of the pint-sized villagers. Their lack of understanding and contempt for the rules make it nothing more than a free-for-all. Every time Daniel stops the match to pull apart opposing players, there's another toss-up. After a few of those, Libby learns to use her knees to keep the little bastards at bay while she slaps the gourd back into play.

Still, by the time the match is finished, she is bitten, bruised, battered, bloody and covered from head to toe with mud. The only positive thing to come out of it is the villagers seem pleased with her. Two of them are leading her by the arms back to the center of the village. Their grip is firm, but they're not pushing or tugging at her. They allow her to walk at her own pace. Two others are holding and leading Daniel along in the same manner. She realizes his status with the villagers is no different than hers. Until then, she presumed he was a missionary, living among these primitive people teaching them about Christianity and western civilization.

"I've got a million questions for you," she says to Daniel, as they walk.

"I'll answer them if I can, but you might want to wait until we're back in our hut."

"Our hut?" Libby asks. He shushes her with a finger to his lips.

She heeds his warning, waiting until they're alone inside the hut where she's been kept during her stay. They sit side by side on a log, which has been debarked and smoothed on top, to serve as makeshift seating.

"What did you mean when you said, our hut? Do all visitors stay in the same hut?"

"That's one way of looking at it, but they don't think of us as visitors. You see, to these people, when they capture an enemy soldier, that person becomes their property. That's how they see us, as property."

"I'm not their enemy, I didn't attack them. I didn't even know they were here."

"I'm afraid it doesn't matter to them how or why you came here. They've kept to themselves for thousands of years. They see all outsiders as their enemies."

"Did you see me when they first brought me here? I must have been unconscious, because I don't remember a thing."

"You took a nasty whack on the head, and had a bout of malaria, as well. It was touch and go for a while there, whether or not you'd make it."

"How long have I been here? What day of the month is it?"

"Doctor Corcoran, look around. Do you see a calendar, anywhere? Day of the month? I'm not even sure what year it is. As far as how long you've been here, I'd say about three weeks."

The more she learns, the more depressing her dilemma becomes. "There were four other people in the group with me. Were any of them captured and brought here?"

"A man was brought here at the same time as you. A white man with a beard. He appeared to be dead. At least I hope he was. His body was badly mutilated during their ceremony afterward. I'm sorry. Was he a friend of yours?"

"That would have been Pierre Dornier, our guide. I wouldn't call him a friend, but he certainly didn't deserve to be killed. Besides him, there were three Dani tribesmen in our group. Did you see anything of them?"

"No, just the one fellow I already mentioned."

"Good. That means they were able to escape and will bring help." Daniel looks skeptical, but keeps his doubts to himself. "What's your story? How did you end up here?"

"I was bringing supplies to the Free Papua Movement in a single-prop plane, flying under the radar, just above the mountaintops, and the engine cut out. I had to make an emergency landing on a rocky slope about four kilometers from here. There I was, thanking Jesus for my bit of luck in getting down without a scratch, and here comes this band of Lilliputians shaking their spears at me, and screaming at the top of their lungs. They were going to kill me straight away, except one of the women interceded and claimed me for herself. As near as I can tell, she'd lost her husband and took me as a replacement."

"So much for your bit of luck. You survived a plane crash, only to be captured by this tribe of pygmy savages. What was the date when it happened?"

"November of 2015."

"Oh Daniel, you've been here for almost two years."

"I didn't realize it had been that long," he replies, in the same dispassionate manner of someone commenting on the weather.

Libby looks closer at Daniel. The length of his captivity is evidenced by his long matted hair, weathered skin and yellowed teeth. He bears scars from abuse, some of which look to be newly acquired.

"How old are you, Daniel?"

"I was born in 1985, so from what you're telling me, I guess I'm thirty-two."

"What happened here?" She points to three cuts on his shoulder, six-to-eight inches in length which look recent.

"If I do anything to displease them, they punish me by lashing me with a switch made from a thin tree branch. It stings, but it doesn't injure me. They've made it clear they don't intend to kill me. They'll keep me alive as long as possible, just so I can do their bidding."

She lowers her voice to a whisper and asks, "Have you ever attempted to escape?"

He reflexively glances at the opening to the hut. "Don't whisper or speak in a conspiratorial tone. They'll pick up on it," he warns. "Just talk naturally, as if we're discussing your poor Aunt Margie's appendectomy, so they don't suspect anything is up. And to answer your question, I've tried on three occasions to escape, but I haven't made it very far. The terrain is so steep and rugged, it's difficult to travel very fast. Each time they've caught up to me by the end of the first day."

"What happens then, do you get another lashing?"

"The first couple of times they did. When they caught me the last time, the woman who owns me, my master, holds an axe over my foot, like she's going to cleave it in half. It was her way of telling me what would happen if I tried it again."

"I can't believe this is happening. It all seems so unreal. You said that you do their bidding. What exactly do they have you do?"

"Not that much really. I carry water, chop wood or tend to their garden. I don't mind the work, in fact I prefer it to sitting in this hut. My master used to come by a few times a week in the evening, so I could service her, if you know what I mean."

"Yes, I understand what you're saying." She wonders if it will be her fate as well to become a sex slave, and have to service the men of the village.

"Anyway, she stopped visiting after you came. I guess, she thought I should save my bullets for when it counts."

Libby is preoccupied with the image of pygmy men forming a line outside the hut, and waiting their turn for a go with her. "I'm sorry, my mind was elsewhere. Did you say something about bullets? Do you have a gun?"

"I was using bullets as a euphemism for sperm. I said, my master didn't want me to waste my sperm on her after you arrived."

"I don't get it. Are you making a joke?"

"It's no joke. Now that they have a male and a female, they plan to breed us. I think they'd like to have a small herd of us someday."

"What! You can't be serious!"

"Lower your voice and stay calm."

"I'll lower my voice, but it is going to be hard to stay calm. What am I to these people, livestock, nothing more than a pig or a goat?"

Suddenly overwhelmed by it all, she begins to cry. Daniel clamps his hand over her mouth to muffle the sound. He wraps his free arm around her shoulder and pulls her closer.

"It will get better," he whispers in her ear. "Just give it time."

# ~33~

Fornicating like a barnyard animal for the amusement and profit of a tribe of pygmies easily qualifies as hitting rock-bottom. Libby can't imagine things getting worse. In the hut, on a bed of dried grass, Libby and Daniel do it at least twice a day. There is nothing remotely romantic about the experience. His breath and body odor are enough to make her gag, and hers can't be much better. She closes her eyes, lies still and pretends she's somewhere else.

Although she derives no excitement or pleasure from it, Daniel appears to. Maybe it's just an act, done for the benefit of the villagers, but Libby suspects otherwise. At least their coupling at frequent intervals keeps the villagers happy. They peek through the opening in the hut to watch each time they hear Daniel making rutting noises. Luckily, the little buggers don't own a camera, otherwise the images of Daniel and her would be all over the internet, by now.

"I can't imagine being pregnant or having a baby in these filthy conditions. I don't see how I could survive it," Libby told Daniel, before the first time they did the deed.

"No worries, I'm shooting blanks. I've had a vasectomy. But, we don't want to let on to the little people, or else they might reconsider your value to them."

"You mean, they might decide I'm not worth feeding and get rid of me?"

"That, or they might use you as the village concubine."

The footy matches still take place two or three times a week, but the little people take it easy on Libby because they feel certain she is pregnant. The women examine her for signs of pregnancy, but find none. For the first three weeks, she receives special treatment, while they wait for her body to change.

Libby's menstrual cycle has occurred regularly, since her early teens. The exceptions to the rule coming during times of extreme stress, and this period of captivity certainly qualifies as one of those. That's why she is startled to feel the blood trickle down her thigh during a footy match. It happens as she stands awaiting a toss-up, and it doesn't go unnoticed by the other

154

players. They realize this means Libby isn't pregnant. Their reaction is one of disappointment rather than anger.

After much discussion among the villagers, one of the tribe's elders comes to visit Libby. He looks like he could be one hundred years old, maybe older. His hair is snow-white, his skin is as wrinkled as a prune, and his hands are gnarled, but his eyes are youthful and bright. He walks through the opening in the hut carrying a basket.

"Is he some kind of witch doctor?" Libby asks Daniel.

"He's sort of a healer, or a medicine man, you could say. He's the one who brought you back from the dead, when you first came here. His name is Tawaka."

Libby sits on the log in the hut next to Daniel while Tawaka squats to examine her. He doesn't touch her. He stares intensely into her eyes as if scrutinizing her inner soul. Afterward he reaches into the basket, takes two drinking cups made from gourds, pours an ounce of reddish-brown liquid into each, and hands one to Libby, and one to Daniel. He gestures for them to drink. Libby raises the cup to her nose. The familiar aroma of certain herbs and spices is present, along with an underlying acrid odor she can't identify. Daniel gulps his down. Libby watches him closely for his reaction.

"Go ahead," he encourages her. "It's just some herbal concoction he's mixed up, probably his version of a fertility drug."

"How exciting," Libby deadpans. "I could end up having triplets, right here on the dirt floor of this hut."

"You best drink it, or the little people will force it down your throat."

"I guess, it can't be any worse than some of the food we've been eating."

She's referring to the insect larvae and forest rodents that are staples of the villagers' diet. She upends the contents of the cup into her mouth and swallows it before her taste buds can object. His task complete, Tawaka leaves them, and they wait for the stuff to take effect, or for their systems to reject it, whichever comes first.

It doesn't take long. Within minutes a transformation begins to take place. Libby enters into an altered state of consciousness, experiencing a heightened sense of awareness of everything in and around her. Her mind is anticipating and processing her thoughts before they can even form.

"It must be some kind of hallucinogen, like magic mushrooms," she tells Daniel. Holding her hands in front of her face, she studies the dirt under her nails, the creases in her skin, and callouses on her palms as if seeing them for the first time.

"It's not like anything I've ever had."

"Maybe it's an antidepressant. I mean, something like that would come in handy if you've got a bunch of depressed captives stowed away."

The concoction's effect on Libby seems to be evolving to another level. Her visual and auditory perception increases tenfold. Her memory function kicks into overdrive. She recalls Bussaba Meesang's experiments with mice, and how she believed the phytochemicals in the berry selectively stimulated brain cells of the mice. Winston mentioned a tribe of indigenous people who perform a ritual involving a berry. A tribe of cannibals that practice black magic, and the neighboring tribes are afraid of them.

"Have you ever witnessed the villagers performing a ritual or ceremony of any kind?" Libby asks Daniel.

"I've seen them celebrating on a few occasions. When they catch something big to eat, like a big monitor lizard or a tree kangaroo, they have a feast. If they kill an enemy, that's cause for a different sort of ceremony. They had one of those when they brought your guide here." Libby grimaces at the thought of Pierre Dornier's body being mutilated for the tribe's amusement.

"I'm more interested in a ceremony involving a particular berry. The berry might be what was in the concoction the witch doctor gave to us."

"Now that you mention it, there was such a celebration. I've only seen it once. It went on for two days. They mixed a few things together and made a brew. When it was done, they poured it into a big drinking gourd, and passed it around so everyone could have a sip."

"Was a pea-sized berry used as one of the ingredients in the soup?"

"I couldn't say for sure."

"Do you remember what time of year it was?"

"Sorry, I can't say with any certainty which year it was."

A plan begins to take shape in her mind. One that includes finding the plant and escaping from the pygmies with it. In the past few weeks, a bond of trust has formed between Daniel and herself. She's certain she can confide her plan to him without fear of betrayal, but that doesn't mean he'll be a part of it. The long period of captivity has greatly demoralized him.

"If I were to attempt an escape, would you help me?"

His eyes show his alarm at the suggestion, but his voice is calm as he says, "I think it's too risky. Even if they don't catch you, there are all kinds of dangers in these mountains. You could fall off a cliff, or be bitten by a snake."

"I can't stay here. I'd rather die than spend the rest of my life living like this."

"Libby, I don't know what I'd do without you." The desperation in his voice tugs at her heartstrings. "You'll get used to it after a while. It will get better."

"No Daniel, it won't get better. I may learn to tolerate my captivity. In time they might break my spirit to a point where I feel I deserve to be dominated and treated like livestock, but it will never get better. Of that, I'm certain."

"I don't know if I can do what you're asking. I know it's not a perfect life here, but it could be a lot worse than it is. If they chopped off my foot and I had to hobble around with a stick strapped to my leg, for instance."

She knew from the start he'd be difficult to convince. Now, she wonders if it's an impossible task. He seems to have lost his desire to return to the world outside the village.

"Where did you spend your childhood?"

"I grew up near Cairns, in northern Queensland, Australia. That's on the east coast, in the middle of the Great Barrier Reef. My dad was a pilot who made a living taking tourists on scenic flights over the ocean. He taught me how to fly."

"Sounds like a beautiful place to live. How did you get involved in bringing supplies to West Papua?"

"All my friends are pilots, or at least they were. There's always talk going about among pilots. You know, someone wants a special cargo picked up somewhere, and taken somewhere else. A pilot who's willing to take the job and not ask questions can make a lot of money."

"What were you carrying when you crashed nearby?"

"For the record, I didn't crash, I made an emergency landing. But, to answer your question, I was carrying unmarked wooden crates. Inside the crates might have been food and medicine, or it could have been drugs and guns."

"When you were captured initially, did they take the cargo?"

"No. I locked the door to it when I saw them coming, so they couldn't get in. They don't have any experience with mechanical things. The first time I tried to escape, I went to the plane. It's still right there where I left it. They covered it with palm limbs, and the grass has grown up around it, so you wouldn't see it if you didn't know it was there."

"Is there any chance the plane would fly us out of here, if we could somehow buy enough time to get there, uncover and start it?"

"Buying ourselves enough time is a big if, by itself. Getting the plane started and taking off from where it is—I'd say the odds of doing that are a million to one against."

"Then, we'll have to think of another way. We'll walk out if we have to, I just need to figure a way to keep the villagers preoccupied for a while."

Libby's sheer determination is slowly winning him over. He yields to her.

"Alright Libby, if I can't talk you out of it, what can I do to help?"

"Thank you, Daniel. We can do this if we stick together. I'm sure of it. It might help if I can find out more about the ceremony with the berry I mentioned. If it's what I think, it would provide the distraction we need."

# ~34~

Winston Cheung has come to realize he's been overly optimistic, all along. He placed such confidence in the thoroughness of his planning and in Libby's ability, he unrealistically expected the search to bear fruit within three weeks—four if there was a delay due to bad weather. Now, seven weeks after Libby, Dornier, Dwe, Addis and Jali left Wamena in search of the berry, his hope for a quick and successful conclusion has vanished.

He and Edgar have invested their life savings, and mortgaged the home inherited from their parents to fund this expedition. The money is being spent at an alarming rate, because of one unforeseeable cost or another popping up daily. Like it or not, they'll be forced to abandon the search, which means abandoning Libby as well, if they don't hear something soon.

On a gray, dreary morning with a steady drizzle of rain outside, Winston and Edgar are in their Wamena hotel room, discussing their predicament. They have a hot plate on which to boil water for tea, a package of rice crackers and two plastic buckets to catch the water dripping from a leak in the roof of the building.

"Winston, I think the time has come to admit we have failed, and go home," Edgar says.

"If only it were that simple. Libby is out there somewhere, and all we can do is speculate on what has happened. I cannot in good conscience desert her."

"It grieves me to consider it, but there may be no other choice. They left here with only enough supplies for three weeks, and would have been forced to return by now. Something bad has befallen the expedition, there is no other explanation."

"There are other explanations. It is a vast unexplored area, where they have gone. There are sources of food and water, even if their supplies have been exhausted. There are a number of possibilities we have not considered. It is far too soon to give up."

"Alright, Winston. What is it you suggest we do? Tell me now, because whatever it is, you need to do it soon."

"I will go find her. I will find the expedition party, or a clue as to what has happened to them."

"Be serious, Winston. You are not physically capable of such a thing."

"And I am not morally capable of doing any less. If Libby's and my positions were reversed, I would expect her to exhaust every effort to help me, because that is the kind of person she is. Until I have done everything within my power to bring her back, I will stay here. Go home, if you feel you must. It is not necessary for us both to stay."

Winston begins hastily pulling clothes from drawers.

"What are you doing?"

"I am preparing to organize a search party, which I should have done two weeks ago. I will lead them to the area where the expedition was to have gone."

"Do not be foolish, brother. You would not last a day out there."

"If you have a better idea, I would love to hear it. Otherwise, sit there and be quiet."

"As a matter of fact, I do have a suggestion if you will stop for a minute to listen." The scowl on Winston's face implies he's not long on patience at the moment, so Edgar proceeds. "The distance between here and there can be covered in an hour by airplane."

"I know a plane can fly over the area, but it cannot land, and it cannot see beneath the thick forest canopy. Do you expect me to drop from the plane by parachute?"

"Winston, we are wasting time arguing. It is the only feasible thing to do. We will go to the airport and inquire about hiring a pilot and plane to fly us over the area."

Winston stews on the suggestion for a moment, then begrudgingly admits, "That is the first intelligent thing you have said, today."

~~~

That afternoon, Winston, Edgar and their Indonesian pilot, Taufik, fly in a Cessna 182, following the Baliem River north along the path the expedition would have traveled. The overhead wings make the Cessna ideal for scanning the ground below, but still they only catch glimpses of the trail between the trees. Edgar sits behind Taufik looking out the window on the left side of the plane. Winston sits on the other side, looking in the opposite direction. Taufik is concentrating on piloting the plane. He can't afford to be distracted by whatever the Cheungs are looking for. There are too many obstacles to worry about, such as mountain peaks obscured by clouds.

160

"Can you find this area?" Winston asks Taufik in Bahasa, as he indicates a spot on the map.

"I can try," Taufik answers. "The visibility may be worse as we get closer to the mountains."

Taufik flies the Cessna at a thousand feet above ground level, circling to get a better look at anything of interest. The plane's fuel capacity allows it to fly for three or four hours before having to refuel in Wamena.

"Can you circle around and make another pass over that area?" Winston asks. Taufik looks carefully in all directions before turning the plane.

"What did you see?" Edgar asks.

"Something white. Maybe a scrap of clothing."

Winston has asked Taufik to retrace his route several times before now. Each time the pilot does so obediently, but thus far they've seen nothing that would merit a closer inspection. The circling has used up more fuel than would be used in a normal point-to-point flight pattern.

"We're down to a quarter of a tank. That's about an hour of flying time left. I'll have to return to Wamena," Taufik tells the brothers, after two hours of scouring the area.

"Please, just a few more minutes," Winston pleads.

"Sorry, I can't take a chance of running out of fuel. In this terrain, with the poor visibility, attempting an emergency landing would be suicidal."

"We can try again, tomorrow, Winston," Edgar says.

Taufik turns the plane toward Wamena, and throttles up to climb to cruising altitude.

Libby and Daniel are gathering wood with the women of the village, a chore which entails picking up deadfall from the forest floor and stacking it to dry. When the Cessna passes by less than five kilometers from them, Daniel is the first to hear the distinctive sound of a low-flying single-engine airplane. He turns an ear toward it. The pygmy women notice his interest, and then hear the plane for themselves.

The villagers have seen and heard jets pass by at fifty thousand feet above them, and occasionally small planes can be seen in the distance, but an aircraft passing by only a thousand feet overhead is rare. Libby can see from their reaction they don't know what to make of it. She acts without thinking, dropping the wood and running to a clearing. Looking to the sky, she spins in a circle, and spots the plane through the haze. It's passing over the village, and she has only a minute to try to catch the attention of its pilot.

Fifty meters away is the patch of ground the villagers have cleared for their games. Libby breaks for it, frantically waving her hands in the air as she runs. By the time she reaches the middle of the footy field the plane is

161

beginning to bank and turn away. She expects the pygmy women to chase and tackle her to the ground, but they don't. Instead, they seem amused by her interest in the plane, like she's a small child seeing one for the first time.

"Wait, go around one more time," Winston instructs Taufik.

"Sorry, I can't. I've already stayed longer than I should have."

"Did you see something, Winston?" Edgar asks.

"I caught a glimpse of a person running and waving their arms."

"The villagers do that often," Taufik explains. "Especially in these remote areas where we don't go as much. They're fascinated by the flying machine."

"I am not sure this was a villager I saw. Can you mark this spot on your aeronautical map. I would like to come back here as soon as possible."

"I can mark it on the chart, but the soonest I can fly back here is the day after tomorrow, and that's if the weather permits."

Libby stands in the middle of the footy field, waiting and hoping for the plane to turn around, but it doesn't. Her spirits sink as it disappears over the horizon. Disheartened, she returns to gather wood with Daniel and the women.

"That was a search plane," Daniel says to her. "It was flying too low for any other purpose. Odds are they were looking for you."

"I hope you're right about that. I need to be ready if they fly over again. Do you have any ideas for how I could signal them? If my friends have initiated a search for me, it won't go on indefinitely. If you were the pilot in the search plane, what would catch your attention?"

"Let's see. If it were me, what would I look for," he says, giving it careful consideration. "Well, it has to be something I could see from one thousand feet in the air while I was flying by at one hundred knots, something that stands out from everything else around it. I'll put my mind to work on it. Whatever we do, it has to be something that won't make the little people suspicious."

As they continue gathering wood, Libby comes upon a gully formed from rainwater running off the mountain slope. Along the bottom of the gully is a sediment of white stones.

"Daniel, I've got an idea. What if we used this white gravel to spell out H-E-L-P?"

Together they carry baskets full of the white stones, one after another, to the center of the footy field and construct the message. When they finish, a large white SOS stands out from the muddy field around it.

"That will get their attention. I'm sure of it."

# ~35~

Two days after they first flew over the area, Winston and Edgar return to the spot Taufik marked on the map, for another look. It's a rare cloudless day in the mountains, and their visibility from the Cessna 182 is exceptional. As Daniel had predicted, Taufik sees the SOS on the first flyover.

"There," he says to Winston. He tips the wings vertical with one pointing at the footy field, and flies in a tight circle around the SOS. The maneuver makes Winston and Edgar queasy, but they can clearly see the message.

"That was put there for our benefit," Winston says.

"Yes, you're right. It's laid out to be seen from the air," Taufik agrees.

"We have to land. She needs our help."

"Impossible, there is no place within sixty kilometers of here to land."

As a practice, the villagers typically spend the hottest part of the day in their huts or under the shade of a tree. From the air the village looks deserted. Libby and Daniel are in their hut when the plane passes by at five hundred feet overhead. She's instantly on her feet and running for the footy field.

The last time she ran to the field to wave at the plane it amused the pygmies. This time around their reaction to it is one of concern. They chase after Libby, but she easily outruns them. She reaches the open footy field, and in plain view of the plane begins waving frantically. The plane is too high to be sure anyone has seen her. Within a minute, two of the pygmy women catch up to her. They've brought along switches, and they lash Libby on her arms and legs, as they push and drag her toward the hut.

"Did you see?" Edgar asks Winston.

"Yes, I saw and I am sickened by it. Are you sure it is not possible to land nearby?" Winston asks Taufik.

"I'm positive it can't be done. Besides, those people look hostile. I'd not only be risking my plane, we'd be risking our necks. A helicopter is the only thing that can land here."

Winston can't think of any way to get immediate help to Libby. If only he could drop a message to let her know they'll come back.

"Make one more pass, as slow as you can safely fly, directly over the center of the open area, where the SOS is."

As Taufik circles back toward the village, Winston assembles his message to Libby. He makes a parachute out of a handkerchief, by fastening the four corners together. Then he attaches her broken Timex watch, the one Edgar had stomped on prior to her departure from Wamena. As they approach the field, Winston asks for the airspeed and height above the ground. He quickly calculates the numbers, and at the right moment drops the handkerchief and watch out the window, hoping it will land where Libby will find it. Taufik banks the plane and heads back to Wamena.

"Do you know where we can hire a privately owned helicopter?" Winston asks Taufik, when they arrive back in Wamena.

"It will take more than just a helicopter to bring your friend out of there. Those mountains are a stronghold for the resistance movement. The rebels are armed, and have been known to shoot at military helicopters. Who's to say they won't shoot at any helicopter they see."

"While I appreciate your insight, you did not answer the question. Do you know of any privately owned helicopters, nearby?"

"The Freeport-McMoRan mining operation has one, but they won't help you. The only other one I can think of is owned by Reverend Clayton Newburg. He's an evangelist."

"Where can we find him?" Winston asks.

"From what I understand, he has a church near Jayapura. You can get more information and contact him through his website."

~~~

Clayton Newburg Ministry dot com states the reverend has been spreading the word of Christ and proselytizing heathens in remote regions of the world for twenty-five years. His efforts are made possible by contributions from the viewers of his television documentaries, the listeners to his radio broadcasts and the millions of recipients of his mailings. According to one of his assistants, a woman calling herself Louisa, he's a very busy man, and unable to personally reply to Winston's email. Winston makes a second email attempt.

Louisa, thank you for the prompt reply. Perhaps if Reverend Newburg knew the urgent nature of my request, he could find a moment to respond.

164

I am currently in Wamena and have a colleague who has been injured in a mountainous region, sixty kilometers northwest of here. The only means of bringing her back here safely is by helicopter. I am appealing to your sense of humanity and Christian ethics to guide your heart, and come to our aid. Winston Cheung

The response comes an hour later.

Mr. Cheung, Reverend Newburg expresses his sorrow for your colleague's misfortune. He will pray for her safe return, but is unable to offer you the use of his personal helicopter due to prior commitments. Louisa

"At the end of the day, he is no different from anyone else we have met here, greedy and self-serving. Let me try," Edgar says, before typing out a third email.

Louisa, please inform Reverend Newburg that our colleague is the famous botanist, Doctor Liberty Corcoran. Your assistance in her rescue would give your organization invaluable worldwide recognition, not to mention millions of dollars in contributions to your cause. Please reply ASAP. Professor Edgar Cheung

Winston reads the message over his brother's shoulder. Before Edgar pushes send, Winston says, "You realize if news of this reaches certain people, it could jeopardize the mission and our entire investment."

"Yes, I considered that, but I place a greater value on Libby's life."

"Then, we are in agreement. Go ahead, Edgar. Send the message."

# ~36~

At twilight that evening, Libby and Daniel walk from the hut to the footy field, because he'd seen something thrown from the plane while the pygmy women were struggling with Libby. The villagers are watching them warily. Libby purposely ignores them. She has whelps on her arms, legs, face and neck from the whipping she received earlier, and is mad enough to choke the life out of the next one of the little buggers to look at her crossways.

"I know it stings where they whipped you, but it won't last long. The pain will go away in a day or two. Try not to think about it," Daniel says, as they walk.

"All I'm thinking about is getting out of this hellhole as soon as I possibly can."

"It fell in this area over here. It looked like scrap of cloth."

"A handkerchief," Libby says.

"It could have been, I guess."

"No, I mean, there it is." She points to it on the ground ahead of them, and picks it up. "It's my broken watch. It's from Winston Cheung. It was him in the plane."

"Why would he have tossed it out of the plane?"

"It's a message, his way of letting me know he'll be back to get me."

Just holding it in her hand comforts her. It's the first she's felt like the end to her ordeal may be near.

"Can I see it a minute?" Daniel asks. He examines it briefly, then says, "It was pretty clever of him to land it on the field, and lucky that I saw it. It could just as easily have caught in the wind and blown into the forest."

"I think it's a sign," Libby says.

"A sign, like an omen?"

"Yes, a sign that we're going to get through this in one piece."

"Uh-oh. It looks like our minders are starting to be concerned."

Libby turns to see two women coming toward them carrying the switches they use to whip their captives.

166

"I'm not taking another whipping without a fight," Libby says, sternly. Daniel can see she means it.

"If you fight them, it could get ugly. Act as if you're afraid of them. Cower and run back to the hut. That should be enough to satisfy them."

After nightfall the temperature drops and the village is quiet, which is the way it is every night.

"I never hear any activity at night. No talking among themselves or moving around the village. Why is that?"

"They're afraid of the dark."

"Seriously?"

"Yeah, I'm serious. They won't come out of their huts after dark. Most of the animals living in the forest are nocturnal. They come out at night to hunt and feed."

"I was told there aren't dangerous predators, like lions and bears, in West Papua."

"There aren't lions and bears, but there are plenty of animals to worry about. You've got venomous snakes, rats the size of a wallaby, monitor lizards and wild dogs."

"So, these people hole up in their huts because of those things? What's to keep us from walking away from here at night?"

"Snakes, rats, lizards and dogs, that's what. Nocturnal animals have night vision. Besides that, they can hear and smell you from a mile away. You and I can't see our hand in front of our face without a flashlight."

"I want to try it. An hour from now, I'm going outside and see how far I can get."

"Why risk it? Your friends will come to rescue you, soon. You said so yourself."

"I just want to see what it's like out there. I'd like to know if it's even remotely possible to escape from here at night. It's a plan B, if the rescue attempt fails."

An hour later, Daniel reluctantly follows Libby out of the hut. All fires in the village are extinguished, but the sky is clear and the moon is full. It sits low in the eastern sky, causing long shadows to stretch west from the forest trees. As the trees move with the wind, so do the shadows. It's an eerie feeling. Libby takes only a few steps before stopping.

"Do you want to go back?" Daniel whispers.

She shakes her head no, takes another tentative step, and stops to listen. The eyes do adjust some, but the ears are better receptors in the dark. She listens to the rustling sounds, trying to distinguish the difference between

167

leaves colliding with one another in the wind, and an animal crawling through the grass.

She catches sight of something moving in the forest. As the wind blows, a shaft of moonlight peeks through the tree branches, and shines upon it briefly. It's one of the pygmies, going somewhere in the dark. She touches Daniel and points. He stares until he sees the figure, heading away from them, climbing up the side of the mountain.

"It's Tawaka," he whispers to Libby. "I can tell from his bent-over posture." They watch the old man ascending the mountain until he's out of sight.

"Do you know which hut is his?" Libby whispers to Daniel. He points toward the edge of the village, where a large hut sits by itself. "I want to see when he comes back. I'm curious about what he's doing up there."

They carefully move to a place where she can't miss seeing him return. An hour goes by, then another. She nods off. He wakes her. He nods off. She wakes him. Somewhere in the distance a melodic howling interrupts the stillness.

"What was that, a coyote?"

"I don't think there are coyotes in West Papua. It must be a wild dog, like a dingo. I've only heard the sound once before. It was on a clear moonlit night, like this one."

"The dog is howling at the moon."

"That'd be my guess."

It's almost daybreak when Tawaka returns. Daniel and Libby are hiding in the shadows behind bushes. He comes down the mountain and slips through the village so quietly, he's almost to his hut before Libby sees him. With a bag slung over his shoulder like a purse, he disappears inside.

"We can go back to the hut now," she whispers.

Once there he asks, "So what did you expect to see?"

"I thought it was suspicious he would go up the mountain at night, especially after what you said about the villagers' fear of the dark. Because of his knowledge of herbs in the region, and because I know certain plants only bloom at night, it all started to fit together. I don't know what I expected to see, but I would love a look at whatever is in his bag."

# ~37~

The Reverend Clayton Newburg's base of operations in West Papua is a sprawling twenty-thousand-square-foot home, located on a hillside overlooking the ocean near the city of Jayapura. It has a huge infinity swimming pool, two tennis courts, and a home theater room to accommodate fifty people. The dining area will seat one hundred guests and the kitchen is equipped to prepare a gourmet dinner for them. There is a stage with a pulpit and a stained glass window behind it in one room, where inspirational orations are videotaped daily, and live-streamed to millions of subscribers.

Each segment ends the same way. Newburg's wife of twenty-five years, Sue Ellen, joins him in front of the camera, with every strand of her platinum blonde hair lacquered in place and a quarter-inch-thick layer of makeup covering her face. Holding hands, they look straight into each other's eyes, and sing "What a Friend We Have in Jesus", while the camera ostensibly pans between them and the thousand-member congregation.

The day-to-day maintenance of the estate and evangelical business is performed by a staff of thirty ministry volunteers who hail from dirt poor, drought- and famine-stricken countries around the world. One of those is Louisa Jalisco, his personal assistant for the last three years. Louisa was orphaned at the age of fifteen, and shortly thereafter, volunteered to serve Newburg's ministry and help spread the word on its behalf.

It was in Bolivia, while the reverend was on a tent revival tour of South America. Louisa walked into the tent barefoot and wearing tattered rags for clothes, as Newburg was near the pinnacle of his performance. He was immediately struck by her natural beauty, and she was mesmerized by his fiery oration.

Newburg is alone in his private study, preparing tomorrow's sermon when Louisa knocks lightly on the door.

"Yes?" he calls out. The door opens just enough for her head to poke through. "Come in, Louisa." She enters tentatively. "Shut the door, and lock it." He comes from behind his desk to greet her.

"Is thees a bad time?" she asks.

169

"No, Louisa. I think this is a perfect time. Sue Ellen has one of her migraines, and is zonked out in the master bedroom. She'll be asleep for hours."

With his arm around her waist he ushers her to the couch. Louisa's butt has barely touched the cushion before Newburg throws himself on her like a net over a butterfly.

"Wait, I have to tell you sometheeng, first."

He pulls his mouth off her neck long enough to say, "Go ahead. I'm listening."

"An email came in a while ago, from a man who says he's in Wamena."

"Uh huh," he replies, as he unbuttons her blouse.

"He asks for your help, and to use your helicopter to rescue a colleague of hees."

"Yeah." He slips his hand under the lacy bra that barely contains her ample breasts.

"I replied to hees email, letting him know that you and the helicopter are not available, due to other commitments."

"Thank you for informing me of the request. That was the correct response. It's what I would have told you to do."

He's struggling to get the front clasp on her bra undone. She unhooks it for him, and he buries his face between the mounds of soft flesh.

Then she says, "The man sent another email after that, saying hees colleague in trouble is the world-famous Doctor Liberty Corcoran. I didn't recognize the name, so I googled it. She appears to be a well-known American botanist. The email deedn't say what she is doing in West Papua. It just implied that rescuing someone with her celebrity status would be good for your image."

Newburg pulls his head from the furrow between her breasts, and begins taking his shoes and trousers off.

"Hmm, an American female celebrity doctor. It does have a nice ring to it. Did you research her background online? What does she look like?"

"She's young, tall and slender. I wouldn't call her beautiful, but she's definitely photogenic."

Newburg imagines the video of him emerging from the jungle, carrying Libby in his arms, and the impact it would have on the viewers of his television documentaries.

"The damsel in distress thing does play well with our congregation. It's worth looking into."

"One other theeng I should mention," she says. "While I was doing the online research, I came across a pornographic video of Doctor Corcoran engaged in sex with another woman."

The mention of this arouses Newburg.

"You're saying she's a sinner? All the more reason she needs our help."

"I'm saying it appears she has some skeletons in her closet we should be aware of."

"Yes, we'll keep that in mind. The woman might have a few bad habits, but then who doesn't. Email the man back, and tell him I'll be at the Wamena Airport in the morning. Then, inform the pilot, my security people and camera crew of the change in plans."

"Yes sir."

She gets up from the couch and begins fastening her bra.

"Wait, what are you doing? I meant after we finish, not right this second."

Louisa pauses with her hands on the buttons of her blouse, unsure of whether to continue dressing or lie down.

"The Bible says I shouldn't be doing thees with you. You are a married man. I don't want to burn in hell."

"You're not married, you've committed no sin. There's no need for you to worry about burning in hell."

"But I'm helping you to sin. What do they call that? I'm aiding and abetting. That makes me guilty, too."

"Look at it this way. If you didn't give me this kind of comfort, I'd have to get it from Sue Ellen. That would make me and her both unhappy. We'd probably split up, which would be bad for my image, and bad for my ministry. What I'm trying to say is, sometimes God is forgiving of small sins when the end result helps so many people."

"Does Miss Sue Ellen know I give you comfort?"

"Of course she does. She's not blind. And I know she appreciates your contribution to my ministry. She just can't tell you so herself. Do you understand?"

"I theenk so."

"Good. Now, hurry. Undress and let's get to it. We've got a lot to do to get ready for tomorrow."

# ~38~

As harvester and guardian of the Chamala, Tawaka knows he has failed his people. When he returned from the mountain early this morning, he felt her presence nearby. It was a mistake to give her the potion, in the first place. The berry's magic is addictive. She'll want more, but the berry is not intended for anyone outside the tribe. He has a vision of the white captives taking the sacred plant and its berries from the mountain to some faraway land, where it is lost to the tribe forever. It would mean the beginning of the end for his people, which is something he cannot allow.

At daybreak he meets with the tribe's elders to confess his mistake and express his concerns. It takes only a few minutes of discussion to decide what must be done. The white captives will have the evil spirits that live within them ceremoniously exorcised. Then, their bodies in which the evil spirits reside will be hacked into pieces and burned, so the evil spirits cannot return.

Libby wakes to the rhythmic sounds of sticks pounding on gourds and ominous chanting. She rouses Daniel.

"What the hell is going on?"

"I don't have a clue. It could be some kind of celebration."

"The harvest celebration," Libby says, under her breath.        "What?"

"The harvest celebration," Libby repeats. "That's when…," she starts to explain, but before she can, several pygmies rush into the hut, grab Daniel and her by their feet, and drag them out.

All the pygmies are gathered around a tree in the center of the village.

The women are pounding on gourds, and chanting, "Bwa bwa poo nya nya," over and over.

The men are wearing costumes made of feathers and fur. Their faces and torsos are covered with paint, and each of them holds a spear.

Libby can't remember ever being so scared. She and Daniel struggle to free themselves, but the effort is in vain. Four pygmies hold them face down in the dirt while others wrap their arms and legs with vines. Two other lengths of vine are tossed over a tree limb. The next minute, they're being hoisted up and left to hang upside down with their heads only three feet off the ground. The pygmies encircle them and continue beating the gourds and chanting.

Periodically one of the men breaks from the circle and charges toward either Daniel or Libby threatening to run them through with his spear, only to pull up short at the last second. After this goes on for a while, Tawaka steps into the circle. He raises his hands, silencing the people, and then he launches into a theatrical oration. It involves a lot of looking up at the sky, all kinds of gesturing and several scathing glances at Libby.

"I've got a bad feeling this isn't going to end well," Libby says to Daniel.

"I won't argue with you there."

Fortunately for the two of them, Tawaka has a lot to say, and on top of that, he seems to be getting a second wind.

"Libby, there's something I have to tell you, while there's still time. I've fallen in love with you."

She looks at him in a way no man wants to be looked at after uttering those words to a woman. Then, she manages a tight smile.

"Daniel, you're an idiot. A sweet and caring man, but an idiot, nonetheless."

"I'll take that to mean you feel the same about me."

She doesn't reply. What's the point? Let him believe whatever he wants. There doesn't appear to be much time left, anyway.

"I wish I could kiss you one last time," he tells her.

"Uh, that's going to be difficult, unless your last name is Houdini. I'll kiss the air and blow it toward you. How's that?"

"If you bend at the waist, and then straighten quickly, you'll start rocking back and forth. We can swing ourselves close enough for an actual kiss."

Daniel demonstrates by doing an inverted sit-up, then letting his head drop. Reluctantly, Libby imitates the move. They repeat the process until they both begin moving to and fro. The vines are green and stretchy. It's nearly impossible to control the distance, speed and direction of the swing. Their heads pass by several times, but never while each is facing the other.

Trapeze artists spend years attempting to perfect their timing, so the trapezes come together at the ideal moment for a leap from one to the other. Daniel and Libby are trying to do it on the fly. As they attempt to maneuver closer, the vines begin wrapping around each other, which causes them to start spinning out of control.

"Libby, I've got an idea. When the vine winds so tightly that we come together, push off me. The vine will act like a rubber band, and propel us in the other direction."

"I don't see what good it will do."

173

"If we can swing out far and fast enough, maybe we can bash a few of these bastards with our heads. If we're going to die anyway, it'd be nice to take a few of them with us."

Libby watches Daniel as he maneuvers his head and torso to build momentum, and get himself swinging in a direction to make the vines wind clockwise around each other. The vines twist tight, and when their bodies come together he bumps Libby with his chest to send her circling the other way. Their speed increases, and the vines wind counterclockwise, tighter than before. They push off again. Their speed increases more, and the arc of the circle widens.

The villagers are amused at the swinging white captives, at first, but as Libby and Daniel spin faster, they become transfixed by it. All the while, Tawaka continues to rant and prophesize to his people, unaware of what's happening behind him.

"Libby, I think the vines around me are starting to loosen. Can you feel it, too?"

"Yes, I can move my arms some."

"The more we spin, the more the vines will stretch. We're liable to pop out of our bindings like a moth out of a cocoon in a minute."

Thirty minutes earlier, Reverend Clayton Newburg's private helicopter took off from Wamena Airport with himself, the pilot, Winston and Edgar Cheung, a camera crew and two security guys aboard.

"ETA is ten minutes," the pilot calls to his passengers.

"Thank you, Bobby," Newburg says. "Go ahead and roll the camera. We'll get some footage from above, while I narrate what we're looking at. It doesn't matter if it's a little rough in spots. We can edit it when we get back."

The camera begins recording, panning between Newburg's smiling face and the mountain. All the while, Newburg is plugging his ministry, and all the indigenous souls of West Papua it has saved in the name of Christ our Lord.

Daniel hears the helicopter as it approaches, "Libby, do you hear that?"

"Yes, I just hope they get here in time. This party looks like it is coming to a climax."

"Try to wiggle free of the vines. If you can get free, run to the footy field. I'll be right behind you."

Libby sucks in her breath and squirms until one arm is free. Tawaka finishes speaking and turns to see what the villagers are gawking at behind him. As he does, Libby reaches out and coldcocks him. He's lying stunned and semiconscious at the feet of the villagers. No one knows what to do, not the pygmies, not Daniel and not Libby.

Then the helicopter appears. It hovers overhead for a minute, before setting down in the footy field. The rotor slows to idling speed. Newburg steps out. The camera is filming everything from behind Newburg, as he raises his arms to greet the pygmies decked out in war costumes, and assembled around the white captives hanging from a tree.

"We are all God's children," Newburg calls out to the villagers. "He loves us all, regardless of our race, gender or size."

There was really no need for the reference to size, Newburg would later acknowledge, but in the end, it probably wasn't what angered the pygmies. Every one of the villagers lets out a bloodcurdling scream and charges toward the helicopter—except for Tawaka, who is still dazed from Libby's punch. The force of the little people running past them sets Daniel and Libby swinging in circles, even faster now. Their already loosened bindings give way and they go airborne, flying several feet before hitting the ground and tumbling several feet farther.

The sight of a bunch of screaming, spear waving pygmies running at you would make most men crap their pants and shriek like a little girl, but not Newburg. This isn't his first rodeo. As calm as you please, he turns his back to the pygmies and smiles at the camera.

"With your help and generous donations, we can continue to save the souls of primitive cannibals like the ones you see here. And if we can save a life or two along the way, like we're doing here with the famous Doctor Liberty Belle Corcoran...," he pauses for effect, then closes with, "It's just a typical day for this humble servant of the Lord."

He holds the pose for a moment, and swipes his hand across his throat to signal the crew to stop filming. The cameraman moves over to make room for Newburg to climb aboard.

"Wait!" Winston cries. "We cannot leave her."

But, Newburg pulls the door shut and tells the pilot, "Get us the hell out of here, Bobby."

Bobby is way ahead of him, throttling up the rotor the instant Newburg is in. They lift off long before the pygmies reach them. A few spears are thrown, but they fall short. At three hundred feet above the ground Newburg says, "Hover right here for a minute."

Meanwhile, Libby is still on the ground waiting for the world to stop spinning, and her eyes to focus. Daniel is on his hands and knees gasping for air, after having the breath knocked out of him when he fell. Tawaka has managed to get to his feet, and is standing, glaring at the two of them.

He reaches into a scabbard strapped to his waist, comes out with a knife and starts toward Libby. She's not aware of him until he's standing over her with the knife raised, ready to strike.

Tawaka looks to the sky and says, "Leehi sheika dya nu moobi—which is probably his way of asking for the spirit's blessing to kill Libby. Then, with both hands grasping the knife, he plunges downward with it, aiming for Libby's heart. She somehow manages to grab his wrist and stop the blade an inch short of piercing her skin, but the little old man is stronger than he looks. He settles his full weight on top of his hands, grunting with the effort, and pushing the knife with all his might.

Just as she feels herself giving out, Daniel body slams Tawaka, knocking him off Libby. He grabs the knife and starts to slit the old man's throat, but Libby stops him.

"We've got to get out of here. They're over there looking at the helicopter, but it won't be long before someone sees us."

"Oh, alright," he says. He delivers three hard blows to the little guy to keep him down, then he gets up and starts running in the opposite direction of the footy field.

"Wait!" Libby calls to him. "Just a second."

In their current predicament, no normal person would have the presence of mind to remember the pouch—the one Tawaka was carrying when he returned from climbing the mountain in the dark. But, being normal isn't what got Libby where she is. She runs to his hut. Daniel doesn't comprehend what she's up to until she emerges from the hut with the pouch hanging by its strap from her shoulder. There's no time to look inside the pouch, because the pygmies have spotted them.

"Come on, Libby. This way."

They run from the village up the slope of the mountain, with the pygmies chasing them like a pack of bloodhounds.

# ~39~

While Newburg and his people have been watching the pygmies below shoot arrows at the helicopter, Winston has been observing Libby through binoculars as she struggles to free herself.

"She is loose, and running in that direction," Winston points, and tells Edgar. "There appears to be a man with her." To the pilot Winston says, "There is a clearing on that side of the village where we can land. I remember it from when we flew over this area previously."

"Not just yet," Newburg says to his pilot. "Let's get more video of the village. Those crude grass huts will play well to our North American and European viewers."

"I cannot allow you to risk Doctor Corcoran's life for your financial benefit," Winston states in his typical phlegmatic manner.

"This is my helicopter and I call the shots," Newburg replies, with equal calm. "The doctor got herself into this mess, and we'll get her out if we can, but there are never any guarantees with something like this."

Newburg's helicopter seats twelve. Winston and Edgar were allocated to the rear of the aircraft before leaving Wamena. It was done to keep them out of the video and audio, as well as out of Newburg's hair. As it turns out, the seating arrangement works well for the Cheungs. No one is paying any attention to them. Edgar nods to Winston. They each raise their walking sticks and point the tips forward.

One of the security guys is sitting in front next to the pilot. Suddenly, he slumps over in his seat. The feather end of a dart protrudes from his neck. A second later, the other security guy who is sitting in the seat behind Newburg slumps over, too. The pilot, camera crew and Newburg haven't a clue as to what just happened or why.

"The effects are temporary. They should regain consciousness in approximately thirty minutes," Winston explains. "Please follow my instructions without delay."

"Now hold on a minute," Newburg says. "Everybody stay calm."

"That is an excellent suggestion, Reverend Newburg. Now do as my brother says, or the next dart is for your pilot."

He points his walking stick toward the helicopter pilot with his finger resting on the trigger located inside the handle, and sights down its length.

"Do what he says, Bobby."

Libby and Daniel get a good head start, but the villagers have home field advantage. They probably know every inch of the area like the back of their hands. Whereas, Libby and Daniel will be lucky if they don't get lost, and end up circling back to the village. Up until a minute ago, they could hear the pygmies screaming and were able to gauge the distance between them by that. The screaming ceases, so they stop running to listen.

"I can't hear them back there anymore. Could it be they gave up?" Libby whispers.

"I wouldn't count on it. They might be flanking us for all we know. I can still hear the helicopter in the distance. At least they haven't left us behind, yet."

"We should keep moving. I feel vulnerable just standing here."

"You're right. Let's change directions. Maybe it will throw them off."

They continue uphill, traveling in a zigzag pattern. As they climb higher up the mountain the foliage is thinner, and the danger of their exposure is greater. Somewhere behind them one of the pygmies is shouting to the others.

"I think he's picked up our trail, and he's telling the others," Daniel says.

"That means they'll find us soon."

"I'm afraid so, unless...," he cocks his head to listen. "The helicopter is coming this way. The sound is getting louder."

"We need to get out from under the trees, so they can see us from above."

"That's going to be risky. As soon as the pygmies see us, we'll be running for our lives. They've got bows and arrows, and spears. All we've got is this knife."

"Daniel, we're out of options. If the helicopter doesn't rescue us in the next few minutes, the pygmies will kill us. We're lucky they haven't already."

"I guess you're right. Hitching a ride on the chopper is our only way of getting out of here alive." He quickly scans the bare mountainside ahead, and makes a decision. "You see that rock outcropping up there? We can hide from the little people on the other side of it. There, they should be able to see us from the air."

"There's no time to waste, Daniel. Let's go."

The rock outcropping is two hundred yards away, a distance which could be covered with one hundred fifty strides in less than a minute on level ground. Between them and the outcropping is a forty-five degree incline, so the going is much slower. Halfway there, they hear the shouts of the pygmies.

"They've found us. Don't slow down. They can't climb as quickly as we can."

Libby is leading the way. She's almost there when an arrow glances off a nearby boulder. Then, another falls a little farther away, and another hits just behind them.

"Don't worry about the arrows, they're lousy bowmen. They've never mastered the craft of selecting and drying the wood properly. Their bows don't bend as they should, and the arrows don't go straight."

"Daniel, I don't think this is the best time for a lesson in bow and arrow making. We have to keep them back until the helicopter can find us."

She picks up a stone and hurls it downhill. It falls well short of their pursuers.

"You throw like a girl. Here, let me show you how it's done." He throws a baseball-size stone at the nearest pygmy, and nails him in the chest, knocking him to the ground. "You gather the stones and I'll throw them."

Libby begins grabbing stones from the ground and handing them to Daniel. As quickly as they are handed to him, he throws them at the advancing pygmies. About half of the stones hit their target. After a minute the pygmies stop to strategize and regroup.

"They're splitting up. One group of them is going that way, and another is going around the other way. They're going to try to get above us. We can't let that happen."

Daniel and Libby resume their climb up the slope, pushing themselves to their physical limits. The helicopter suddenly appears above them.

"There they are," Bob, the pilot says.

"I count ten of the tribesmen chasing them," Edgar says.

"There are more on the other side of the mountain slope. Set the helicopter down, as close to Libby as possible," Winston instructs.

"I can't land it on a slope that steep. I'd kill us all," Bob argues.

"Bobby's right, Mr. Cheung," Newburg says. "We have to wait until they reach a level piece of ground."

"The tribesmen are too close. We have to pick them up, now."

Edgar points his walking stick toward the pilot. "You leave me with no other choice. I am prepared to die, rather than leave Libby to be killed by those savages."

"Wait, please," Bob pleads. "There's a rope ladder stowed under the reverend's seat. I can get down low enough for them to grab it. I swear to you, it's the only way to safely extract them."

"Why aren't they landing?" Libby asks, but Daniel understands their dilemma.

"He can't set it down on an incline like this, and I don't see anywhere around us where the ground is level enough. We've got to keep going up. Otherwise, the little bastards will catch us."

They climb farther, managing to keep themselves an ample distance from their pursuers, but there is still nothing other than sloping terrain for as far as they can see. Libby increases her pace, scanning the mountainside as she goes, and then stops abruptly.

"What is it?" Daniel asks, from a few paces behind her. She doesn't reply. Her line of vision is focused down and in front of her. He understands why when he reaches her. They've come to a drop-off into a large gorge. Were they to take three more steps forward, they'd fall for hundreds of feet into what looks like a bottomless abyss. They look to both sides for a way across, but see none.

"Looks like we've come to the end of the line," Daniel says.

"Not yet. Look!" She points at the ladder dangling from the helicopter, which is descending toward them.

"When it's close enough, grab onto it and hang on tight. Climb up it and don't look down."

It's a difficult maneuver for a helicopter pilot to pull off in the best of circumstances. The updraft from the wind blowing against the side of the mountain and the downdraft from the rotor makes it twice as tough. The ladder swings away from Libby, out over the abyss and then back toward her. Bob has to take care so the ladder doesn't catch on a rocky crag, and snap in two.

The camera crew of two are stationed on each side of the helicopter door. They're wearing safety harnesses to keep from falling out. "Grab it!" one of them shouts to her.

She pushes away the thoughts of all the bad things that can happen, and wraps her fingers around a rung. Immediately, she is pulled into the air before her feet are on the ladder, and she dangles over the gorge for what seems like an eternity. Finally, her foot finds a rung, and she climbs up the ladder. They pull her aboard, and Newburg straps her into the seat beside him.

Out of breath, and in a state of shock, she cries, "Daniel!"

"We'll get him," Newburg assures her.

As Daniel stands at the edge of the cliff waiting for the ladder to swing back toward him, the pygmies come into view fifty feet behind him. He makes a desperate leap, managing to grab the bottom rung, as arrows whiz past. The pilot increases the rotor speed in an effort to get out of range, while Daniel pulls himself up hand over hand, until his feet find purchase. Before the aircraft has risen out of range of the pygmies' bows, an arrow digs into Daniel's back.

"Hang on!" shouts one of the camera crewmen.

"Daniel!" Libby shouts, and tries to get out of her seat, but Winston restrains her.

"One more rung," the cameraman says.

He leans out the door of the helicopter reaching down, but Daniel is weakening. His eyes are unfocused and slowly closing. One hand lets loose, and then the other. His body arches back and he comes off the ladder like a diver from the high board. From the helicopter they watch him slowly descend to the floor of the gorge.

"We lost him," Bob says, somberly.

No one utters another word, as they hover for a while over the gorge. Then, Libby's sobbing breaks the silence. Winston tries to console her.

"He was so close to being free, after two years of captivity," she wails.

"What was his name?" Newburg asks.

"Daniel Jones. He was a pilot who had to make an emergency landing near here, in November of 2015. The pygmies have kept him captive ever since."

"Dear Lord," Newburg begins, without preamble. "We ask that you welcome Daniel Jones into the eternal kingdom of our Lord and Savior, Jesus Christ. His time on earth was short, but he was a good man and a faithful servant. May he rest in peace."

The ladder is pulled up and stowed. Libby's metabolism slows as the adrenaline rush diminishes. She's completely spent, bruised and battered. What a lousy end to a horrible experience. Winston wraps his coat around her, and pats her shoulder.

"It is so good to have you back," he tells her, but she doesn't reply.

"Do you need immediate medical attention at a hospital?" Newburg asks her. She shakes her head in response. "Take us back to Wamena, Bobby."

# ~40~

*Five weeks later*

Although safe and sound back home in Taos, Libby has difficulty getting over the nightmarish ordeal.

"Libby, I would never dream of trying to pressure you into doing something you didn't want to do," Jessica begins. "You know this, don't you?"

"Yes, I know you're just looking after my best interests." Not true. Jessica is her agent. She would say or do anything to further her own cause. It's what agents do.

"Sooner or later, you're going to have to pick yourself up, dust yourself off and get back on the horse."

It's one of a dozen metaphors Jessica is fond of using. Personally, Libby prefers the direct approach, where people say exactly what they mean, instead of wrapping the ugly truth in a pretty package with a bow on top, leaving it on your doorstep, ringing the bell and hiding.

"You're right. I've got to get back in the saddle," Libby says, to humor Jessica.

"I'm going to come right to the point."

"That would be refreshing."

"Do I detect a trace of sarcasm in your tone?"

"I'm sorry, Jessica. It's just that we've had this conversation before, and nothing has changed. I'm still not ready for any public appearances."

"As your agent, it's my duty to tell you the public's interest in you won't last forever."

"As my agent, you already have, several times."

"Are you still seeing your therapist?"

At Jessica's suggestion, Libby began seeing a psychologist when she returned from West Papua.

"You mean my shrink? No, I have an appointment with her this afternoon, but I'm going to cancel it and tell her I'm through with therapy. It doesn't seem to be helping."

"Maybe you should ask her about upping the dosage of your medication."

"I'm not taking any medication. She recommended an antidepressant. I read about it, and saw suicide is high up on the list of side effects. Now, I'm not a medical doctor, but I know the recovery rate from suicide is way less than it is from depression. I told her I'd skip the pills and take my chances."

"Well, drugs aren't for everyone, or therapy either, for that matter. Sometimes we know what's best for ourselves, when no one else does. I really believe you need to get back into the routines you were familiar with prior to this incident in West Papua. Get back to being the plant doctor who helps people with their gardening problems and endorses herbal products. It might be the only thing that will help."

"It might be, but I'm not ready, yet. And, I'm not scheduling anything until I am."

Libby can't fault Jessica for trying. Literally millions of dollars have been turned down because of Libby's steadfast refusal to be seen in public. The odd thing about it is, for every offer she says no to, there are two more coming in. She gets requests for interviews from newspapers and magazines, and requests for her to appear on nationally televised talk shows. There's even been an inquiry about a book, and another for the movie rights to the story of her ordeal at the hands of the pygmy savages.

At the heart of this mass hysteria surrounding Libby's West Papua experience is the video footage taken during her rescue. Newburg's people not only had the camera on while Libby and Daniel were hanging from the tree, and the horde of pygmies were charging the helicopter, they filmed Libby on the ladder as it dangled from the helicopter during the final stage of the rescue. The most sensational part of the video is when Daniel takes an arrow in the back while climbing the ladder and falls into the gorge.

Although the incident is profoundly tragic, the camerawork is award-winning stuff. It's one of those things that's difficult to watch, but at the same time impossible to look away from. Libby didn't see it when it happened. Newburg's organization included the video in their live-streamed broadcast the day after it was made. By the time she got back to the United States, six days later, Liberty Belle Corcoran was probably the most talked about person in the world. Once she was home, Libby forced herself to view the video, while Diane held her hand.

"Are you okay?"

"I will be in time. At least I made it home alive. I can be thankful for that."

"Why were all of those naked children chasing you, and where were their parents while all of this was taking place?"

"Those weren't children, they're pygmies. None of the tribesmen are more than three or four feet tall."

"How weird!"

"It was way beyond weird."

Though he never said it in so many words, Winston holds himself responsible for what happened to Libby. After the rescue, when they returned to Wamena, he personally looked after her for the two days they remained there, never leaving her side for more than a minute. He swabbed and bandaged her wounds, spoon-fed her, helped her bathe and brushed the snarls from her hair with the care a father might show for his terminally ill daughter. During those two days, Libby didn't speak, laugh or cry. She turned inward, completely shutting out the world.

As they packed and readied themselves to leave Wamena for the long journey home, Libby came across Tawaka's pouch among her things. She forgot about it. Winston was curious about its contents, but hesitated to ask for fear of stirring up bad memories for Libby. She ran her fingers over its leathery surface, and studied the drawstring as if trying to decide. Then, she opened it to look inside. For the first time since leaving Taos, a genuine smile stretched across her face.

"I did it," she declared. She took the cluster of berries from the pouch and held them out to show Winston.

"Yes, you did," he said. Then, his stoic veneer cracked and he began sobbing uncontrollably.

The Cheung brothers accompanied Libby on the return trip to Taos. There, they divided the ten berries from the pouch, giving Libby six and Winston four. The purpose for divvying up the berries was so a thief couldn't get all of them at once. As an added precaution, Libby keeps her share in three separate safes, in three different locations. The process of studying the berries has been delayed because of Libby's inability to focus her attention on any one thing for more than a few minutes.

"The hardest part is done. You have found the berry," Winston tells Libby before he and Edgar return to Hong Kong. "The research can begin when you are ready, and if you need to communicate with Edgar or myself, use this email address." He gives her a piece of paper on which he's written it. "Set up an email account for yourself under a fictitious name. Use an internet connection that cannot be traced back to you."

"I expect to begin studying the berry soon," she tells Winston. "In fact, I'm eager to begin the research. It will be therapeutic for me to get back to work in my lab."

"Forgive me for telling you something you obviously already know, but you should exercise caution at all times," Edgar says. "Be wary of strangers who come to your home or office."

"I have to say I am in agreement with my brother, Libby. The news of your rescue in West Papua was broadcast around the world. Everyone has heard of it, including all of your friends, and all of our enemies."

Prior to getting involved with the Cheungs that bit of advice would have seemed like nothing more than the overactive imagination of a person suffering from paranoia. Now it makes perfect sense. Starting immediately, she needs to beef up security at home and at her office. Early one morning she calls the only member of her security staff.

"Are you awake?"

"I am now."

"For reasons I can't go into, I want to take some additional protective measures around here."

"How come?"

"Didn't you just hear me say, for reasons I can't go into?"

"I mean, how come you can't tell me?"

"Quentin, if I told you why I can't tell you, I'd be telling you."

"You lost me, there."

"I'm not surprised. Let me explain it to you in another way. I'm going to give you some instructions, that I want you to follow without questioning them. Do you understand?"

"Of course I understand. I'm not an idiot."

"We'll save that discussion for another day. Right now, I'd like you to do what I ask without voicing an opinion or objection. I've arranged for a company to install cameras, motion detectors and some other stuff. Most of the work will be done at night after the employees have gone home, so I need you to supervise them."

"You don't trust them?"

"Trust is for those who are too lazy or naive to take the necessary precautions. The installers are people I've never met. I pulled their name from the Yellow Pages. I can't believe I'm saying this, but I trust you more."

"When are they coming to do this? Or is that something I'm not supposed to ask."

"They're scheduled to be here at six p.m. today. The job might take all night. I'm counting on you to stay awake and keep an eye on things."

185

"How will I know if they're putting things where you want them?"

"I faxed them a diagram showing the layout of the buildings. The spots where I want the monitoring devices placed are clearly marked."

"Maybe it would be better if you supervised them. That way you'd know it was being done the way you wanted."

"While the work is being done, I'll be sleeping, so that I'll be rested enough to do my job tomorrow. The bottom line is, I can't do everything myself. You're the night watchman, so an installation taking place at night would be your responsibility. Don't you agree?"

"It sounds like you're giving me extra work, but no extra pay for doing it."

"That's one way to look at it. Another way to see it is, I'm giving you an opportunity to prove your worth to me, so I won't continue to wonder why it is I keep you around."

# ~41~

Libby's alarm clock sounds at four a.m. the next morning. She reaches over and hits the snooze button, then immediately falls back asleep. Ten minutes later, it happens again. Ten minutes after that, when the alarm clock sounds for the third time, she throws her legs over the side of the bed and staggers to the bathroom.

She empties her bladder, washes her hands and face, and then stands for a moment looking at her image in the mirror. The scars from the lashing she received at the hands of the pygmies aren't deep. Her dermatologist says they'll go away completely, in time. The loss of body fat makes her ribs show, and gives her a gaunt appearance. Her posture sags from the malnutrition she suffered. Those things too, will get better in time.

One's thirtieth birthday is a significant milestone for most. Libby's occurred during her period of captivity. It wasn't until after she was home in Taos that she realized the big event had come and gone. In some ways, it's as if the pygmies stole a year from her, and not just the two months they kept her. Although the desire to reclaim her former life has been there, the motivation has been missing, until now.

"The first order of the day, Doctor Liberty Belle Corcoran," she tells her mirror image, "is a hot cup of black coffee."

It's the third week of October. The temperature outside is twenty-five degrees Fahrenheit, and inside the house it's close to sixty. Libby puts on her terry cloth robe and fuzzy slippers to make her way into the kitchen. She flips on the light and gets the coffee maker going, then she pours a glass of orange juice to drink while she waits on it to brew.

As she raises the glass to her lips, a beam of light reflects off it. She follows the line of the beam back to its source, which is a flashlight shining through a gap in the drapes on the door to her patio. She parts the drapes enough to see Quentin on the other side of the door holding the flashlight.

"What do you think you're doing?" she asks. His reply is muted by the closed door between them. She opens it a crack. "What do you want?"

"They finished installing the security stuff, thirty minutes ago. I saw your light on, so I came over to tell you."

"Thanks, for that. Now, stop shining your flashlight in my face, please."

"Oh, sorry." He switches it off. "Is that coffee I smell?"

"I don't know, Quentin. Is it?"

"Could I have a cup?"

"Are you out of coffee at your place?"

"No, I have coffee. I don't have any water. My pipes are frozen."

"If I give you a pitcher of water, will you go away?"

"Come on, boss. What's it going to hurt to let me have a cup of coffee?"

"If I give you a cup of coffee, will you go away?"

"Have you got company? Is that why you're trying to get rid of me?"

"None of your business. Now help yourself to coffee and leave."

At six a.m. Libby is in her office, with her hair pulled back into a loosely braided ponytail and just enough makeup applied to hide the scarring. She's wearing black slacks, rubber soled loafers, a white lab coat and horn rimmed glasses. No one else will be in for another two hours. When they do arrive, she wants her presence known to them. She wants them to see her looking like her old self, the message being she's back in charge of her life and business.

Before the employees arrive, she goes around inspecting the installations made overnight. Motion detectors and cameras have been strategically located around the perimeter of the compound, and everywhere inside the different buildings. The ability to monitor activity anywhere on the grounds and detect intruders gives her an added measure of comfort. Hopefully, she can now focus her full attention on her research.

As she scans her email, an hour before anyone else is due to arrive, her personal phone sounds an incoming call. She checks her screen to see it's Gunter. She hesitates. They haven't talked since she got back from West Papua. She picks up on the fourth ring.

"Hi Gunter," she says cheerily. "How have you been? It's good to hear your voice."

"Yes, Libby. It is good to hear yours as well. I was so sorry to hear of your unfortunate experience in West Papua. Zat must have been terrible for you to lose your lover like zat."

Some of the news reports following Daniel's death depicted Libby and him as lovers, who'd been abducted by a tribe of pygmies while hiking in the mountains of West Papua. Libby wants to set the record straight before the conversation goes any further.

"It was a bad experience for sure, but the man who was killed, Daniel Jones, wasn't my lover. We were captured at different times, and being held by the same tribe."

188

"On zee news zat was not made clear," he says, as if relieved to know Libby wasn't Daniel's lover. Or at least it sounds that way to Libby.

"I'll be making personal appearances, soon. Several of the things reported in the news weren't totally accurate. I hope to correct some of the misconceptions."

"Zat will be good," he says, then he not so subtly switches topics. "Were you able to locate zee plant before you were captured?"

She hates to lie to him, but she's not going to betray Winston. Besides, she won't know what she has until she can perform a few experiments.

"Sadly, our search was cut short. The guide leading me to the area was killed before we reached it. I didn't have the strength to try again after the rescue."

"Zat is too bad. If zee plant can be found, it will be worth a lot of money."

"If there's another search organized, I don't think I'll be a part of it. A word of advice, if you go looking for the plant. Watch out for pygmies."

"Don't worry. I won't be going to West Papua. I am not as adventurous as you are."

"Speaking of adventure—will you be adventuring my way any time soon?" she asks, in a flirtatious tone. There's an ever so slight pause before he speaks, which makes her anxious.

"I have nothing planned at zee moment, but you never know."

She knows she shouldn't push, but she wants something more out of him. Not a lot, just a few kind words.

She tries again, "I'd love to see you." It comes out solicitous. There's another pause, and she wishes she hadn't said it.

"I am very busy between now and zee end of zee year. Maybe after zat, I will have business zat brings me close to New Mexico. It was good to talk with you. Take care of yourself, Libby."

"Yes, you do the same," she says, trying to sound more upbeat than she feels. "Bye, Gunter."

As soon as Gunter disconnects he punches in another number. Duc Nguyen, CEO of Khon Kaen Pharmaceutical, picks up in Thailand.

"Did you get the information I requested?" he asks Gunter.

"Not yet, but I will have it soon."

"Then why are you calling me if you have nothing to say?"

"Zee payment for my expenses has not been wired to my bank as was agreed. I am informing you of zis oversight."

"So far, the information you have provided has been of little use. We can discuss your expenses if and when you have something worth paying

189

for. Besides I have someone else working on it, because I am beginning to wonder where your loyalties lie."

"But, we have a deal. You cannot back out, now," Gunter says, but Duc Nguyen has already disconnected.

~~~

The last Libby was wholly engrossed in a lab project was almost a year earlier. She had forgotten how much she enjoys the process of breaking down and studying a specimen. Part of what makes her so good at what she does, is her innovative approach to it. From what Libby has seen of her notes, Bussaba Meesang had a unique approach, as well. The notes she made, and the conclusions she arrived at are interesting, and may be helpful in some way, but the methods used are outdated. Libby will have to start from scratch.

She sets up in a laboratory room with all the proper equipment, and tells her staff she's not to be disturbed, which draws a curious glance or two from the lab technicians. Their typical routine is repetitive most days, and the notion of something different taking place intrigues them. However, for the time being, Libby wants to keep whatever she discovers about the berry confidential. In the privacy of the room, walled off from distractions and interruptions, she can totally immerse herself in the project without the worry of someone seeing something she'd rather they didn't.

From a vault, she takes one berry sealed in a plastic container to the room. She begins by taking several photographs of the whole berry with a high-resolution camera. Every step of the procedure will be documented in this same way. Next, she carefully cuts out a section of the plastic textured outer skin of the berry, to place under a microscope which is equipped with another camera. The process is repeated with other sections of skin and pieces of pulp beneath the skin. In the very center of the berry is an oval-shaped seed, as colorless and transparent as glass. After photographing it, she puts it in a separate sealed plastic container to be placed back in the vault.

Now comes the process of extracting DNA samples to be sequenced to form a barcode. The barcode will allow her to compare the berry to other existing plants, and possibly identify its species or a close cousin. The DNA extraction process will destroy the berry's value for many other research purposes, so it's important that she be patient and get it right the first time. It starts with pulverizing a sample of the pulp and putting it in a solution of salt water and dish detergent, to break down the cell membranes and free the DNA. While the pulp is soaking in the solution, Libby takes a break.

# ~42~

Before leaving the lab, Libby locks the door to the room where she's working, which is something that has never been done previously. There is nothing of value in the specimens they work with, so there's no need to secure them. Mae Lee witnesses Libby locking the door.

"That must be something pretty important you're working on, to keep it under lock and key," she comments.

"It's something I'm doing as a favor for a friend. I don't want it accidentally mixed in with our paying clients' jobs," Libby replies, nonchalantly.

"Is it something I can help with? I'm not terribly busy, right now."

"I don't need any help, yet. I have a limited amount of material to work with, and it's irreplaceable if I mess up anything. For now, I think fewer cooks in the kitchen is best. I imagine Percy can help you find something to fill your time."

Mae Lee doesn't appear interested in consulting Percy for his suggestions. She was hired a month earlier while Libby was still recovering. Beth was out on an extended maternity leave, and Scott quit suddenly without giving notice, leaving the lab staff short-handed. Gwen used an employment service to find another lab technician. Mae Lee was hired as a result of their search. Even though Libby hasn't been around her, there's something about her that rings hollow and insincere.

"Percy," Libby calls. "Is there something Mae Lee can assist you with?"

"Uh, sure. I can find something for her to do."

Libby turns her back to Mae Lee and leaves the lab without another word.

"Is she always like that?" Mae Lee asks Percy.

"Like what?"

"Superior acting, as if she is the most important person in the room."

"Well, she owns the company," he says. "Around here, that makes her the most important person in the room. She can be a little cold sometimes, but in her defense, she's very busy. Besides that, she's been through a rough period. You might want to cut her some slack."

192

Mae Lee doesn't appear placated. She sidles up to Percy, giving him a flirtatious smile.

"Do you have a key to the room where she's working," she asks, in a conspiratorial manner.

Percy reflexively glances around before saying, "No, I don't. Why would you even ask?"

"I'm just wondering what kind of project she's got going. Aren't you?"

"Not in the least, and my advice to you is don't even consider going behind her back—on that or anything else—that is, if you want to keep your job."

"Alright, don't be so paranoid. I was just curious. I won't do anything to get us in trouble,"

She gives the word **us** extra emphasis.

"There is no **us**, if you do something I've already told you not to."

"Oh, I see," she says, pushing her lower lip out as if hurt by his words.

"We should get busy. Libby will be back in a minute. You want to help me tag these samples?"

"Okay." They work without speaking for a minute, then Mae Lee asks, "Have you seen the latest 'Star Wars' movie?"

"No I haven't. I've heard it's pretty good. Lots of special effects and stuff."

"I've heard that, too. It's playing in town, tonight. Would you like to go?"

That one seemed to come out of left field. Mae Lee has never expressed any interest in him before now, but maybe she's been working up to it.

"Yeah, uh…, sure. That sounds great."

Libby comes back into the lab, going directly to the room where she's been working. Percy doesn't seem to notice. He's engaged in a conversation with Mae Lee, who glances at Libby for a brief moment before turning back to Percy.

The next step in the process is to put the solution that's been soaking into a centrifuge to help separate the liquid from the solids. The liquid containing the DNA is then mixed with alcohol to precipitate out the DNA. This part of the process takes Libby two hours, twice as long as the procedure normally takes, due to her constantly checking and rechecking everything she does.

The final product of the precipitation is a clear goo, which she separates into four small test tubes, designed to fit in the automated sequencer machine. The time required for sequencing varies greatly from one sample to another. When the job is completed, the machine prints out the results.

Once the samples are in the machine, Libby decides to take lunch at her house while the sequencing is being done.

Diane is sitting at the kitchen table in flannel pajamas, a robe and slippers, with a cup of coffee in front of her, when Libby walks in near noon. She's wearing an expression on her face that discourages conversation. Libby has seen it before, so she goes about making herself a salad as if there's no one else in the room. After a minute of that, the silence apparently gets to Diane.

"Where have you been?" she asks, in a thick voice. Libby takes her salad over to the table, to sit across from Diane.

"I've been working in the lab all morning. I decided to get back into my old routines, the ones I was familiar with before the Papua thing. You're not looking so jazzy. Are you sick?"

"No, I'm just tired. I was out sort of late, last night. I had a date."

"A date? You mean like a date, date? A dinner with a guy, sort of thing?"

"I met a man who asked me out. We had dinner, and drinks afterward, and then he took me to his place. You can figure the rest out for yourself."

"Wow! That sounds kind of impulsive."

"Because I slept with him on our first date, I'm impulsive?"

"I was talking about him. It was impulsive of him to ask you to his place. You accepting was just you being yourself. Where'd you meet this guy, anyway?"

"At the supermarket. He's a butcher. He gave me a good deal on pork loins."

"I won't ask what you gave him in return."

"It wasn't an exchange. He gave me a deal because he's a nice man. Do you think I'm going to sleep with him for a pork loin? A T-bone steak maybe, but not a pork loin."

"That's the Diane I remember," Libby says sarcastically, and pushes her salad aside.

Diane reaches across the table and plucks out a cherry tomato. "Don't be such a prude, Liberty. You're the one who brought up the subject of me giving him something in trade."

"You're right, I started it. My bad, I should have known better. Tell me about him. What's his name? How old is he? What does he look like? Where'd you have dinner?"

"His name is Reggie. He has medium length brown hair, brown eyes and a mustache. We ate at Sorrento's Grill." She takes another morsel from

194

Libby's salad bowl. Libby pushes the bowl across the table and hands the fork to Diane.

"The color of his hair and the fact he has a mustache isn't much of a description. Did you get a good look at him before the lights went out?"

"Yes I did. I looked at him for a few minutes before he asked me out, and decided he was good enough to take me to dinner. If you want a better description of him, go to the supermarket and see for yourself. You'll find him in the meat department."

"I might just do that, the next time I'm in town." She glances at her watch. "But right now, I need to go back to work. Will you be around later?"

"Probably not."

"Another date with Reggie, already?"

"It beats sitting around the house watching TV."

"That's true, I guess. Well, you kids have fun. Should I leave a light on?"

"Not unless you're afraid of the dark."

The lab staff is still at lunch when Libby returns. The sequencing machine has completed its task, and the pages of results are waiting for her in the printer tray. She searches through every plant DNA barcode reference library she knows of, but by the end of the day cannot find anything close to a match. That supports her working theory it is most likely an undiscovered species of plant, and debunks the hypothesis it is a naturally occurring hybrid.

The next day Libby prepares to begin another set of experiments dealing with genetic engineering, an area of botanical science in which she is well-versed. A typical application of genetic engineering for her is to manually transfer the genes of a donor plant to a host plant. Normally, this is done to modify the traits of the host plant in a positive manner. Libby's reason for mixing the DNA of the berry with that of other plants is to see how the host plants react. The experiments may take weeks to complete, but hopefully she'll see some encouraging preliminary signs long before that.

"How's it coming along?" Mae Lee asks, as Libby locks the lab room door at lunchtime.

The girl always seems to be nearby every time Libby leaves the room on a break. And besides that, she's far too interested in what Libby is doing.

"Just fine," Libby answers, then diverts Mae Lee's attention away from the subject. Indicating the leaves and pieces of oranges on the workbench beside Mae Lee, Libby asks, "Are you making any progress with the citrus tree job?"

"Yes, it's coming along well. I've identified four types of fungi in the leaf specimens they sent. None of those are the problem. And I've found insect eggs in a large enough quantity to indicate an infestation is a possibility. I'm working on identifying the insect, now."

"Well, keep up the good work. I'll see you after lunch."

Mae Lee turns back to her project. With her peripheral vision she watches Libby leave.

"Are you ready to break for lunch?" Percy asks.

"Not yet. I've got two more tests to run first. You go ahead without me."

Once she's alone in the laboratory, Mae Lee goes to Libby's lab room door and tries the knob, but it's locked. It's a deadbolt, not a spring-loaded latch she might slip a plastic driver's license behind to gain access to the room. Without a key, there is no way in that won't leave visible damage to the door or lock. She'll have to think of something else.

With her new security system, Libby is able to remotely view what the cameras are recording using a special app for her smartphone or iPad. As she is heating a bowl of clam chowder in her kitchen, she sees Mae Lee attempting to enter the lab room where the Chamala research is taking place. Her suspicions are now confirmed.

# ~43~

Within a few days of beginning research on the berry Libby is convinced of its potential. Under a microscope she observes what happens when cells of the Chamala are introduced to those of various fungi. In every case, the fungus cells are stimulated, and begin reproducing at an accelerated rate. While this is an exciting phenomenon to witness, Libby realizes it is only a glimpse into the myriad of possible uses for the Chamala. Winston Cheung's ultimate hope is for the Chamala to be used in biopharmaceutical drugs which benefit mankind.

It's a noble goal to aspire to, not to mention lucrative for those involved in developing the plant's potential. The problem for Libby, Winston and Edgar going forward is they can't do this by themselves. Libby's knowledge of research involving pharmaceuticals designed for human consumption is limited. Winston and Edgar's knowledge of such things is practically nonexistent.

Libby has a working relationship with a pharmaceutical company with the necessary resources to take over and advance the research further, but it would mean giving up a large share of the profits, as well as control of the project. However, if they don't form a limited partnership with a pharmaceutical company, the project may stall out. Checking her watch, Libby sees it's noon, which means it's two a.m. in Hong Kong. The lab staff appears to be at lunch as she locks the door to the room.

"I have a few errands to run," she tells Leslie, as she passes through the front office on her way out. "I'll probably be gone for a couple of hours."

Libby dons sunglasses and a ball cap, to avoid being recognized while in Taos. She drives to a bistro on Gusdorf Road to use their Wi-Fi connection. The place is not busy, as this is the off-season. While she is enjoying a plate of quesadillas, she composes an email to send to Winston, which reads:

Winston, the work is progressing nicely. The next stage will require a third party with resources I don't have. I have an idea of how to involve another party while retaining overall control of the project. I can apply for a patent for the Chamala, calling it a hybrid plant, and using the DNA I have extracted from the berry as an identifier. This would mean no one could use, grow or profit from the plant without a license from us to do so. If you are in agreement, I have a business relationship with a pharmaceutical company, and would like to contact them about performing the next stage of research. Let me know as soon as possible. Libby

She puts cash on the table for her bill and returns to work. There's a strange vibe in the lab building as she enters. Percy and Mae Lee are at their respective stations acting as if they're too absorbed in their work to look up. So, Libby continues to her lab room without speaking. As soon as she enters the room and shuts the door behind her, she knows someone has been in the room while she was gone. A trace of a woman's perfume or a man's cologne lingers in the air.

Her pad with all the project notes she's made is sitting exactly as she left it—closed with the last page she wrote on bookmarked with her pen. It's the same with her laptop. It's closed and turned off. She turns it on to check the system logs, and finds it was last used forty-five minutes earlier, while she was at the bistro in Taos.

Angered by the intrusion, she starts for the door, intent on confronting Mae Lee. She stops with her hand on the knob. What proof does she have of wrongdoing? The longer she considers it, the more questions arise. Such as: How did Mae Lee gain access to the room? And, where was Percy while Mae Lee was in here? Libby decides she needs to be sure it was Mae Lee, and determine her motive, and if anyone else was involved before showing her hand. She uses her smartphone to check the security camera footage for the period in question.

The laptop system logs show someone used it at one twenty. Libby scrolls back to where the timestamp on the security video feed says one o'clock, and plays it forward. At ten minutes after one Mae Lee and Percy come back from lunch. Together they look around the lab building, and then knock on the door to Libby's lab room. After a minute, Percy takes a set of keys from his pocket and unlocks the door. Mae Lee goes in while Percy stands guard outside. She remains inside the room for approximately fifteen minutes. There is something small in her hand when she comes out. Probably a thumb drive or storage device.

Firing Percy and Mae Lee would bring work in the lab to a standstill, but how can she keep them on if neither can be trusted. There's no other option, she decides.

"Percy. I'd like to speak to you."

She walks to a corner out of earshot of Mae Lee and beckons for him to follow.

"Do you have a key to the room where I'm working?"

"No. Why do you ask, did you lose yours?" he answers casually.

"I watched you on the security camera unlock the door for Mae Lee to go in the room."

"I don't know what you're talking about. What camera?"

"The one I had installed recently." Percy glances around trying to see the camera. "Don't bother," Libby says. "It's camouflaged and too small to detect."

"I..., uh...,"

"Why did Mae Lee want in the room?"

"She said she was curious about what went on in there."

"What was she carrying when she came out of the room?"

"Nothing," Percy says, without conviction. "I mean, I didn't see anything."

Libby looks over at Mae Lee, who's been watching the exchange between the two out of the corner of her eye. "Wait right here."

"How's it going?" Mae Lee says innocently, as Libby approaches.

"Not well for you at the moment," Libby replies. Mae Lee looks puzzled. "I want whatever it was you took from that room."

"I don't know what you're talking about," Mae Lee says, indignantly.

"Yes, you do. My security camera recorded you coming out of that room with something in your hand that looked like a small storage device. The laptop system logs show you used it at one twenty. You're busted. Now, empty your pockets and your purse onto the table."

"You can't make me do that, and I don't have to put up with this shit."

She snatches her coat and purse, then turns to leave. Libby grabs her shoulder to stop her. Mae Lee whirls around swinging her purse from its strap with both hands. It catches Libby on the side of her head, knocking her to the floor. While Libby lies there dazed, Mae Lee flees the building. Percy helps her to her feet.

"Libby, you've got to believe me. I didn't know she was like this," he says.

But Libby doesn't seem to hear. She's too consumed by rage. Pushing Percy aside she charges after Mae Lee and catches up with her in the flower greenhouse. Mae Lee is halfway to the other side of it. Over her shoulder she sees Libby gaining on her. Afraid she can't outrun her, Mae Lee stops and prepares to slam Libby with her purse again.

Her timing is off and the swing is late. Libby easily ducks the purse and tackles Mae Lee to the ground, toppling a hybrid rose bush in the process. They wrestle around for a moment, each struggling for leverage over the other. Mae Lee gets her hand on a branch of the rose bush, and manages to rake it across Libby's neck. Then, she rolls on top of Libby, and tries to pin her arms. After that, all Libby can see is the pygmy woman lashing her with the switch.

"You horrible little bitch," Libby growls.

She winds a lock of Mae Lee's hair around her left hand, pulls her off and plants a knee on her chest. While she's immobilized, Libby pummels Mae Lee's face with her fists until she stops moving. Before getting off her, Libby goes through her pockets, then she finds Mae Lee's purse and dumps its contents onto the ground. As she suspected, there's a thumb drive among the stuff.

"Whoa! That's some punch for a girl." Libby follows the sound of the voice to a cluster of rose bushes where Quentin was sleeping prior to the ruckus.

"What are doing in here, Quentin?"

"Until you started fighting with Mae Lee, I was taking a nap and having this really awesome dream. I was back in California on my board, riding this big wave, with two sharks after me."

"Quentin, I really don't care about your dream, right now. Give me a hand here."

"What are you going to do with her body?"

"She's not dead, just unconscious. She stole something from the lab." Libby shows him the thumb drive she retrieved from Mae Lee's purse.

"Those things aren't very expensive. This looks like excessive force to me. She can probably sue you, and retire on the money she gets."

"Don't be an idiot, Quentin. It's not the thumb drive she stole. It's the information on it. Help me take her to the lab building. I want to tie her to a chair and ask her some questions."

"Cool! I saw this movie where they used a battery charger to torture this dude, so he'd spill his guts and tell the bad guys where he hid the drugs."

"Let's hope it doesn't come to that."

# ~44~

Libby drives into Taos early the next morning to use the Wi-Fi connection at a coffeehouse. She scans the email reply from Winston as she sips a steaming mocha latte.

Libby, although I have reservations over involving a third party at this stage, I agree that it will be difficult to achieve our ultimate goal otherwise. I will defer to you on this matter. Make the necessary decisions with our full support. Winston

~~~

On the previous day, questioning Mae Lee produced little of any value. She maintained her innocence, saying she entered the lab room because she was curious. She went on to say she did nothing more than look while there, and that she didn't even remember having the thumb drive with her—a claim that was discredited when Libby inserted the thumb drive into her laptop to view its contents. Percy professes to be ignorant as to Mae Lee's intentions, and Libby believes him. Men like Percy are easily manipulated by women like Mae Lee.

"You are both terminated, effective immediately," Libby says, after the questioning. "Quentin will escort you to your vehicles. If you're caught on the premises at any time after this, I'll have you arrested for trespassing."

"You haven't heard the last of this," Mae Lee threatens. "I'll sue you for firing me without cause, assault, slander and anything else my attorney can come up with."

"You'll be speaking to your attorney through the bars of a jail cell, if you're not off this property in three minutes," Libby replies.

Percy can't bring himself to meet Libby's eyes. "I'm sorry about this," is all he can say.

"No more than I am."

Quentin returns to the lab afterward to tell Libby.

"They're out of here. Percy was cool about it, but Mae Lee spun her tires throwing gravel everywhere as she left."

"We're going to have to be extra vigilant around here, now. Mae Lee was after information on something I brought back from West Papua. I doubt she is working alone, and I think we can believe her when she says we haven't heard the last of this."

"It's time to get serious about security around here, boss."

"You're not getting a gun, Quentin, and that's final."

"How'd you know I was going to say that? And how am I supposed to protect us against an armed gang without a gun?"

"I knew you were going to say it, because it's what you say every time we talk about security. I don't want you or me to confront armed men. That's why I had the cameras and motion detectors installed, so we see them first. I'll show you how to monitor the cameras on a laptop or smartphone, and how to receive an alert if one of the motion detectors is tripped. If necessary we can call the police, but I'm not comfortable with you having a gun."

"What about a Taser? I'd rather have a gun, but a Taser would be better than nothing at all."

"Let me think about that, and get back to you."

~ ~ ~

The Davin-Boyd Pharmaceutical Company specializes in the development and manufacture of plant-based drugs. Libby has maintained a working relationship with them since college. In fact, they offered her a high-paying middle management position after she received her master's degree, which she respectfully declined in order to begin her own business. The mutual trust stemming from their dealings together is the reason Libby chose to approach them first with the Chamala.

The contract signing takes place in the Taos office of Libby's attorney, Wes Steiner. Two lawyers representing Davin-Boyd read over the terms of the contract while Herb Lawton and Libby converse in another room. Lawton is someone Libby has known on a professional level for a few years.

"I was surprised when you called. I heard about the thing in West Papua, and thought you'd be taking a breather for a while. I guess, I was wrong about that," Lawton says.

"I took a month off when I got back. It still haunts me, but working in my lab is therapeutic for me. How's your family?"

"Good of you to ask. They're doing fine. My daughter Haley idolizes you. She's viewed the video of you climbing the ladder into the helicopter more times than I can count."

"That's flattering. How old is she?"

"Haley's twelve, going on thirty-two. She tells everyone who will listen she's going to be a doctor of botany like Liberty Corcoran. When you write a book on your experiences, I'll be first in line for an autographed copy."

Simply stated, the contractual agreement between Davin-Boyd and Libby's company gives them the right to study the berry to determine its medicinal value. At the same time it gives Libby control of the plant's reproduction. After the contract is signed and notarized, Libby turns over two Chamala berries sealed in an air-tight container, to Lawton.

Keeping the results of the research confidential is a task that becomes more difficult with each new person involved. Libby has plenty of incentive not to publicize her findings too soon. It adds an element of risk to the mix she can do without. Davin-Boyd on the other hand, is a publicly traded corporation, with more than a billion shares of stock outstanding. Rumors, whether true or false, good news or bad, can have a billion-dollar effect on the company's stock between the market closing on one day and its opening on the next.

That's why Libby isn't surprised when she enters the word Chamala in the Google search box and gets several hits. This is only two weeks after the contract with Davin-Boyd was signed. The first time she searched for Chamala online was shortly after she returned from Mahé, and then it turned up nothing. What this all boils down to is the demand for the Chamala will be created long before the research is completed and the product is ready to be marketed.

With that in mind, it's time for Libby to focus her attention on the supply end of the equation, and concentrate on growing the plant. She'll use one of the custom-made grow light enclosures to attempt to get one of the seeds to germinate. That will give her the ability to control the temperature, light, air, water and nutrients given to the plant. After giving the two berries to Davin-Boyd, there are four seeds left to work with.

The first obstacle Libby encounters is finding extra time in her schedule. After firing Percy and Mae Lee, and with Beth out on maternity leave, she's down from four lab techs to one—herself. If she works sixteen hours a day, seven days a week, her output will almost keep up with the work coming in. But, that leaves her with no time for the Chamala research, and completely exhausted, besides.

"I contacted the employment agency we used to find Mae Lee, but they won't place anyone with us after the thing with her," Gwen explains to Libby.

"Because I fired the lying bitch?!"

"Don't take it out on me. I'm just repeating what they said. Apparently, they get a percentage of the first six months of pay from the person they place with a company. By terminating Mae Lee before the end of that six-month period, you violated some clause in the contract, and it cost them two thousand bucks—which you'll be billed for, by the way."

"Well, screw them anyway for sending us Mae Lee in the first place. What about another employment agency?"

"I've tried them all. Evidently, our name has been blacklisted because of the incident."

"Crap! What about Beth? Isn't her baby due, soon?"

"Ethan Jr. is two months old. Beth took an extension on her leave, which is due to expire in a week. Though she hasn't officially said so, I don't think she plans to come back to work. Her firstborn, Deidra is almost three. The cost of two kids in day care is enough to make her think twice about having a career."

"What if she brings her kids with her? Maybe that would offer her an incentive to return."

"If you'll pardon me for saying so, Libby, you're not thinking this through. I know you don't have children, but have you ever been around babies or toddlers? They're only cute if you don't have to put up with them for any longer than a few minutes."

"You're being cynical, now. It can't be all that bad, and besides we don't have a lot of options. Call Beth and run the idea by her."

As it turns out, Libby was right about it not being that bad if Beth brings her kids to work—it is far worse. Childproofing the laboratory building was difficult enough. Rigging every door, cabinet and container in the complex to prevent an inquisitive three year old from gaining access was an enormous and expensive undertaking. She has to hand it to Beth for being able to accomplish as much work as she does, in spite of stopping every fifteen minutes to tend to the needs of her kids. Motherhood is excellent training for multitasking. Beth being there won't free up Libby entirely, but it should give her the opportunity to break away and check on the Chamala's progress at regular intervals.

"What's that?" Deidra asks Libby, while pointing at a piece of lab equipment.

"A sequencer," Libby replies tersely.

"What's that?" Deidra asks, pointing at something else. Libby tries to ignore her, thinking Deidra will lose interest and go away, but Deidra repeats the question until Libby gives in.

"A centrifuge," Libby says.

"What's that?" Deidra asks, pointing to a third item of interest. Libby looks to Beth for help, but Beth is someone with the unique ability to enter data into a computer and breastfeed her baby while texting her husband about dinner. Not only can she perform those functions simultaneously, she can do it all while tuning out Deidra's one hundred twenty decibel shriek.

"Ethan has a friend who's going through a divorce," Beth tells Libby during one of those rare moments when both kids are napping, and they can converse without shouting to be heard. "He and his soon-to-be-ex-wife have three children, ages four to ten."

"No," Libby says, slowly and clearly.

"No what?" Beth asks.

"I'm not going out with your husband's drinking buddy, whose wife threw him out."

"It's not like that. He's a really nice guy, and he's not bad-looking."

"The answer is still no. And for the record, saying he's not bad-looking is the same as saying he's not good-looking. It's like a glass being half full or half empty sort of thing."

After a few days around Deidra and Ethan Jr., Libby begins checking into a tubal ligation procedure for herself. But on the positive side, she is able to plant the first of the four Chamala seeds. Now, begins the days, or weeks, or possibly months of waiting for it to germinate.

# ~45~

A couple of weeks after firing Mae Lee and Percy, Libby is awakened around two a.m. by a thumping sound coming from somewhere in her house. She gets out of bed, puts on her robe, and takes a flashlight and a pepper spray canister from a drawer beside her bed. The thumping stops. Diane has been staying at Reggie's most nights. Libby is home alone.

The thumping starts again. It gets louder as Libby moves toward her kitchen. She's afraid to open the drape on the patio door, because the glass on the door gives her little protection from someone with a gun. The thumping stops again. After a minute of silence, she eases over to the patio light switch and flips it on.

"I'm armed!" she shouts. There's a barely audible muffled response to her warning. She stands to the side of the door and parts the drape just enough to peek through.

Quentin stares back at her. His eyes plead for help. Duct tape covers his mouth, and binds his arms and legs. She opens the door, and looks all around before stepping toward him.

"What happened?"

"Moompha mumpha," he replies. Libby grips a corner of the tape and pulls. A clump of hair from below his lower lip sticks to the tape as it comes off. "Owww! You could have been a little gentler. Look what it did to my soul patch."

"I'm sorry. Now, what happened?"

"Somebody snuck up on me, and clubbed me with something. When I woke up I was like this. I had to hop all the way over here."

Libby cuts Quentin loose and calls the Taos County Sheriff's Office to report the assault.

"Do you have any idea how many of them there were, or what they were driving?" the deputy asks Quentin.

"Sorry, no. The cameras might have gotten a picture of them."

"He means the security cameras. I had them installed inside and outside the buildings."

She uses her smartphone to review the overnight camera feeds. Two figures dressed in black with ski masks covering their faces are seen breaking into the building and the lab room where Libby conducts the Chamala study. As they emerge from the room they're carrying the journal containing all of her research notes.

Two officers do a cursory search around the perimeter of the building, but find nothing left behind. Before leaving, they fill out a report, and give her an email address she can use to send the camera images of the culprits and update the list of items stolen if necessary. Quentin has a knot the size of a baseball on his head where he was clubbed. Libby gives him a bag of ice to put on it.

"Do you think it was Mae Lee and Percy who did it?"

"The guys we saw on the camera feed were bigger and bulkier. It looked to be two men, both at least six feet tall."

By the time the deputies have gone and Quentin returns to his quarters, it is only two hours until daybreak. Libby showers, dresses and eats a bite before going to her office. She goes first to the lab building. The door to her room has been pried open by the men in black. Her journal is gone, but she already knows this after viewing the security video. The rest of the lab building seems untouched.

The most likely scenario is that these guys are associates of Mae Lee. She would have told them about the cameras. That's the reason for the ski masks over their faces. They were wary of other security devices, so they went straight to the lab room, ignoring everything else. It is difficult to understand why they would risk breaking in just to steal the journal. It contains notes she made during her research, but that in itself is of no value. In fact, without the berry, the journal is completely worthless.

Around ten Jessica Rawlins calls Libby on her personal phone.

"Good morning," Libby answers.

"For you, maybe, but not for me. You see, I have this client who is keeping me in the dark about everything that's going on in her life, which is making it very difficult for me to give her the high level of representation I give my other clients."

"If it were me, I'd kick the ungrateful bitch to the curb," Libby replies.

"Don't tempt me, Liberty. When were you planning on telling me about this miraculous drug, you're developing from a plant you've recently discovered? Don't you realize what kind of impact this could have on your career? This is the sort of thing on which empires are built."

"Jess, if I don't tell you something, it's because the information is not meant to be released to the public. Where did you hear about the plant?"

207

"You're all over the internet. And this plant—what's it called, Chamala?—it's a hot topic on social media, complete with pictures and information."

"I knew there were rumors, but I didn't know it had gotten so big. Any pictures of the Chamala are phony, and most of the information, if not all, is speculation. This added publicity is proving to be dangerous for me, my employees and associates. Last night someone broke into my lab. All they took were some lab notes."

"And, you think they were looking for the plant?"

"Who knows what they wanted. The point is, the fewer people who know about the Chamala, the better for me." Libby's phone sounds another call coming in. Glancing at the screen she sees it's Gunter Schneider. "I've got another call, Jess. We'll talk again later." She clicks off before Jessica can object. "Well, this is a nice surprise."

"Yes, I was thinking of you, and called to see how you are doing."

"Does that mean you miss me? It would be nice to hear you say it, if that's the case."

"Of course I miss you, dear girl, but I have to be honest with you and say zat it is not zee only reason for my call. I am in a bit of a spot. I have promised something to someone zat I have failed to provide. Zis person has paid me for information zat I have not given, and now zey are angry with me."

"I'm sorry to hear of your trouble, Gunter. How much are we talking about? I can loan you enough money to get you off the hook with this person. Would that help?"

"Zat is kind of you to offer, but it is not money he wants, it is information—information zat you can provide. How is zee study of zee plant coming along, Libby?"

As strong as her feelings for Gunter are, it doesn't override her resentment at being manipulated by the man for his own selfish purposes.

"Plant?" Libby replies coolly. "Which plant are you referring to? I study several different plants every day."

"You know which plant I mean. I will cut to zee chase, as you Americans like to say. Zee party I mentioned has paid me for zee location of zee plant. Zee whole world knows it is in West Papua, but zat is a big place. If you can give me zee GPS coordinates of where you found zee plant, I will pass zem on and split zee money with you."

"This party you mentioned, are they responsible for the burglary of my business, last night? Is Mae Lee working for them?"

208

"I know nothing about a burglary. Your place was robbed? What did zey steal?"

"They took some lab notes from one of my ongoing projects. They probably mistook them for something else, because the notes are of no value."

"You were not hurt when zis happened, I hope."

"No, I wasn't, but one of my employees was injured. If you know who is responsible, now is the time to come clean with me."

"Libby, I am truly hurt zat you would suspect me of being involved in something like zat. I would never be a part of anything zat brought harm to you, your business or your employees. Please tell me you know zis is true."

*If you weren't so damn good-looking*, Libby thinks. She can hardly believe the words come from her mouth, when she says, "I know you wouldn't."

"I have told you about zee feud between Khon Kaen Pharmaceutical and Winston Cheung. And, I know zat you feel a certain loyalty toward Winston, but you and I should not get in zee middle of zis. Duc Nguyen, who owns KKP, feels zat Winston owes him something. He will stop at nothing to get what he wants."

"Is he the one who had my place burglarized? Does Mae Lee work for him?"

"I honestly do not know, but it is possible. Zis is why I am asking you to give him what he wants, so he will not hurt you or Winston. Zis plant is not worth it. Tell me zee GPS coordinates for where you found zee plant, and I will give zem to Duc Nguyen. After zat, I can assure you he will not bother you again."

If not for Winston's courage and persistence, she'd still be in the hands of the pygmies, or dead. Libby would never consider betraying him, but it serves no purpose to tell Gunter that.

"I didn't have any kind of device to know the exact longitude and latitude, while I was held captive, but I'm sure I can calculate those numbers if given the time."

"It would be wonderful if you could do zat for me."

"For you?"

"I mean, for us. Do zis for us, Libby."

The word "us" has such a hollow ring to it, as Gunter says it, just now. And the image of them as a couple is starting to fade for Libby, as well. The conversation itself is making her sad, and she needs to end it before she starts to cry.

"Alright, I'll work on calculating the coordinates, and email you with those when I'm done."

"It would be better if you give zem to me over zee phone. I will call you later today."

"Alright, then. Look, I'm sorry, but I've got to go, now. We're very busy here, and I'm short-handed. Take care, Gunter."

When Gunter calls back, Libby gives him GPS coordinates for a spot approximately twenty miles west of the pygmy village. They will probably realize she's lied to them in time, but it will give Winston and her some breathing room until then.

# ~46~

Only a month after taking possession of the berries, Herb Lawton calls Libby with the good news.

"There is no question about the plant being a significant discovery. Our lab techs are bouncing off the walls, they're so excited. In fact, it might represent the biggest find of its kind since penicillin."

"My associates and I feel just as strongly about it."

"As I'm sure you know, it involves thousands of man-hours, and sometimes years of testing to have a product ready to market. So, before we make that sort of investment, we have to do a feasibility study to keep the stockholders happy."

"That's a little out of my realm. What does a feasibility study entail?"

"We do a cost analysis and an estimate of potential revenues. We can come up with a number for the revenues, based on the sales history of other products. We need your help with the cost analysis. Can you give us an idea of what it will cost to produce the berries?"

The concise and honest answer to the question is no, but Libby knows that's not what Herb wants to hear. Instead she says, "I'll need a little time to work on that. How quickly do you need an answer?"

"Yesterday, if not sooner. At least that's how our CEO would answer that."

Libby feels like she has to give him something, so she makes an educated guess.

"Because it will take a few years for the growers to build their facilities and establish their Chamala crop, initially the cost per berry will be significantly more than it will be later."

"Bottom line, Libby. Give me a number you feel comfortable with. There's nothing etched in stone here, and I won't hold you to it, but I need a ballpark figure."

She pulls a number out of the air she thinks is high, because she knows it's always easier to lower rather than raise the price, later.

"Five hundred dollars a berry, which computes to approximately three thousand dollars per ounce."

211

Lawton gives a low whistle in response. "More than the price of gold, but far more valuable if the preliminary findings are true."

"Like I was saying, as the number of plants increases the cost will likely drop."

"To be honest, I'm not sure my people want to see that happen."

"You've lost me there, Herb. You don't want the cost to decrease?"

"What we don't want is for the plant production to increase so rapidly the bottom drops out of the market. In other words, if every small dirt farmer in South America is growing Chamala plants, the berries will be practically worthless, and so will the drugs we make from them. Ideally we'd like to control the production of the berry, thereby stabilizing the market for the drug. Because this is a hybrid plant for which you have a patent pending, you can theoretically control who grows it."

"Yes, basically that's true. In order to grow the Chamala for commercial gain, a person or entity needs my written permission."

"I'm sure you're probably aware there has been a lot of chatter online concerning the plant. Some people are talking like they have one growing in their backyard. We're assuming it isn't true, but I'd like you to confirm that."

"I can tell you without fear of contradiction that ninety-nine-point-nine percent of what you've seen online regarding the Chamala is fiction."

"That's what I thought, but it's still good to hear it from you. Let me ask you about something else that came up in a meeting yesterday. Would you consider selling the patent for the Chamala to Davin-Boyd?"

"This is the first time that question has been raised. Actually, I haven't even thought about it, until now."

This is true. She hasn't considered it because she doesn't know if it is even an option, given the patent probably won't stand up to close scrutiny. The idea of patenting the Chamala as a hybrid plant was a sham from the start, designed to conceal its origin from the likes of KKP.

"Well, I advise you to start thinking about it. In fact, I'll give you something to stimulate the thought process. Ten million dollars."

"Ten million dollars? What's that?"

"That's our starting offer for the patent."

"Uh..., wow!" is all she can say.

"Is that a yes?"

"No, it's not a yes, but I will give it serious consideration. How would it work? Is this a cash offer, or are we talking about shares of Davin-Boyd stock."

"It's a cash offer, only we'd prefer to make it a cashier's check. The way it works is we schedule a closing, at which time we sign the agreement and give you the money. Ahead of that, you give us a copy of the patent application and the plant, so our people can verify its validity."

The last part of that might be a problem, Libby realizes, but ten million bucks will go a long way toward fixing it.

"Put the offer in writing. I'll have to take it up with my investors."

Eager to pass on some good news for a change, Libby goes back to the bistro in Taos during her lunch break, to email Winston about the offer from Davin-Boyd. Her local celebrity status has yet to run its course after the publicity surrounding her rescue in West Papua. So, she ties her hair back, and dons a ball cap and sunglasses before getting out of her SUV. With an order of quesadillas on the table in front of her she composes the email.

Winston, I have something exciting to report. My contact with Davin-Boyd called to update me on the Chamala berries. Apparently, their preliminary findings far exceeded their expectations, because by the end of our conversation he made an offer on behalf of the company. They are offering ten million dollars for the patent to the Chamala plant. I don't know how familiar you are with the patent process for hybrid plants, it's somewhat complex to explain. Owning the patent on the plant that produces the Chamala berry would give Davin-Boyd total control over who grows it or uses it in their product. In other words, they would have a monopoly on drugs made from the Chamala, for the length of the patent. Please give me your thoughts on this offer from Davin-Boyd. Libby

~~~

When it comes to battling problems of a botanical nature, Libby's supreme confidence in her ability is easily the strongest weapon in her arsenal, and the only one as it pertains to the task of growing a Chamala plant from seed. The textbook method of tackling this undertaking doesn't apply. There is nothing known about it, and thus no established perimeters or starting point.

Two weeks earlier, she planted the first Chamala seed in a special potting soil mixture with a miniature camera buried next to it, so she can monitor its progress without uncovering it. The camera takes time-lapse images of the seed which Libby views daily. There's been no visible change during this period. Patience may be a desirable attribute for a gardener, but not one that works in Libby's favor in this case. She is working against the clock, and the pressure is building with each passing minute.

With the second of her four remaining berries, Libby runs a different set of experiments, using what she calls the common sense approach. In West Papua the plant grows at an elevation of eight to nine thousand feet above sea level, where the air is thinner and the temperature ranges between forty and one hundred degrees Fahrenheit. The climate of the area is humid, with rainfall averaging one hundred inches annually. The number of hours in a day it is exposed to sunlight is an unknown. Likewise with the soil composition surrounding it. Those are questions she'll attempt to answer.

After dissecting the berry, she isolates the seed to examine it with a magnifying glass. It resembles an oval-shaped piece of glass. The outer hull is transparent, which allows her to observe the embryo inside of it. The embryo itself is in the primary stage of development, the point where it is most fragile, but also the point where it is most sensitive to stimuli.

She runs a series of tests to see how the embryo responds to differing degrees of artificial and natural light. There is no reaction. It's as if the light doesn't penetrate the hull. When she holds a light over it pointing down at her workbench, the solid shadow of its shape confirms no light passing through. This is a phenomenon she has never before witnessed, or heard of—a surface transparent enough to see through, but opaque enough to block out light.

She carefully measures exactly two hundred milliliters of rainwater into a beaker, immerses the seed and leaves it to soak for thirty minutes. Later, when she takes it out, there are still two hundred milliliters of water in the beaker, which means no water penetrated or was absorbed into the seed hull. The surface of the hull is waterproof.

"So, how does an embryo develop within an encasement which is watertight, airtight and opaque?" Libby wonders aloud.

The answer to that question she decides, is the Chamala embryo must be able to develop without outside stimulus. All the nutrients it needs are contained inside the hull. It would be helpful to know the chemical composition of the embryo and any fluid inside the hull. But breaking through the encasement would kill the embryo. It is the equivalent of taking a fetus from the womb prematurely. It would leave her with one less seed, which ultimately may be of critical importance to the success of the project.

Her scalpel hovers over the seed as she considers piercing the hull. Then, her phone sounds an incoming call, interrupting her. It's Gunter, which probably isn't good because it's almost midnight in Austria.

"How are you, Gunter?"

"My dear Libby," he says, flamboyantly. His voice is loud, the words are slurred, and there is a lengthy pause between each phrase. "You disappointment me."

"I disappoint you? Is that what you said?"

"Yes, zat is what I said." There's silence for a moment, then, "You gave me zee wrong coordinates…, and I think it was intentional."

"I thought they were the right ones. If I made a mistake, it is certainly easy to understand how it would happen. I didn't drive in or out of the area with a GPS on my dash. I made a guess, which I thought was at least close."

"No, Libby. I don't think you are being truthful to me."

"Gunter, have you been drinking? Because if you have, you might want to have this conversation another time. Otherwise you might say something you really don't mean."

"We will have zis conversation now." He pulls the phone from his mouth to belch. Libby hears what sounds like ice clinking against glass. "Your lie cost me a lot of money."

"It cost you a lot of money? What happened to us? Remember, I gave you the coordinates for us, or so you said."

"And…," he says dramatically, "it is not just zee money. Now…, you and I are on Duc Nguyen's shit list, which is not good."

"Getting involved with KKP was your own doing, don't blame me. And don't call me to complain when things don't go the way you plan. I don't want to talk to you while you're drunk and belligerent like this. Sober up before you call or don't call at all. Goodbye, Gunter."

# ~47~

Duc Nguyen is a ruthless, self-serving man who isn't burdened with a conscience or sense of fair play, but he is not stupid. He knew Doctor Liberty Corcoran was not the sort of person who would betray Winston Cheung for money, even though Gunter Schneider had assured him she would. While Gunter worked on getting the information from Libby, Duc sought it out from another source. The pilot who flies the helicopter for Reverend Clayton Newburg will be able to pinpoint the location on an aeronautical chart, and he will probably do so for very little money. If not, there are other ways to get the information from him.

Newburg's helicopter is serviced, fueled and stored in a hangar at Sentani Airport near Jayapura. Bob the pilot has a one-room efficiency apartment as his living quarters in the rear of the hangar. Duc sends Mae Lee there to speak with him. Mae Lee arrives at the hangar looking like a Bangkok whore. She plans to seduce Bob and extract the information while he is under her spell. He answers her knock on his door with nothing but a towel wrapped around his waist. Behind him, a boy no older than twelve lies under the sheets on the only bed in the room. Bob glances nervously at the boy, then back at Mae Lee. With one hand holding the towel in place, he straightens to his full height and moves to block her view of the room.

"Can I help you?" he says.

Thinking quickly, she responds, "I'm with Indonesian Child Protective Services," having no idea whether any such agency even exists. "I'm investigating a reported sexual abuse involving a young boy."

Bob looks her over. "Dressed like that?"

"You don't like the way I'm dressed?" Mae Lee says flirtatiously. "Oh, that's right. You prefer young boys."

"Wait a minute. You've got the wrong idea, now."

Mae Lee lets him sweat for another minute before saying, "Alright, I'm not really with CPS. I just said that to see how you'd react."

"If that's your idea of a joke, you've got a strange sense of humor."

"Yeah, everyone tells me that. Actually, I came here to ask for your help with something."

"What sort of help?"

"Some friends of mine want to do some backpacking and mountain climbing in an area of West Papua that you're familiar with. We were hoping to get directions from you."

"You've got me confused with someone else. I don't do backpacking tours."

"But you piloted the helicopter that rescued that woman, Doctor Liberty Corcoran. My friends would like to go there."

"You best tell them to go somewhere else. That place is tough to get to, and besides that the natives in that area are hostile to outsiders."

"My friends have their hearts set on going there, and believe me, they can take care of themselves. You needn't worry about them."

Bob is anxious for Mae Lee to leave so he can go back to what he was doing before she got there. Mae Lee senses this. From her purse she takes a topographical map with longitude and latitude lines drawn on it, and unfolds it for him to see.

"What's that?"

"It's a map of the area we're speaking of. I was hoping you'd make a mark on the spot where Doctor Corcoran was being held."

"Look, I don't know if I want to do that, and right now, I'm kind of busy. So, why don't you run along and leave me be." He tries to shut the door in her face, but she blocks it with her purse.

"Bob," Mae Lee says, sweetly. "My friends will be very disappointed if I don't get what I came for, and I hate to disappoint them, so I'm going to do everything I can think of to make sure that doesn't happen. Now, I don't want to cause trouble for you by alerting the proper authorities to your perverted sexual practices, but if you don't do what I ask you leave me with no other choice."

Bob takes the map and studies it. Mae Lee hands him a pen. After a moment, he makes a small mark on it.

"You're sure that's right?"

"It's close enough. They won't have any trouble finding it from there." He shuts the door, and this time Mae Lee doesn't try to stop him. She has what she came for.

~~~

For only the second time in the forty-thousand-year history of their tribe, a mysterious flying machine hovers over the pygmy village. As some of the villagers grab spears and others nock their arrows in preparation for

217

battle, six paramilitary soldiers rappel to the ground on ropes. The fifty-plus pygmies are liking their chances against the six enemies, and are already salivating over the celebration which will follow their victory. Then their opponents open fire with automatic rifles, killing half the villagers in the first volley. That evens the odds significantly. When the rifles finally fall silent, not one tribesman remains alive in the village. Most die fighting the intruders. A few escape into the jungle.

The helicopter lands on the bare piece of ground where the pygmies once played footy. Duc Nguyen and an assistant step out. He walks through the village surveying the scene, and looking inside each hut, but finds no trace of the plant he came for.

"You have killed them all," he says to the commander of the team of mercenaries. "Do you have a method of interrogating dead men?" A rhetorical question, the commander realizes. He answers with a shrug of his shoulders. "See if you can catch any of those who fled into the jungle, and bring them back."

The search for the little people who ran into the jungle turns up nothing. Duc's frustration is evident. All the time and money spent chasing the mysterious berry, has netted KKP zero results. Winston Cheung is a thief. He is to blame for all of this, and Doctor Liberty Corcoran is his willing accomplice. In a rage, Duc orders the mercenaries to burn every hut in the village, before they leave.

~~~

One news source reports a package of three capsules of Chamala selling over the internet to a wealthy Chinese businessman for the equivalent of one million US dollars. It's only one of hundreds of incidents just like it. They occur in spite of warnings of blatant and widespread fraud. For many of the buyers, the allure of a pill that will grant a miracle, is too great to resist, even when the pill is being sold online sight unseen. Ads touting the Chamala's power, claim it will stimulate nerve cell growth, allowing the blind to see, the deaf to hear, the demented to think clearly and the paralyzed to walk.

A Davin-Boyd spokesperson releases a statement to the press. It is carefully worded to denounce the Chamala products selling on the black market as bogus, while at the same time letting the public know authentic Chamala products will be available through Davin-Boyd, soon. On the heels of that press release comes another from Khon Kaen Pharmaceutical announcing they too will have Chamala products in the near future.

Try as they may, law enforcement agencies across the globe are at a loss as to what to do about it. There is so little known about the Chamala, or how to determine the validity of the pills and capsules being sold. And truth be told, the buyers don't seem anxious to prosecute the sellers. To admit they've been duped would mean accepting there is no cure for their condition.

Libby suspects Davin-Boyd is at least partially responsible for starting many of the rumors surrounding the plant. She has been monitoring the trading price of their stock. It has risen almost twenty percent in the last month. The cynic in her warns it might have been their intention from the first. Hype the new discovery and make a fortune on the front end, without investing a jillion dollars on research. From that perspective, the offer of ten million for the patent makes perfect sense. Meanwhile, she continues trying to get the Chamala seeds to break out of their dormant state, and show signs of life. Thus far, she's had no success.

In a foul mood after her lack of progress, the dismal news, and the depressing conversation with Gunter, Libby takes it out on Diane that evening as Diane prepares to leave.

"How come you're spending so much time with Reggie? I hardly see you anymore."

"Oh Liberty, make up your mind. One minute it's, when am I going to leave here for good, and the next minute it's, why don't I spend more time with you."

"There's no reason to get testy. I was just asking."

"Me testy?! You're the one who's been cranky lately."

"I won't deny it. I've been under pressure at work, and a little overstressed because of it. I'm sorry if I've been difficult to be around. Is that why you spend your time elsewhere?"

"No. I spend my time elsewhere because I get bored with sitting around here. I know you like this place, but living in the sticks isn't working for me."

"We could go out together occasionally. We can have dinner in town or see a movie."

"Let's see. I can go to a movie with you," Diane says, as she holds her left hand out, palm up. "Or," she continues, holding her right hand beside the other, "I can spend time with a guy." Her right hand drops from the weight of it. "Sorry Liberty, it's no contest."

"Nice to know where I am in order of importance in your life. You know, I saw Reggie the last time I was at the supermarket. He doesn't strike me as your type."

"I didn't realize I have a type. He's a man with all the necessary equipment. I'm not as picky about the other details as you are."

"You can say that, again."

"Liberty, stop it. Alright, do you want to know why I prefer to spend my time with Reggie, rather than you? It's because Reggie doesn't criticize every little thing I do."

"Questioning what you do or why you do it isn't criticism. It's just verifying that you've given it due thought."

"Call it what you like, but it's a constant reminder of how little you think of me."

"Do you ever wonder if I was switched at birth, and you're not my biological mother?"

"That would explain it. Wouldn't it?"

# ~48~

The email was sent from Yan Chai Hospital in Hong Kong. In the subject line it says, from Edgar Cheung. It reads:

Dear Libby, Please forgive me for delivering this news in such an impersonal way. I am in the hospital recuperating from serious injuries, and am unable to do much without assistance. Winston and I were victims of a home invasion. I am sorry to report Winston did not survive his injuries. The burglars demanded the one thing Winston was not willing to part with. I think you know what I mean. I am alive only because I gave them what they wanted. I hope you understand when I say, I want nothing more to do with the project. It has been a curse on our house and brought me only sorrow. I urge you to abandon the project before it is too late. Edgar

Flying halfway around the world to comfort Edgar while he tries to cope with the loss of his brother is the least Libby can do. And Edgar is probably the only person capable of understanding how Winston's death affects her. As she walks down the long corridor of the hospital, she tries not to let her gaze linger too long on the injured and ill people she passes or let herself dwell on their suffering.

Instead, she concentrates on the numbers above the door to each room. She has to stay strong, and have an expression on her face which masks her sadness when she reaches room three forty-two. Edgar shares a room with three other men. He is in a bed against a wall with no window to view the outside world from. He has a cast on each arm, and a bandage wrapped around his head.

"Libby, you should not have come," Edgar says, as she enters the room. "It is too far to travel, and there is nothing to be done, now."

"I couldn't bear to think of you being alone during this terrible time."

"But I am not alone." He gestures to the others in the room. "I have my friends Jaco, Denny and Rason." The other men don't speak when introduced. "They do not know a word of English," Edgar explains.

"I'm so sorry it happened. Do you know who did this to you?"

221

"Yes, I know."

"Is Duc Nguyen responsible for Winston's death?"

"Let it go, Libby. It is not important now. We cannot bring Winston back, and he would not want you or me to avenge his death, or to mourn his passing. He is at peace now."

She knows this to be true. Winston wouldn't want her to be unhappy in any way. It makes her question the decision to come here.

"Then, can I do anything for you while I'm here?" she asks.

"Please, sit and talk with me. That is all I want."

So she does. They talk for two hours, without once mentioning the Chamala berry, West Papua or KKP. Mostly they share memories of Winston.

After that, Edgar says, "I am tired, and wish to nap now. Go home, Libby. It was good of you to come, but there is no need for you to stay any longer."

She kisses his cheek, manages a smile and bids farewell.

~~~

Eventually common sense would have prevailed. People would have seen the hype surrounding the Chamala as just that, and nothing more. The adage, if it seems too good to be true, it probably is, applies here. Greed led thousands to participate in the cruelest of hoaxes, and con thousands of others to buy into it. One news report estimated the street sales of phony Chamala products to be in the billions. Even if the figure is accurate, it only represents a fraction of the total losses, when considering the effect on the stock market and the lives taken or ruined.

At their pinnacle, shares of Davin-Boyd stock sold for one hundred forty-eight dollars each on the New York Stock Exchange. Before trading was suspended, pending an investigation into insider wrongdoing, shares of Davin-Boyd stock were selling for thirty-nine dollars and change. Every other pharmaceutical company on the NYSE was sucked into the vortex as the Davin-Boyd stock price plummeted.

"I wanted you to hear this from me first, rather than read it in an impersonal letter delivered by special courier," Herb Lawton begins his explanation to Libby. "The consensus among the company brass is we acted on the Chamala research prematurely. The board voted to rescind the offer to buy the patent. I'm sorry Libby."

It didn't come as a shock to Libby. She's been expecting it, looking forward to it, actually. Everyone had such high hopes for the Chamala plant.

Carrying the weight of being the one responsible for making it all happen has been a burden too great to bear.

"I appreciate you taking it upon yourself to call and tell me. I'm not surprised to hear it. I've been following the reports of Davin-Boyd's financial troubles in the news. Between you and me, I'm somewhat relieved. The pressure to develop a plant suitable to a commercial growing environment was getting to me. The ten million would have been nice, but with my time freed from the Chamala research I'll be making more personal appearances, which pay well and will make my agent happy."

"You've got a great attitude, Libby. It's been a pleasure working with you, and I hope our professional relationship can continue when I get settled in at my next job."

"Your next job?! You're quitting Davin-Boyd?!"

"Quitting wasn't an option. I'm being terminated, or laid off as they put it, along with two thousand others. Can I give your name as a personal reference on my resume?"

"Seriously?"

"Yes, I'm serious. The name, Doctor Liberty Belle Corcoran is well known, and carries a lot of weight in most circles."

"In that case, I'll be proud to tell anyone who asks that Herb Lawton is a dear and respected friend of mine. Take care of yourself, Herb. Drop me an email when you get situated with the next company."

The Davin-Boyd Pharmaceutical Company sent the official notice of their intent to cancel the agreement with LBC Botanical Research to Libby's lawyer, Wes Steiner.

"There's a clause in the contract that allows either party to cancel with proper notice. You have no legal recourse in the matter," Steiner tells her over the phone.

"I'm not interested in pursuing it, anyway. The Chamala has been nothing but trouble from day one. I'm sorry I ever got involved."

She's even sorrier when she receives a notice to appear before the Securities and Exchange Commission to testify in the investigation into illegal insider trading of Davin-Boyd stock.

"Have you bought, sold or received Davin-Boyd stock in the last year?" Steiner asks, when she shows him the notice.

"I've never bought, sold, been given, seen, owned or handled Davin-Boyd stock at any time in my life."

"Then, you won't need legal representation. And if something comes up, and you do need an attorney, I'm not qualified. It's a federal matter. I can recommend someone, but let's wait and see what transpires."

"Well, if I haven't been involved with their stock, why am I being called to testify in an insider trading investigation?"

"Again, this is all out of my area of expertise, but insider trading is when executives of a corporation profit from good or bad news by buying or selling shares of stock prior to that information becoming public. The laws regarding this also extend to people outside the company who accept money to aid the inside traders. For instance, if you had information you knew would affect their stock price, and they paid you to keep it quiet."

"That didn't happen. First of all, I haven't received money from Davin-Boyd in the last year. The research I've been involved in with them is in the early stages. There is nothing certain about my findings. I suspect someone who works for Davin-Boyd might be responsible for starting rumors which affected the stock prices, but I don't have any proof of it."

"I'd advise you to keep that sort of speculation to yourself. There's a chance this has something to do with the ten-million-dollar offer. As slow as organizations like the SEC move, it's likely they sent the notice to you before Davin-Boyd officially rescinded the offer."

"It's hard to believe that losing a ten-million-dollar deal might be a blessing in disguise."

# ~49~

Libby knows as soon as she reads the first line of the email it was sent by Daniel's mother.

Doctor Liberty Corcoran, My name is Katherine Jones of Cairns, Queensland, Australia. I was referred to you by Reverend Clayton Newburg. Friends of mine who watch his television broadcast regularly saw the filmed segment of your rescue in West Papua, during which a man identified as Daniel Jones died. I believe he was my son. I was hoping he might have said something to you that would confirm this. I would appreciate a reply, either way. Katherine Jones

Libby can't bear to think about Daniel falling to his death, but feels the woman deserves to know her son's fate, after two years of uncertainty. Her reply reads:

Katherine, The man who died during the rescue introduced himself as Daniel Jones, and in a conversation said his father is a pilot in Cairns, Queensland, Australia, where he was from. He told me, he was held captive for about two years, following an emergency landing of his plane, while delivering supplies to the Free Papua Movement. He was as brave a man as I have ever known, and instrumental in my survival in captivity, as well as my escape. I hope knowing what happened to Daniel will comfort you in some way. I am so sorry for your loss. Libby

Only a few hours after receiving the reply from Libby, Katherine sends another email.

Libby, I can't thank you enough for your kind words about my son, and for giving me the relief that comes with finally knowing. I was curious about the Free Papua Movement, and tried to find out more about them. They have a website they use to raise public awareness of their plight, and on it there are pictures of a village they claim was recently destroyed by the

Indonesian military. The village looks very much like the one in Reverend Clayton Newburg's video of your rescue. I could be wrong, of course, but I thought you would want to know. Katherine

Libby searches for the website Katherine referred to, finds the pictures mentioned, and peruses them for something familiar. The first few show piles of ashes where huts had been with the trees adjacent to them scorched. The next set of pictures, according to the caption, are the skeletal remains of the village inhabitants, after the vultures and jungle scavengers finished with them. Some of the bones are scattered across the field where the pygmies played footy. That's when she realizes Katherine's hunch is right.

The pygmy village had indeed been raided, and it appears as if most were killed. As inhumane as the genocide of the tribe might be it's no more so than her treatment at their hands. She won't weep for the little savages, but the demise of the tribe could mean the secret of where and how the Chamala plant grows is lost forever.

With that thought looming heavily, Libby takes the last Chamala berry from the safe, and dissects it to remove the seed. It's after work hours, and she's the only one in the building. She has tried everything she can think of to get one of the seeds to germinate. This seed represents the last chance. Failure would mean the time spent on research, her ordeal in West Papua, the Cheung brothers' investment, and Winston's death are all for naught. Maybe their expectations were unrealistic from the beginning. She examines the seed, hoping to see something she hasn't seen before now, but cannot.

"I can't do this anymore," she says aloud.

In one corner of the lab, there is a container for organic waste. Everything and anything botanical in nature to be discarded goes into it, whether it's a leaf, flower petal or banana peel. She takes the seeds and remaining parts of the four berries, and throws all of it into the container. Nothing good has come from having and studying the berries, only bad things. It's time to put an end to this.

~~~

"I can't tell you how excited I am to have you back to your old self," Jessica Rawlins tells Libby, ahead of her first personal appearance since returning from West Papua.

"I'm still not sure I'm ready, not one hundred percent, anyway," Libby replies.

226

"Trust me on this, Liberty. You're a natural. Once the red light atop the camera comes on, all your apprehension will disappear."

They are sitting in a room at the Albuquerque NBC affiliate TV station at nine a.m., waiting for Libby to be called onto the set of "Rising Stars of New Mexico", hosted by Grayson Whitney. Jessica has come along to give Libby moral support, or so she says. Fifteen minutes earlier, when Grayson comes into the room to say hello to Libby, Jessica wraps herself around him like an octopus on a clam, and plants a sloppy kiss on his lips.

"It's so good to see you again," she tells him, in a sultry tone.

"Have we met?" he asks.

"Oh Grayson, you're always such a tease," she replies, with a laugh.

"Liberty!" Grayson enthuses, as he extricates himself from Jessica. "I'm so glad you agreed to come back on my show. Ever since we announced it I've had a ton of emails, all supportive and saying how eager they are to hear from you."

As soon as his arms are free enough to do so, he embraces Libby like an old flame. She feels the blood rush to her face. Over his shoulder, Jessica gives Libby a wink and a thumbs-up.

"I'm glad for an opportunity to be on your show again, Grayson."

"Have you had a chance to look over the questions I plan to ask?"

"About those," Jessica interjects.

Libby cuts her off saying, "I'm sure they'll be fine, Grayson."

"Spectacular! This is going to be a great show, one of the best ever. Just sit back and relax until we're ready for you, about twenty minutes from now."

Standing in the wings waiting to go on, Libby listens to Grayson's introduction.

"Folks, our next guest needs no introduction, as the video of her courageous escape from a tribe of cannibals has been viewed online more than one hundred million times. I am honored to have her on our show. Please welcome the fabulous Doctor Liberty Belle Corcoran."

The sound engineer flips a switch for the prerecorded applause, turns the volume to max, and then flips another switch for whoops and whistles as Libby strides onto the set. She waves to the imaginary audience and air kisses Grayson's cheek, before they sit down and the applause fades.

"I have to say you look great, Liberty. Doesn't she look great?" Grayson says to the camera. The sound engineer plays whoops and wolf whistles.

"Why thank you, Grayson. You're looking pretty good yourself," she says with a wink.

He gives her his patented thousand-watt smile, then turns to face the camera for the benefit of the viewers.

"Liberty, I have so many questions, there isn't enough time to ask them all. I'll start with asking you what it was like to be held captive for two months by a tribe of primitive cannibals, not knowing whether you'd survive another day?"

"It was very difficult. I was at the point of giving up several times during my captivity."

"How did you cope? Where'd you find the strength to keep going?"

"My dear friends, Winston and Edgar Cheung were not far away. I had faith they'd find me in time. And Daniel Jones, another captive helped me to survive in the meantime."

"As I understand it, a romance evolved between you and the other captive you mentioned, Daniel Jones, during this period."

"That's not completely true. We formed a bond the way two soldiers in combat would. We helped and were dependent on one another. Had it not been for him, I'm sure I wouldn't have lived through it. My heart goes out to his family and friends in Cairns, Australia, as they struggle with their loss."

"According to what I've heard your reason for being in West Papua was to lead an expedition in search of a particular plant. Is that true?"

"Yes. Our purpose was to find this plant, and learn more about it. I was able to locate berries from the plant, but my efforts to get the berries to germinate failed. As a result, the expedition, unfortunately was a complete failure."

Jessica watches the show in the waiting room. She is on her phone when Libby comes out afterward.

"What did you think?" Libby asks.

Jessica holds up a finger to quiet Libby while she finishes her conversation.

"That was Upward Magazine on the phone. They want to do a feature story about you. Your face will be on the cover, which means on the shelves of newsstands and checkout lines all over the world. Isn't that incredible?"

"Incredible," Libby replies in a monotone.

"Why aren't you as excited as me at that?"

"I am, I'm just a little tired."

"Liberty, you need to embrace your new celebrity status. It's here to stay."

"I'll work on it. Now can we go, or were you planning to stick around and try to grope Grayson, again?"

"Speaking of," Jessica says, looking over Libby's shoulder.

"Liberty, I'm glad I caught you before you left," Grayson says. "Thanks again for doing the show. Jenna says it's already being talked about on social media."

Libby straightens her spine to stand erect and bring herself closer to eye level with Grayson, who is four inches taller. Jessica crowds in close so she's not left out.

"It was my pleasure, Grayson. I thoroughly enjoyed being here," Libby says.

"Listen," Grayson says, taking Libby's arm and steering her away from Jessica to speak privately. "I seem to remember you saying, the last time you were here, that if I found myself in Taos some weekend to give you a call. Does the offer still stand?"

Libby doesn't attempt to hide her delight with his sudden interest in her. "Why, of course it does, Grayson. Anytime you like."

"How does this Saturday look for you? We could have lunch in Taos, and after that you could show me around town."

"That sounds great, Grayson. I'd love to do that."

"Then, I'll see you Saturday."

"What was he telling you in there?" Jessica asks, as she's driving away from the station with Libby in the passenger seat.

"He asked me out."

Jessica swerves, running a wheel up on the curb and almost taking out a pedestrian.

"No way! You're serious? Grayson Whitney asked you out. I can't believe it. What did you say?"

"I said yes, of course. He's coming to Taos this Saturday to take me to lunch, and then we're going to do some sightseeing around town."

"I am so fricking jealous I can't see straight."

"Maybe I should drive, then. I don't want to die in a car crash before the big day."

# ~50~

Sunday before Thanksgiving, Libby is relaxing at home in her den with a glass of wine, while thumbing through the latest issue of Botany Quarterly Magazine. The previous six months have been the most tumultuous of her entire life, but things are slowly returning to normal. The brouhaha surrounding the Chamala has faded, her business is running smoothly, her appearance schedule is booked full and her love life has never been better.

Diane enters the room, and takes a seat across from Libby. Neither of the women speak initially. Things between them have been somewhat strained as of late, but that's nothing new. Their relationship has always run hot and cold, for as long as either can remember.

"I have some good news for you," Diane says, after a beat.

"A little good news would be nice for a change."

"I'll be moving out next week. I bet you thought that would never happen."

"I'll admit there are days when I wondered if we'd be together from now on, like two old spinsters. Next week, you say. Where are you going?"

"Back to California. Claude has asked me to marry him, and I said yes."

"The same Claude you broke up with earlier this year? The same Claude you said you never wanted to see again? That Claude?"

"Yes, him. He called to tell me he couldn't live without me. He's a different person than before. I could tell, just from his voice over the phone."

Diane has made more than her share of impulsive decisions such as this, and most have turned out bad. Then again, it's her life. They are both adults. It's not for either of them to hand out advice. Nor is it the responsibility of one to repair the damage when the other screws up.

"Am I invited to the wedding?" Libby asks, hoping it doesn't sound cynical.

"We'll probably just say our vows in front of a judge, without a ceremony. We haven't talked about it yet, but he's been married twice before, and we're not teenagers, after all."

"Well, I guess congratulations are in order." It sounds more like a question than a statement.

"Oh Liberty," Diane sighs. "I know you think I'm making a mistake, and hell, who knows, maybe I am. But, it won't be the first one, nor the last, so just wish me luck and leave it at that."

"Good luck, Diane. I never thought I'd say this, but I'm going to miss having you around."

"You're a terrible liar. You always were."

Libby feels a lump forming in her throat. Diane looks like she's on the verge of tears, too.

"You want a glass of wine?" Libby asks.

"No thanks. I've got a date with Reggie. We're going to have dinner, and rent a movie to take back to his place." Libby tries, but fails to hide her utter amazement at what she's hearing. "Close your mouth, Liberty, before a bug crawls in there."

It's something Diane used to say when Libby was a child, and found herself stupefied by something her mother had done. She can't help but laugh at the memory.

"It's good to see you laugh, Liberty. You should do it more often. I'd better go now. I don't want to keep Reggie waiting. Don't wait up."

"Don't worry, I won't."

~~~

On Christmas Eve Libby sits alone at her home in the Miranda Canyon, watching a flame flicker in the fireplace, and sipping from a mug of hot chocolate. Outside, a dusting of snow covers the ground. Christmas was never a big deal when she was growing up. Diane didn't fuss over it like the other mothers. They didn't put up a tree, decorate the house, sing carols or exchange gifts. And because such traditions weren't practiced then, Libby has never felt the need to start doing those things since.

Her new beau on the other hand, grew up in a family that pulled out all the stops for the holiday season. The celebrating began each year during the week of Thanksgiving, and lasted through New Year's Day. That hasn't changed for his parents, but now that he's grown, with a career and other obligations, he only makes it home to Georgia for a few days at a time.

He wanted her to come with him this year, but Libby declined. He is the youngest of four kids, and the only one who is unmarried and has no children. Sitting at the table over Christmas dinner, with all eyes scrutinizing her dress, hair, makeup and every movement, waiting for her to slip up and

231

embarrass herself is a recipe for a reoccurring nightmare. If and when she meets his family, it will be done one at a time and with an engagement ring on her finger.

Her phone sounds the ringtone designated for him. She's been expecting the call.

"Hello handsome," she answers.

"Why hello yourself, darling." His soft, Southern-tinged baritone sends shivers up and down her spine. Then, he says, "I miss you," and she turns to mush.

"Are you having fun with your family?"

"I always have fun with them, but I'm anxious to get back to New Mexico. This is the first time since we started seeing one another that we've been this far apart, and I don't mind telling you, I don't like it at all."

"I know how you feel. I've gotten used to having you close."

"If you remember, I did ask you to come with me."

"I remember, and I think it was the right decision for me to stay here. We haven't known each other that long. Bringing a girl home to meet your parents, and at Christmas, no less, is a big step."

"My family is really laid-back. It wouldn't have been a problem," he assures her.

"Is that right? Did you happen to mention you have a new girlfriend?"

"I probably did. When my family gets together, everybody is talking at once, so I don't hear half of what's said, or remember half of what I hear. It's the same for the rest of the crew."

"You're being evasive, now. I'm beginning to think you're ashamed of revealing our relationship to your family."

"Now Liberty, you know better than that. I'm in love with you, and that's not a word I kid around about."

In the background Libby hears someone say, "Grayson hon, who's that on the phone?"

Grayson makes an attempt to cover the mouthpiece, but Libby can still hear him say, "It's no one mother, just a buddy from work calling to wish me a Merry Christmas."

"The kids are waiting on you. They want to open some presents, so tell your friend you'll call him later, and come along."

"I'll be there in one minute," he tells his mother, then to Libby he says, "Sorry about that. Now, where were we?"

"You were trying to convince me you love me. And, from what you told your mother, you've got about thirty seconds left, so make it good."

"I love you, Liberty.  I miss you terribly, and I hope this is the last Christmas we spend apart."  She doesn't respond, so he prompts her.  "How'd I do?"

"On a scale of one to ten, that was a twelve.  Hurry home, Grayson."

# EPILOGUE

There's a light rap on the door to the patio, which can only be one person. Libby lifts herself from the couch where she'd been speaking on the phone to Grayson a minute earlier. The sound of his voice still lingers in the air.

"I'm in a good mood," she tells Quentin, as she opens the door. "Please don't do or say anything to spoil it."

"The last thing I want to do is make you mad at me. I just came over because it's Christmas Eve and I know you're here by yourself. I thought you might want some company."

It isn't her first choice for how to spend Christmas Eve, but Quentin is all bundled up, and looking cold, lost and lonely, so she invites him in.

"You want some hot chocolate?" she asks.

"Sure, that sounds good."

"I thought you might go home for Christmas," Libby says, as she heats a cup of water.

"No reason to. My parents are out of the country somewhere, and the servants are all off for the holidays. It's that way every year. They lock up the house and leave. Have you heard anything from Diane?"

"Not a word since she moved. But, that's probably a good sign. It means she hasn't gotten into trouble she can't get out of by herself." She hands the hot chocolate to him. "Come on, let's go in the den. I've got a fire going."

"Cool! Do you have any marshmallows?"

"Sorry, no."

"What about weenies?"

"No weenies, either. How about a baked potato? I could wrap a couple in foil and roast them over the coals."

While she gets those ready, Quentin sheds his coat and makes himself comfortable on the couch in the den. Libby brings the potatoes and nestles them into the hot coals. While they roast they watch TV and talk about this last year—the trip to Mahé, the people like Diane, Gunter and the Cheungs who have come into their lives.

"Thanks for letting me hang out with you," Quentin says, at the end of the evening as he gets ready to leave. "And thanks for the potato. It was pretty good cooked that way."

"You're welcome, Quentin. I actually enjoyed the evening."

"We should do this again," he says.

"Let's not rush into anything."

She walks with him to the patio door to lock it behind him. As soon as she does, he raps on the door.

"What now, did you forget something?"

"Yeah, I forgot to give you your gift."

"Quentin, you didn't need to buy me a gift."

"I didn't. I found it." He pulls the item from his pocket, and holds it out. "It's a really awesome ornament. Somebody threw it away."

Libby recognizes it immediately, but can't believe it is real until she holds it in her hand and feels its energy course through her.

"Where did you find this?"

"It was in that heap of garbage behind the lab."

"The mulch pile?"

"Yeah, there. The moon was full and straight overhead. I thought it was a piece of glass, until I picked it out of the pile and saw it has its own little light inside. That's got to be the world's smallest light bulb."

The mulch pile is where the organic waste from the lab ends up. The Chamala seeds that didn't germinate were discarded there, and by some miracle of nature, one has begun to grow. For whatever reason, the Chamala responds to the environment created in that mulch pile.

"Quentin, I want you to take this and put it back in the exact same spot where you found it. Would you do that for me, please?"

"How come?" Libby gives him a look which says don't ask. "Alright, I get it. I'm supposed to just do it, without asking why."

"Trust me, Quentin. This is one of those times when the less you know the better."